THE CARTEL 7
ILLUMINATI

ALSO BY THE AUTHORS

The Cartel 6: The Demise

THE CARTEL 7

ILLUMINATI: ROUNDTABLE OF BOSSES

ASHLEY & JAQUAVIS

ST. MARTIN'S GRIFFIN 🙞 NEW YORK

This is a work of fiction. All of the characters, organizations, and events portrayed in this novel are either products of the authors' imaginations or are used fictitiously.

 Printed in the United States of America. For information, address St. Martin's Press, 175 Fifth Avenue, New York, N.Y. 10010.

www.stmartins.com

The Library of Congress Cataloging-in-Publication Data is available upon request.

ISBN 978-1-250-06700-5 (trade paperback)
ISBN 978-1-4668-7491-6 (ebook)

Our books may be purchased in bulk for promotional, educational, or business use. Please contact your local bookseller or the Macmillan Corporate and Premium Sales Department at 1-800-221-7945, extension 5442, or by email at MacmillanSpecialMarkets@macmillan.com.

First Edition: July 2017

10 9 8 7 6 5 4 3 2 1

THE CARTEL 7
ILLUMINATI

Chapter 1

The beautiful skyline of Kolkata, India, astonished as they all stared out of their windows. The tall buildings' structures were advanced and bright lights lit up the sky as they prepared to descend for landing. Carter looked on in amazement, never having seen anything so beautiful. The scenery reminded him of New York at night back home in the States, which was shocking to him. Never would he have thought the country could be so modern and picturesque.

Everyone was well rested, except Carter. He had stayed up the majority of the flight, wondering what he had been sucked into. *This some movie shit,* he thought to himself after thinking about the tactics they went through to recruit him and his counterparts. Ghost stepped from the cockpit, where he and the pilot were during the flight.

"Good evening, everyone. We are approaching the city

of Kolkata. This is where my team of scientists are located and waiting on your arrival. They are currently duplicating the drug we call Lolita, which is derived from the Rebe flower, as I explained before. This will guarantee the well-being of your lives, kids, and grandchildren. Generational wealth is inevitable. Welcome to the future," he said smoothly just before he disappeared back into the cockpit and closed the door behind himself. It seemed as if he disappeared before any of them had the chance to ask questions or reply. As always Ghost was smooth and mysterious and his persona and his name matched perfectly. His ghost-like characteristics gave him a mystique and essence that were unfamiliar to them all. His ability to convince successful drug lords to come together and not create a hierarchy or totem pole was brilliant.

"Is that nigga smooth like that all the time?" Brick asked, breaking the quiet tension within the aircraft. Everyone chuckled and it broke the ice among the group of strangers. Brick was a heavier set man with a dark, full beard and raspy voice. He wore dark Versace shades to hide his eyes as he displayed his smile and looked around. Small chatter began as all the different personalities began to discuss their new venture.

* * *

"You think this shit is really legit?" a man asked, as he put the question on the floor for discussion. He wore a well-tailored shirt with the tie slightly loosened. The cut of his pants was perfect and obviously costume fitted. His slim frame and broad shoulders were athletic and his salt-and-pepper beard suggested he was a gentleman of a certain age.

"Shit, it has to be. Our meeting was in the fucking *Vatican,*" Millie said as she emphasized the sacred venue that their initial meeting was in.

Carter Jones remained silent as he sat in the back of the aircraft and listened closely to the open conversation. Not being the one for small talk, he was interested in seeing what was to come from all of this. He had other things on his mind, such as his wife, Miamor, his son, and the cartel organization as a whole. He decided to keep mum, so he could feel everyone out before engaging in the fraternizing. He did notice one thing, though: the older of the two ladies, Anari, was sitting back listening as well. She didn't say too much and they kept locking eyes with each other, both trying to figure the other out. Only time would tell the relationship that these two would incur. *Friend or foe?* both wondered, feeling the power that the other one held. It was something about a powerful person that was radiant and they both felt it.

The aircraft landed smoothly on the private runway and five black SUVs were awaiting their arrival—one for each person. They all stepped off the jet to a red carpet that led them to the row of cars. Each door was open and a chauffeur stood there, all of them wearing black suits and shades. They all were of Indian descent, hired guns by Ghost and his board members. Ghost stood at the top of the plane's stairs as all the bosses reached the bottom.

"Your personal cars are waiting for you and will take you to your next location," Ghost said loudly so everyone could hear him loud and clear.

* * *

"Right this way, ma'am," one of the chauffeurs said to Anari as she was the first to get escorted to her vehicle. Everyone else followed suit and got into the luxury truck that had champagne and fruit awaiting them in the backseat. Once everyone was secure in their car, they exited in a single-file line, heading to a resort where they would rest for the night. After a short ride, they arrived at a private estate that was surrounded by a lake. It was in the hills of Kolkata where the air was moist, but warm. As they all stepped out of the cars the huge castlelike mansion was before them. The beautiful gray brick mansion had a wraparound driveway that seemed to be the size of a football field. The gargoyle statues on top of the castle gave it a dark, Gothic appearance. The moon seemed as if it was shining directly onto the historic place for their viewing pleasure.

"Wow. This shit keeps getting better and better," Brick said as he stepped out of the car and nodded his head in approval of the palace. One by one, they all stepped out and stood side by side. Ghost was standing in the driveway, waiting for them. He began to walk toward them and stood front and center. They all were surprised he had made it there before them and they never even saw him get off the plane. Ghost stood with his arms crossed and his legs shoulder width apart as he waited until all eyes were on him before he said a word.

"Welcome to your place of residence for the next two weeks." Ghost unleashed a small grin. "Allow me to show the place," he said just before he led them in. A doorman was standing at the door in a tuxedo awaiting their entry. As they filed into the house, the pleasant smell of flowers invaded their nostrils and shiny marble floors were at their feet. The high ceilings and space were high-end and luxurious. The porcelain staircase and handcrafted podiums were marble and added a cherry on top of the already astonishing place. The mansion was immaculate to say the least.

Ghost continued to host the bunch, intoning, "This was the great emperor's home and this will be our haven on this brief trip. So, rest up guys. Get rest and relax—tomorrow I will be taking you to the lab so you can see how everything is made firsthand. Your rooms are assigned to each one of you individually and your name is on the door." Ghost straightened his tie and looked at each of them in their eyes. His strong jawline and impeccable posture made him look presidential and solid.

"Oh, how could I forget? Each of you has a personal masseuse, for your tension or whatever stresses you guys need worked out of your body," Ghost said while growing a smirk on his face. He then clapped twice, loudly, which echoed throughout the home. Within seconds a line of women appeared at the top of the stairs, all of them wearing sultry lingerie and standing with a model's posture.

They all smiled and were of Indian descent. All of them were different sizes, but equally beautiful.

"Fellas, the ladies will help you get that tension out," Ghost said as he smiled and winked at the guys. "And of course, for the ladies . . ." Ghost clapped again and two well-built, shirtless men appeared in the line as well. Both had perfect smiles and tans that were sun kissed.

"Whoa, homeboy. I think you have me mistaken," Millie said as she stepped forward, showing off her fit body. She wore a casual sweat suit, but her curves were still noticeable. "I don't play on that side, feel me?" she said, letting her sexual orientation be known. Everyone began to chuckle at her bluntness.

"I want lil' mama right there," she said as she looked up at the tall, slim woman in line. They both locked eyes and the sexual energy was created instantly. Millie ran her tongue across her top lip and smiled, displaying her perfectly straight pearl teeth.

"Well, I guess that's that," Ghost said while smiling and rubbing his hands together. "Each of you has a suite upstairs and a twenty-four-hour chef is on staff. Just simply pick up your room phone and tell him what you want. Other than that, the night is yours. I suggest you guys relax and rest up. We all have a full day tomorrow. Tomorrow is the beginning of a new regime." Ghost walked toward the exit. "I'll be staying in the guest home, just across the lot. A cell phone is on each nightstand and my number is saved in each one. Any questions or qualms, don't hesitate to text me. Good night," he said. And just like that, he was gone.

Carter stood back and watched. He wanted to see who would jump first. He wanted to see who had the vice of sexual pleasure. He personally had no desire to be with another woman for two reasons. One, he was madly in love with Miamor and felt that he was the reason she was in jail. The thought of being with another woman while she sat in a small cell was unsettling. Two, he was here to get to the money. He was interested in what Ghost was offering and the fact that he had offered to pull strings for Miamor's release had Carter committed to the proposal. Carter watched as everyone headed up the stairs, grabbing a girl to accompany them as they disappeared into their quarters for the night. He noticed that Anari didn't even give the men a glance as she brushed right past them and headed to her room. *Who is she?* he asked himself as he watched her closely.

A lone girl stood at the top of the stairs, waiting for Carter as he stood there and thought to himself. "Sweetheart, I won't be needing your company tonight unfortunately. Have yourself a good night," Carter said as he gave her a half smile, smoothly sliding both of his hands into his slacks' pockets. He slowly climbed the stairs and walked past the lady in red. Although he had no plans on utilizing her services, he did, however, get a peek at her voluptuous body through the see-through lingerie. Her erect nipples pointed directly at him. Her dark areolas were on full display and her glossed lips made her that much more enticing. However, Carter held his ground and walked right past the olive-colored beauty.

He retired to his room and was taken aback as soon as he stepped in. The marble floors looked like a sea of blue water with a black lining throughout. It was simply amazing. The canopy bed had sheer fabric draped over the California king–sized mattress. The room was spacious and resembled a luxury hotel. Carter walked through the room, observing each nook and cranny. He made his way toward the rear and the double doors that led to the balcony. The moonlight shined through the curtains, providing illumination to the scenery. Carter opened the doors and stepped out onto the balcony and saw that it was a view of the lake in the back. The moonlight bounced off the water and Carter stepped to the edge and admired the view. The cool air soothed him and he closed his eyes and tears began to form. The thought of Miamor being in a cold cell tormented his soul and beautiful views like the one he was currently witnessing only flooded guilt into his heart, knowing that hers was that of four cement walls. Miamor was truly the love of his life and his heart ached for her. Although she was the strongest woman he had ever known, he knew that prison wasn't humane.

"I love you with all my heart," he whispered as a single tear flowed down his cheek. He quickly wiped it away. He thought about his son as well and it was hard being away from little C.J. However, it was easier to deal with knowing that his sister Breeze was watching over him, or so he thought.

He stared into the lake and assessed the current dilemma. He began to think about the things Ghost had presented to them and how he said he had major political connections regarding the success of moving the new drug. Carter began to wonder if Ghost could use those same connections to help his situation with the FBI, Miamor, and reuniting his family. He quickly turned around and went back into the room, looking for the nightstand and the cell phone that Ghost had referred to earlier. He walked over to the phone and saw the BlackBerry just as described. He picked it up and began to look through the contacts. Ghost's name was already stored in it and that's when Carter sent the text.

I would like to speak with you alone if possible.

A few moments later Carter got a return text from Ghost, instructing him to walk across the yard and meet him in his personal villa that sat about one hundred yards away from the mansion Carter was currently in. Carter sat on the bed and took a deep breath, trying to figure out the best way to approach Ghost and ask him about his personal family situation.

* * *

Anari let the steaming-hot water run on her head and down her body as she enjoyed the water's massage. She rested her hands on the stone-tiled shower walls and thought about the opportunity at hand. She was a retired drug dealer and that came with no pension or retirement plan. Her money had been running low and although she'd vowed to never enter the drug game again, this opportunity was much needed and seemed to have low risk. She kept replaying the words of Ghost over and over in her head trying to make sense of the proposition. She was a street legend back in the States and her name held power. Many rappers, entertainers, and celebrities within the black community acknowledged what she had done in the streets for years throughout the Midwest. She had been one of few throughout history that had been on the feds' radar and escaped a guilty verdict. She was the female Teflon Don in every sense of the word. She was bulletproof. Not for nothing either—she was highly intelligent and moved to her own beat and drum. She and her husband had become urban legends. Anari stepped out of the shower and quickly wrapped herself in the oversized terry cloth towel. She walked out of the bathroom and opened the closet door. It was fully stocked with new clothes and as she began to thumb through it, she noticed that every piece of clothing was her exact size.

"Wow, they really did their homework," she whispered to herself as she picked out a pair of silk pajamas and headed toward the bed thinking about what she had fallen into. She then exited the room and walked throughout the house, getting more comfortable with her surroundings. She reached a den that sat in the middle of the beautiful home and saw that there was a table with an ivory chess set. Being a big chess fan, she sat down and began to play a game with herself.

What is this guy's angle? Is this shit real? Anari asked herself as she pushed the pawn up two spaces. Ironically, she felt as if she was a pawn in the grand scheme of things, a position she felt very uncomfortable in. Although Anari was a woman, she had always played the king of the board. She was determined to get to the source of Ghost's intentions. She knew that he wasn't the main guy, because if so she wouldn't have seen him. She knew and understood fully that power moved in silence.

* * *

Carter exited the place and looked across the yard and saw a small building with a light on. He began to walk over. He looked at the end of the long driveway and toward the gate entrance and saw two gunmen standing guard with assault rifles. He didn't know if they were keeping people from getting onto the property or keeping the guests in. He shook his head and focused on the small villalike building across the lawn. He approached the front door and gave it a few knocks and waited for a response. Moments later, Ghost answered the door. He was shirtless and sweating. A gym towel was draped over his shoulders as he breathed heavily, while using the tip of the towel to wipe the sweat beads from his forehead and smiling.

"Hey, man. Come in," Ghost said as he stepped to the side, clearing the path so Carter could walk in.

"Thanks," Carter said under his breath as he proceeded to walk in. He observed the small studio apartment. It only had a treadmill, a small kitchen, and a bed. The floors were made of wood and the room had four brick walls. The marble countertops and dark wood cabinets that matched the floors were modern and resembled a high-end Manhattan apartment.

"You have to excuse me. Just got a five-mile run in before bed," Ghost said as he walked over to the dresser and pulled out a T-shirt.

"No worries," Carter said as he leaned against the wall and slid his hands into his pockets.

"What's up? Is everything ok?" Ghost asked just as he slid the shirt over his head and onto his body.

"No, not really. I want to talk to you about something," Carter began.

"Okay. Shoot," Ghost answered as he walked closer to Carter and folded his arms in front of his chest.

"Well, I remember what you said back at the Vatican about you having connections and political ties, right?" Carter quizzed.

"Yeah, of course."

"Well, you see, I have a problem back home that I need help on. It's my wife—"

"Miamor," Ghost said, cutting him off midsentence.

"Y-yeah," Carter answered, confused, wondering how Ghost had read his mind.

Ghost chuckled as he walked over to the kitchen and reached on top of the refrigerator.

"You drink scotch," Ghost said as he then pulled two glasses from the cabinet.

"Sure," Carter said as he stood straight up and began to rub both of his hands together. Ghost poured them both a drink and then handed Carter a glass. They took sips simultaneously, both looking each other in the eyes. Ghost continued the discussion.

"I know what you are going through with your wife and family. Like I said, my partners and I have been watching you all for years and we know about the trouble that she has gotten herself into."

"Yeah, it's been a bumpy ride. Can you really help me?" Carter asked with skepticism.

"I believe I can. There are ways we can make things disappear. The law is much more lenient to our establishment and the people who are in business with us. You see, you have a unique situation because Miamor is already convicted. However, there is more than one way to skin a cat," Ghost said just before he downed the remainder of his scotch and walked over to the kitchen counter. He sat the glass in the sink and reached into a kitchen drawer, pulling out a legal-sized manila folder. He walked back over to Carter and handed him the envelope.

"What's this?" Carter asked as he accepted the envelope and looked down at it in confusion.

"Go ahead. Take a look," Ghost answered as he once again folded his arms in front of his chest. Carter opened the envelope and reached into it, pulling out a stack of photos. He began to look through the pictures and frowned in perplexity. He didn't recognize anybody in the pictures.

He did notice that each picture had a similar character, a thirty-something white man.

"I don't get it. I don't recognize anyone. What am I looking at and what does this have to do with my family?" Carter asked.

"You're looking at the DA that prosecuted your wife. Also, that's him taking bribes from various criminals over the past two years," Ghost said with no emotion. Carter instantly began to realize why the pictures were so important.

"Oh, yeah?" Carter said under his breath as he continued to flip through.

"That's right. This changes everything and turns the odds in your wife's favor. If we can prove that the DA was soliciting illegal funds during your wife's trial, it's a big chance that we can get a retrial and from that point, we have the resources to sway any juror that's in that courtroom. We have our ways to make people see things our way, if you know what I mean: a random audit, pressure from local police, or monetary compensation for their cooperation. Whatever needs to be done to get her free, we will handle it." Ghost slowly paced the floor. Carter watched closely and studied his calm demeanor and looked into his eyes, trying to find an inkling of him lying—but he couldn't. Ghost was the real thing.

"So, you think you can really get Miamor released?" Carter asked with blatant skepticism in his tone.

"I don't think . . . I know we can. Like I said, if you help us with our goal we can help you with yours," Ghost said as he stopped right in front of Carter, while confidently looking into his eyes.

"This is unbelievable," Carter said as he shook his head.

"Well, believe it. This isn't what you are used to. This is what white America calls nepotism and political power. This is foreign to people with brown or black skin. People like us can't make calls to the higher-ups to make things go away or use a political connection to our benefit. This is what you call *absolute power,* my friend."

"Well, I'm all in," Carter said as his heart began to beat rapidly. He held his chest feeling his heart being tender. He knew that after his previous injuries he would never be the same, so he tried his best to deal with it without exposing it. He smiled and downed the rest of his scotch, ready to do whatever to free the only woman he had ever truly loved.

* * *

Anari was still playing chess with herself, trying to make sense of it all. She leaned forward and studied each move as if it was her last. Her index finger rested on her temple as she squinted and looked at the chessboard. Something was bothering her and she couldn't quite put her finger on it. She hated the fact that they were cut off from the world and stuck with people she didn't know from Adam. She began to question the real reason she was handpicked by this secret organization. "What is the motive, Anari?" she whispered to herself as she made her next move. She then spun the board around, so she could see the game from the imaginary opponent's view. She realized that was exactly what she was trying to do in real life at that moment.

Carter entered back into the house and saw Anari from afar as she sat and played chess. He wasn't tired so decided to walk over and join her. As he approached her, her eyes never lifted from the chessboard and she was laser focused as she whispered to herself.

"Mind if I join?" Carter said as he stood over her.

"You can do what you want to do, sir. This isn't my house," she said, not even giving him the respect of looking at him when she talked. Anari was a gangster effortlessly and it oozed off her. She was feminine without exploiting her sexuality but well aware of the power only a woman could possess.

"I will take that as a yes," Carter answered with a smile. He sat across from her and watched as she continued to analyze the board. "So where are you from?" he asked as he placed his hand on the knight and made a move. This made Anari break her concentration, sit up, and look at him. He snickered and her brow furrowed at the arrogant smirk that crossed his face. She would have to concentrate to win this battle. She sensed genius behind his smooth, dark skin as she studied Carter, who was now focusing on the board, thinking about his next move.

"I'm a citizen of the world," Anari finally answered vaguely as she made a move on the chessboard.

He peered up, meeting her gaze. It had to be more than irony, the fact that they were bred the same. They were predators, which meant they were more alike than different. Carter wasn't sure if it was a bad or good thing but he respected the fact that she was guarded with her information. Letting the wrong person in could lead to self-destruction and he knew that like himself her trust was earned. She reminded him of his wife, only more calculating. Miamor may have been deadly, but Anari was bossed up. She reveled in her queendom. Carter recognized royalty when in its presence.

"This shit crazy, right?" Carter whispered as he leaned in closer and looked around.

"Yeah, I'm still trying to figure out their angle. It has to be an angle," Anari said, sharing her thoughts.

"That's what I've been thinking," Carter agreed as he nodded his head in confirmation.

Just then a short man with all white on came from the rear of the place, wearing a tall white chef's hat. He approached them with a big smile. His fat cheeks seemed to be greased as they shined in the light.

"Good evening, my name is Victor and I am the resident chef. May I prepare something for you or bring you a beverage?" he asked while maintaining his larger-than-life smile.

"Hello Victor. I'm good for now," Anari responded as she looked at him and gave a fake grin. Carter just simply shook his head no. Victor nodded his head in understanding and disappeared back to the rear of the house. Just like that, he was gone.

"You see that shit?" Carter whispered.

"See what?"

"This shit is unreal. It's like some real secret society shit. This big-ass house, chefs popping out of nowhere to serve us. A meeting at the Vatican. This doesn't seem real."

"Man, tell me about it," Anari said, finally letting her guard down and looking Carter in the eye. They shared a smile and the ice was finally broken.

"So, what's your story? Where did they get you from?" Anari inquired.

"I'm from the States but I was over in Barcelona when everything went black."

"Barcelona, Spain?" Anari asked in confusion.

"Yeah, I had to lay low over there. The feds were on me back home so I had to go into hiding. I was doing my thing in Miami and then I tried to go legit in Vegas. You know how that goes, though," Carter said as he moved a piece on the board.

"You're Carter's son, right?" Anari asked as she looked closely at his facial features. Also, she knew that anything that moved in Miami was under the umbrella of the Cartel. Their reputation rang bells throughout the country as the biggest and most organized crime syndicate in the South. If drug dealing was an art they would be the Picassos of it. They simply were the best to ever do it.

"Yeah, that's my father. Never met him though," Carter admitted as he dropped his head and focused on the chessboard.

"Oh, I see," Anari said, not wanting to ask any more questions. She had heard nothing but good things about his father during her time on the streets. Her husband, Von, used to do business with him and he held Carter in high regard.

"I heard you used to make it snow in the Midwest. I grew up hearing your name for years. Tony, right?" Carter said as he called her by her street alias.

"Yeah, I did my thing back in the day," Anari confirmed as she moved a chess piece. "Check," she added just before looking at Carter.

"If this is anything like Ghost says it is, we are set for life. This is what them privileged conglomerates have been doing for years. They sell legal drugs and we never seem to get a piece of the pie. They only leave us with the product that comes with a life sentence if sold," Carter explained.

"It's too good to be true. However, I'm thinking that we didn't have much of a choice. Ghost made it seem like the option was ours, but I truly beg to differ. You see what happened to ol' girl once she declined? I'm pretty sure I would have been right there with her if I chose to decline. They put it in front of us like they are presenting us an opportunity but did we really have a choice?" Anari said just before she stood up. "Checkmate," she added as she trapped his king and walked away.

Her words lingered in Carter's thoughts as he began to digest the situation at hand. It was a new world order and he was a part of it. Frankly, he felt as if he was in a dream but the stakes were high, especially for him. He had no choice but to play the game, hoping that he didn't let it play him in the end. Carter could do nothing but smile and shake his head in disbelief and admiration. He knew there was something special about Anari.

Chapter 2

What is time? It's a concept of measuring one's day, measuring one's steps, measuring one's life. It's man-made. An idea made up to hold one accountable for the way they fill their day. At least that was what Miamor tried to tell herself to cope with the fifteen years she had been sentenced with. Miamor stood behind the wooden defense table as the man in the black robe stared down at her. He was perched up so smugly on his judicial throne as he condemned her for the next decade and a half. Even in this moment, fear didn't exist within her. Rage, yes, but fear, never. She would be lying if she said there were no feelings of regret. Miamor was being taken from her son, from her husband, from her family. Remorse for the choices that had led her to this moment was a natural feeling, but still she refused to let it weaken her.

So, she erased the concept of time from her mind. In

that moment, it did not exist. She would not count the times that the sun rose and set in the sky, she wouldn't acknowledge the years that would age her against her will. She would just be. She would just exist. She would just survive, until the day came when she would be a free woman again. Miamor held out her hands as steel clasped around her wrists, binding her. She looked behind her in the crowd. Not one familiar face was present. They couldn't be. Everyone affiliated with the infamous Cartel was a target. Carter was on the run. Aries had gone back underground where Miamor hoped her dear friend would stay. Breeze was taking care of the children and Monroe was dead. They were weak. The era of supremacy that they brought to the streets was no longer. The day that they had all tried to avoid for years had finally come. The Cartel had been brought to its knees at the hands of the federal government and the media was out to document the fall from grace. No amount of money could get Miamor out of this predicament. She did not cower or cry as the cameras flashed in her face.

Her heart beat rapidly as she was escorted by two federal agents to the awaiting transport vehicle outside. They held semiautomatic weapons and were dressed in full protective gear in anticipation of a getaway attempt. All their efforts were for naught, however. There was no grand escape plan. She would take those years on the head. They had offered her a deal to flip on Carter, but she never flinched. Miamor was too solid. She would do every single day they had given her without complaint because she was serving them for the man she loved. She would do a lifetime for Carter Jones.

Miamor eyed the other women that sat solemnly on the bus. They each shared the same fate. They were being shipped away and most of them would be forgotten, but Miamor knew that if no one ever spoke her name again, there was one person who would always remember her. As long as they both breathed, the universe would connect them. Carter and Miamor. Their love story was epic and to separate them was to go against the very fabric of God's plan. Neither time nor space could dilute what they shared. She sat down in the back and stared straight ahead to avoid being caught by the cameramen lurking outside the window.

Day one of fifteen years, she thought as the bus pulled away from the courthouse. Staring at the bleak, dark journey ahead of her would only make life seem unbearable. She had to block everything out and keep her mind strong to survive. This was the first day and the last day she would count, until they let her go. She promised herself that.

* * *

"You're going to have to do some time. Our best bet is to enter a plea agreement with the government."

The words were spoken, but they couldn't be true. Breeze was the most innocent of them all. Her father had kept her that way; her brothers had kept her that way; even Zyir had understood the value in keeping Breeze away from the flame. Still here she was, burnt by the game, just like the rest of them. As she sat at the cold, metal desk, handcuffed to her chair, she sighed deeply. Einstein was the best lawyer on the East Coast and had defended the Diamond family for years. If he was admitting defeat, she knew she stood no chance.

"How much time?" she asked.

"I can get it down to three years for tax evasion. They don't have anything drug related to hold over your head, but the money . . . the money is very dirty and well, since you're the last one standing, the burden is yours to carry. I'm sorry," Einstein said sincerely. "With good behavior, you will be out in eighteen months." A year and a half was nothing to the common criminal, but to a pampered princess like Breeze, it seemed like an eternity. She was paying for sins that were not her own.

"This is bullshit," Breeze whispered. Tears stung her eyes, but Breeze choked them down. There was no room for weakness in this moment. "I'm pregnant. My nephews need me. This baby needs me. What's going to happen to them? There is no one left! Where are they?"

"Right now, they are at your home with the housekeeper. If you can't make arrangements for their care, Social Services will take the boys and your daughter after she is born. . . ."

"No," Breeze replied as she pulled against the handcuffs in frustration. She was shackled like an animal, being arrested for a crime that was not hers to pay for. It all seemed so unfair. There had always been someone in line before her to take responsibility for her family's dirty deeds. How had blame fallen on her? "No! They can't do this. You have to get me out of here."

Breeze could see the sympathy in her attorney's eyes. She wasn't getting out of this unscathed. The pretty Diamond princess would be held accountable for every dirty dollar she spent. "They didn't choose this life," she pleaded.

"Neither did you, but this is where we are," Einstein replied.

"I need time to turn myself in. I need time to say goodbye to them. I don't want to have my daughter in prison. Can we work out some type of arrangement with the government that gives me more time? My baby is due in four weeks. That's all I need."

"I don't know if—"

"We've paid you millions over the years. I don't want to hear anything except yes, I will make it happen," Breeze demanded. Einstein nodded and then stood to leave the room. "Oh and Einstein," she added. He paused in his tracks and turned to face her. Breeze's normally demure demeanor was extinguished and replaced with a rage he had never seen from her. "I need an attorney from your firm to expedite my divorce. If I'm going to prison, I'm going wearing my father's last name, not the name of a snitch."

Einstein nodded and left the holding cell. When she was alone, Breeze's chest heaved in distress. The world felt like it was caving in. She was alone and her back was against the wall. She had become so accustomed to her family handling things. Even when the men were exiled in Saudi Arabia, Miamor had taken the lead. Now it was all on her. Everything, every responsibility had fallen into her lap by default. She now owned every burden and for the first time she realized how heavy the crown truly was.

Breeze wished that her parents were alive to help her. She wished her brothers were alive to help her. Being the last one standing wasn't a privilege at all. Breeze was sickened. She couldn't wrap her mind around the idea of going away and leaving the children without protection.

Hours passed. Federal agents came and went. They didn't want Breeze, they wanted Carter, but she lived by a code that even Zyir had not been strong enough to uphold. She wasn't telling, not even to save the future generation of Diamonds. The federal agents used every tactic within the law to get her to break but she held firm. Hours passed before Einstein came to her rescue.

Breeze sat chained like an animal, her head resting on the table. She was disheveled and if she didn't get out of the small room fast she was going to go crazy. Einstein entered the room with Agent Rivard. "We are giving you seventy-two hours to get your affairs in order. You will surrender your passport. Do not try to run, do not try to skip town. I will have eyes on you. We will be kicking in your door at hour seventy-three so don't try anything. This is a courtesy, Mrs. Rich—"

"Diamond," Breeze corrected.

"Well, Ms. Diamond, this is a courtesy. If I feel at any time that you are attempting to evade the law, I will arrest you and the three-year plea will be out the window. I'll have the prosecutor go for maximum sentencing," the agent said. "Am I clear?"

"I'm not running," Breeze answered.

The agent removed the handcuffs and Einstein wrapped his suit jacket around Breeze's shoulders as he whisked her away.

Breeze would be lying if she said she didn't think about running. It would be so simple for her to hop on a jet and put thousands of miles between herself and the law, but she would be exiled. Breeze would never be able to come back and a three-year sentence wasn't worth a lifetime of looking over her shoulder. Even though she didn't want to, Breeze would have to sit down for a while. It was a part of the game she never thought she would see, but inevitably it had come to pass. When they pulled up to her home she sat there silently, as she wondered how she would tell her nephews the bad news. *They have been through so much,* she thought.

"I will be here to pick you up and take you back to turn yourself in," Einstein said.

She nodded and then exited the car. The house was still as Breeze crept inside. Her housekeeper, Rosa, was asleep on the couch. Breeze walked over to her. "Rosa," Breeze whispered.

"Oh, Mrs. Rich! Thank God you're back. I didn't know what to do. The boys were worried. I stayed because I couldn't leave them here alone, but my daughter is home by herself. . . ."

"I know Rosa, thank you for staying. You can go,"

Breeze said. She rushed over to her purse and reached inside, pulling out her wallet. "Here is a little something extra for your troubles."

"Thank you, but is everything okay?" Rosa asked.

"No, everything is fucked up," Breeze admitted as she sniffed away her tears. She brushed her messy hair out of her face. "You can go now, Rosa."

Breeze saw the woman to the door and when she was alone she rushed to her phone. She thumbed through her contacts until she saw the name she sought.

"Aries," she whispered. She never thought she would call on Aries for a favor. Their tumultuous past hindered them from ever truly forming a real bond, but Breeze had no one else to turn to. She needed someone to take C.J. and Mo. Eventually, she would need someone to take care of her daughter. Aries was ruthless, but she was a good mother. Breeze knew that there was no safer place for the kids. Aries wouldn't let anything happen to them. Breeze pressed the Call button. She waited with bated breath. "Come on Aries, pick up," she urged.

"The number you have called is no longer in service."

Breeze sank to the floor and covered her mouth to stop herself from crying too loudly. Aries was her last hope. Carter couldn't come back. Zyir was incapacitated. Miamor was gone. There was no one to step up in her absence. Her desire to leave town in that moment overwhelmed her, but she was eight months pregnant and in no condition to go on the run. She would have to face her fate and accept the fact that for the next few years her family would be torn apart.

Breeze inhaled deeply and closed her eyes as her father's voice echoed in her mind: "Diamonds are forever." She could hear his deep baritone in her ear as if he were standing right in front of her. "You aren't built to break. It's in your blood to be strong." She calmed herself and stood to her feet, wiping the evidence of her emotion from her face. Breeze climbed the stairs to her home. It was late and the boys were asleep, but she couldn't help but wake them. Time couldn't afford to be wasted. Not when she was counting every hour until they took her away.

She opened the door to one of the guest bedrooms and allowed the light from the hallway to spill inside. C.J. and Mo looked so innocent, but their entire world was about to be stripped from them for the second time. She turned on the light, interrupting their dreams.

"Get up boys," Breeze said sternly.

"Aunt B, you're back!" C.J. exclaimed.

"What time is it?" Mo asked as he rubbed his eyes. C.J. squinted in confusion as he peeled off the covers.

"It's late, but I have something important I need to tell the two of you. Meet me in the basement please," Breeze said.

She heard their groans as they climbed from bed and then went to the basement. She hated what she was about to do, but it had to be done. She didn't want them thrust onto the streets of Miami without knowing exactly who they were or where they came from. No one would be there to protect them and they would have to use their instincts to navigate through the next few years. She was about to tell them the story of the Cartel, starting with their grandfather, Carter Diamond.

As the boys descended the steps, Breeze sat stoically, her heart heavy with angst.

"I'm going to jail," she said bluntly. The revelation stopped them in their tracks. "I'm not sugarcoating it because no one in this world is going to make anything easy for you. Especially now. Social Services will come and take you away. I have to go away for a few years but while I'm gone the two of you are all each other have. You are family and family sticks together, always."

Breeze grabbed them both by the chins and alternated her gaze between them. "Look at me. Family is all there is. You take care of each other and never let anyone come between you. Do you understand me?" she asked.

They nodded, but remained silent. She saw fear in them and sadness filled her. "This family comes from the streets. You both are sons of the Cartel, and because of that people will test you. You have enemies that were made way before you were even born so you must judge everyone with your third eye. Trust no one but family. Our family is in the drug business. You're not even old enough to know this, but if you're going to be out there without cover, you have to know it. You have to grow up fast and I'm so sorry for that, but it is important that you move smart. That's how you survive. You outthink everyone around you."

Breeze could see in their eyes that they were overwhelmed, but she had to put it on them. They had to absorb things in only hours that had taken her decades to learn. She walked over to the mahogany desk that sat in the corner. Opening the bottom drawer revealed a safe. She opened it then retrieved two 9mm handguns. She placed them on top of the desk.

"Come here," she said.

Mo's eyes widened in curiosity. Breeze loathed guns. Everyone she had ever loved had died by the gun. They terrified her, but she had learned to shoot like a marksman at the age of fourteen. Her father had taught all his children how to handle a firearm, but Breeze rarely pulled triggers. She was the only girl in a family full of brothers and an army of goons behind them. Her protection had been inherited since birth. Still, she remembered the nights of shooting beer cans on the Diamond estate, until she could put a bullet right through the middle.

"Pick them up," she said.

C.J.'s hands were so small that they barely fit around the handle. Mo handled it a little better, but still they were both clueless. Breeze stood. "Follow me outside," she said. They walked around to the back of the house and gathered on the patio. Starting with Mo, she stood behind him and wrapped her arms around his body, placing her hands around his. "Press the button on the side to release the magazine." She pulled out the empty clip and then handed Mo the bullets. "You place them in one by one," she continued. She remembered her father, teaching her this same routine. "Once it's full you put the magazine back, push it until you hear the click." She turned the gun around. "This is your safety. If it's up and you see this red dot, you can shoot. Red means dead. Remember that. If you don't see red, the gun won't shoot. Always make sure the safety is off when it's time to use it," she schooled. Breeze couldn't believe she remembered all of this. Word by word she was telling them what Big Carter had once told her. "This is your slide. You pull the slide back to put a bullet in the head. You hold the gun in your right hand and secure your left hand under the bottom," she said. "This isn't a movie. Don't hold your gun sideways. You hold it straight, steady. Look out over the top and find your aim. You see these two little pieces on top of the barrel?" she asked.

"Yeah," Mo answered.

She turned and looked at C.J., who was quivering but listening intently. "Come over here so you can see too," Breeze instructed. "Those are your sights. The front sight should be directly between the grooves of the back sight. If they are aligned you're ready to hit your target. You concentrate. You breathe. You find what you're trying to hit and close one eye to lock in. Never let your nerves talk you out of pulling a trigger. Once you pull a gun, you be ready to use it. It'll be loud and that's okay. It'll kick back on you and that's okay too. Pull the trigger."

BANG!

The gunshot was so loud that Mo dropped the gun instantly. Breeze had expected it. Feeling the power of a gun for the first time was intimidating. Her heart raced at the sound. She gritted her teeth, hating that she had to be the one to teach them this. She was the least skilled and most inexperienced in gunplay out of their family, but she was all that was left.

"Pick it up and fire again," she instructed.

Mo reached down. "But I can't even see the tree. It's too dark."

"You think niggas will only come for you in the light? You find the target and you hit it. Dark or not," Breeze stated. Mo's wrist shook nervously. "The pistol is yours. You don't have to be afraid of it. What you should fear is the pistol that the person you're aiming at could be getting ready to fire at you. You pull your trigger before your enemy pulls his. Hesitation gets you killed. You don't hesitate. You breathe and you—"

Before Breeze could finish her sentence, Mo pulled the trigger. She leaned down and kissed the top of his head. "Good," she whispered as a tear fell from her eye. She turned to C.J., who looked up at her with angst. "Your turn."

* * *

She spent three days telling them about their past, teaching them to handle a weapon, and making sure they understood that loyalty among family was everything. In her heart, she knew it wasn't enough. They were merely boys. They had so many questions and if she was honest with herself she had to admit that she was the most unqualified of all the Diamonds to answer them. She did the best she could and as she rode with Einstein to drop the boys off with Social Services, she prayed.

God, please keep them together. Please watch over them, she thought. She sat in the backseat between them so that she could hold their hands. "I won't see you for a while," Breeze said, her voice cracking against her will. She was sending her cubs into the wild, hoping they didn't get eaten alive.

"We know," C.J. answered. The woe in his voice put a weight on her heart that she would carry with her until they were reunited. She hadn't even been able to focus on her strife. The fact that she would have to survive in prison on her own had been an afterthought. She was too consumed with preparing her nephews to make it on their own.

"I love you both so much and as soon as they free me, I'm going to come get you. We are family and I promise you we will be together again," Breeze whispered. The frog in her throat stopped her from going on further.

"We're here," Einstein said.

"I love you Aunt B," Mo whispered.

"Oh, I love you too, Mo," Breeze cried, her tears falling now as she hugged him tightly. She pulled C.J. closer to her, bringing him into her embrace as well. "I love you both so much, and I'm so sorry for all of this." She kissed the top of their heads. "Diamonds . . ."

"Are forever," Mo replied.

C.J. looked up at her with sadness reflected in his eyes. "But my daddy ain't a Diamond."

Breeze shook her head and gripped C.J.'s chin. "Your daddy is a Diamond, baby. He is the first-born son of

Carter Diamond. It doesn't get any purer than that," she assured. Einstein opened the back door and they all climbed out. Breeze was a mess. She couldn't help herself. This was it. It felt like the final chapter was closing on her family's story. She knelt before them and pulled them both into her, their heads locked in a circle. She closed her eyes. "You use your name. You won't have much out here. In fact, you have nothing, but this is Miami. We owned this city once upon a time and the Diamond name is worth something on these streets. Use it when you have to and keep your name clean always. There are men on these streets who will go to war for you behind your name alone. Many men owe debts to our name and they will be your allies when you need them. Your names are all you have but if you use it right, it's all you'll need. Be strong my boys."

"They have to go, Breeze," Einstein said reluctantly.

Breeze nodded, wiping the tears from her face as a woman came to separate them. She stood fiercely like a lioness protecting her cubs. "You take care of them," she said passionately.

"Come on boys, this way," the woman stated. They didn't take their eyes off Breeze. They kept looking back at her hopelessly as they were ushered away and when they disappeared into the glass building, Breeze broke down.

She placed a hand over her mouth and cried hysterically as she climbed into the passenger side of Einstein's car. It was time to turn herself in and for the first time in days Breeze thought of her fate. Breeze was paralyzed with dread as Einstein pulled up to the federal building.

"How did it come to this?" she asked.

"As soon as the eighteen-month mark hits, I'll start working on a release for good behavior," Einstein assured. "Just keep your head down until then."

"You find my grandfather, Emilio Estes. He went off the grid when all of this went down, but he will send someone for the kids. You have to use whatever resources it takes to contact him," Breeze urged.

"I will exhaust all options," Einstein assured. "But it's time you start worrying about yourself. Where you're headed, you can't afford distractions, Breeze."

"I'm not worried. Miamor is there. She will have my back. There is no one out here watching out for them," Breeze said.

"Miamor will not be where you are headed. You are being transferred to South Carolina. The facility is maximum security," Einstein informed.

"What?" Breeze was shocked. "I don't want to be locked away with murderers and rapists without my family there to protect me!"

"It was a part of the three-year deal. You must do hard time, Breeze. The prosecutor insisted," Einstein said.

Breeze was relying on her family's reputation to see her through her bid. The Diamond influence would have been heavy in a prison in Florida. It wouldn't be the same if they moved her across state lines.

Never did she think she would be the one in this position. It was such a heavy price to pay for spending the dirty money that her family had accumulated. The pedestal that she had lived on her entire life had come crashing down and there was no one around to cushion her fall.

* * *

Breeze held her head high but her chin quivered uncontrollably. She had never been so scared in her entire life but she refused to show it. She walked into the prison praying that she made it out alive. Her nerves were so bad that she couldn't seem to control the shaking of her hands as she held out her wrists for the warden.

"Welcome to South Sonoma Correctional," the warden said. He was tall with the palest skin Breeze had ever seen. His bumpy skin and receding hairline accompanied the stern expression on his face. "Your reputation precedes you, but let me warn you now. Your affiliations outside these walls don't mean anything in here. If you start trouble in here—"

"I don't want any trouble. I just want to do my time," Breeze answered, clearing her throat to stop her voice from revealing just how vulnerable she was. If any one of these guards or inmates knew exactly how soft Breeze was, they would use it against her. She needed to keep to herself and remain low-key.

She felt like property as she was transferred from the warden to a guard before she was led into a private room.

"Take off your clothes and put all your possessions in this bag."

Breeze hesitated. "Is there a room or a curtain?" she asked.

"Sure, princess, I got a private suite for you too with a king bed."

Breeze didn't miss the sarcasm. She turned around and stepped out of her dress.

"This ain't your personal wardrobe, Diamond, speed it up," the guard said as she threw the khaki-colored uniform at her. Breeze bit her tongue and bent down to pick up the clothing before putting it on. The polyester made her skin itch. Breeze was accustomed to a certain lifestyle. She would have to expect nothing; that way, whatever was not received couldn't be missed.

When she got down to her wedding band she asked, "Will I get this stuff back?" She hadn't been able to take it off, even after discovering his deceit. She couldn't help but wish that she had visited him in the hospital. He needed her. A bullet to the brain had erased every memory of her from Zyir's mind and Breeze hadn't wanted to remind him. She wanted to move on with their baby by herself and leave him in her past. She couldn't help but think this was her karma for abandoning him.

"When you process out, all your items will be returned," the guard said. Breeze closed her eyes and kissed the ring before placing it in the bag. It was a slim chance she would ever see the six-figure diamond again. *Don't think about him. Don't think about anything or anybody outside of this place,* she thought. She was cuffed again and escorted onto B block. "Welcome to your new home, princess. As long as the institution isn't overcrowded you will have your own cell while you're pregnant. Don't get used to it. As soon as you pop out that kid, we'll move someone else in," the guard said, handling her roughly as she removed the cuffs and then nudged Breeze into the cell. The walls immediately felt like they were closing in on her. It wasn't what she envisioned it to be. There were no bars, only white brick walls, steel doors with electric locks, and fluorescent lights. A bunk bed with a stained mattress and a toilet that smelled were the only amenities. Breeze was afraid to move. The thought of laying her head on the soiled bed made her skin crawl. The flutter in her stomach caused her baby to kick and Breeze knew she would have to control her emotions. *I can't break in here,* she thought.

She sat down on the bottom bunk and cringed. Breeze knew nothing about struggle. She didn't come up rough. She didn't have roaches and she had never dealt with mice or fought with jealous girls on the block. There had been no syrup sandwiches or hand-me-down rags. Breeze knew nothing about making something out of nothing and behind these walls that would be a weakness. Coming from the top would make the bottom feel lower than low. She bent over and rested her elbows on her knees. The walls were so tight around her that it felt like she would suffocate. Breeze was in a desperate way and it would take everything in her to make it out of prison alive.

Chapter 3

The whir of the ceiling fan was the only sound that could be heard as Bernice Jackson filled out the intake paperwork in front of her. Office hours had come and gone, yet here she sat, under strict orders to process these two kids tonight. She looked through the one-way window, observing the young men who sat in the room. They had no idea they were being watched, their movements and every word recorded for later review. Bernice had been working for Florida Social Services for twenty years and she had never had so much urgency placed on her shoulders regarding the handling of incoming children. The U.S. attorney himself was headed all the way to her office to personally oversee the placement of these two boys. She couldn't help but wonder who they were and why they garnered so much interest.

She sighed in frustration. She wasn't particularly happy

that she was working overtime and as she hammered out the work she waited impatiently for the U.S. attorney to arrive. It was quite odd that someone from such a high level was even getting involved at all. The sound of the electronic doors opening let her know that the man of the hour had finally arrived. She stood from her desk as two suits entered the room.

"That's them?"

The entitlement of white privilege entered the room as the prestigious man didn't even bother with the formality of introductions before getting down to business.

"Yes, that's Monroe Diamond II and Carter Jones Jr.," Bernice replied.

"Ages?"

"Monroe is twelve and Carter is eight. If I may ask, sir—"

"You may not," the U.S. attorney said. He turned and looked at the security cameras. "Turn those off."

"Sir, I can lose my job for that. Every second that these kids are here needs to be recorded. I can't just shut it off," Bernice responded.

"This is above your pay grade. Shut the cameras off please."

Bernice reluctantly followed the instructions. *What the hell does he want with these kids? Who are they?* she thought. She had immediately assumed they were the sons of drug-addicted parents, perhaps an abusive mother or deadbeat father. She had seen so many different scenarios of neglect in her line of work but none of her previous cases had received such high-ranking attention.

"Where is the paperwork?"

The U.S. attorney didn't even look at her as he spoke. His eyes remained glued on the window as he watched them intently. She hurriedly retrieved their folders and handed them over.

He flipped through the pages, briefly scanning the documents before he turned to her and said, "There are one of two things that can happen to you tonight. You can forget what you are about to see and I will call in a personal favor to promote you, or you can take the moral road and be fired right now, on the spot. The choice is yours."

Bernice felt cornered and her stomach sank because she wasn't sure if she wanted to be involved in whatever plot was about to unfold. "They are only kids," she whispered.

"They are pawns and they are going to help me catch the king," he answered before walking into the room.

* * *

Mo's face twisted in mistrust as soon as he laid eyes on the man in the stiff suit.

"Hello Monroe, hello Carter, I'm a friend of your family . . ."

C.J. looked at Mo for confirmation and Mo simply shook his head, letting C.J. know that this man was not an ally of theirs. Mo sniffed out the hidden agenda instantly and his guard was up.

"I'm sorry about what happened to your father, Monroe. I'm sorry you had to see that. I know that must have been hard." The U.S. attorney was trying the sympathetic route first, but there was nothing he could say to Mo and C.J. to get them on his side.

"Don't talk about my dad," Mo said in a low tone. He could feel the dull ache that formed in his chest. Every time he thought about the bullets that had ripped through his father it made his heart feel tender. He didn't know that it was sadness that gripped him and he was uncomfortable with the vulnerability that came along with the memories.

"I know it's hard for you to speak about. No child deserves to see their parent—"

"I told you don't talk about my dad!" Mo said as he looked the grown man square in the eye. The look on his face was filled with hurt and fury, but still the attorney pressed.

"You boys belong with family. I need you to help me find your father, Carter," the attorney said, hoping to get better luck with C.J. "If we can just contact him, he can come and take you both home. You don't have to stay here. If we can locate a relative, you can go home."

The smile plastered on his face didn't quite reach his eyes as he looked back and forth between the boys. Monroe avoided the man's intense stare as he flipped his hoodie over his head and crossed his arms.

"What do you say, Carter?" the man pushed.

"I ain't got nothing to say either," C.J. answered.

The U.S. attorney nodded, losing patience. "Okay, you little shits." He grabbed Mo around his bicep, squeezing so tightly that it felt like it would snap.

"Ow, man! Let me go!" Mo shouted as he tried to pull away, kicking and pushing the man to no avail.

"Get off him!" C.J. was out of his seat in the blink of an eye, throwing futile punches. If one fought, they both fought. It was how they were raised. Protecting one another was always their first instinct even in an unwinnable situation. It was what made them close. They were more like brothers than cousins and to be sitting here in this office with this strange man who was desperate to take down their family put them on the defense. They were being ripped apart, from the very top of the food chain down to the small fish. They were throwing kicks and fists trying to defend not only themselves but their family. Their frustrations had mounted and this was the result.

"Can I get some help in here?" the attorney shouted as he pushed C.J. with full force. C.J. lost his balance and fell headfirst into the metal table. The metal corner connected with his temple and a loud crack echoed throughout the room. Suddenly everything in his line of sight turned white.

Blood spewed and C.J. reached for his head as he cringed in pain. He felt wetness, blood, he assumed, as it seeped through his fingers and he blinked repeatedly, trying to make his surroundings appear before his eyes again. "I can't see! I can't see!" he shouted, frantically, the sudden blindness scaring him. It was like someone had shined a light directly in his face. He stumbled, dazed from the blow, as dizziness disoriented him. His heart was racing so fast, adrenaline coursing through him as he struggled to stand to his feet. He was confused and it felt like bolts of lightning were going off inside his head. He fell back against the wall. "I can't fa—fa—fa—" C.J.'s speech became incoherent as his body shuddered violently. He was seizing from the impact of the blow.

"What did you do to him? What you do to my cousin, man?!" Mo shouted in anger as he struggled against the attorney's grip. "Help him! What did you do?!"

Bernice rushed in and hurried over to C.J. The sight of him convulsing uncontrollably terrified her. "Call 911," she screamed urgently as she kneeled over his body. She looked back over her shoulder and noticed the U.S. attorney's hesitation. "If you don't want to explain this boy's death, I advise you to pick up the phone and call for help now!"

Still, he took his time, knowing that an explanation would be required to excuse what had happened.

"Sir!" Bernice insisted. *This boy is going to die in here and I'm going to lose my job,* she thought.

She pulled out her cell phone and dialed for help.

"They were fighting and while trying to separate them, he fell and hit his head on the table," the attorney said. "You got it?" He stared intently at Bernice, who nodded her head while looking on in fear at C.J.

"You're lying, you did this! You pushed him!" Mo shouted, defensively.

The U.S. attorney bent Mo's arm behind his back, twisting it so far that it felt like it would snap.

Bernice watched in horror. She didn't want to lose her job trying to save two boys she didn't know, but the entire situation felt wrong.

Mo stretched out his arm across the desk and grabbed the first thing he could get his hands on. When his hand wrapped around the pencil he stabbed backward, hitting the U.S. attorney directly in the eye.

"Agh!"

Mo was tackled to the ground with force and he grimaced as a knee was put into his back. Suddenly there was chaos in the room as paramedics and police officers entered moments later. "C.J.!" Mo could barely breathe. The weight from the grown man holding him down was constricting his lungs from filling with air. He felt the pinch of the metal cuffs as they shackled him before pulling him off the floor. The U.S. attorney was being loaded onto a stretcher as another team of paramedics worked on C.J. "Is he okay?" Mo cried, his heart filled with worry. They were the last two standing and if something happened to C.J., Mo would be alone to navigate through the world.

"You need to worry about yourself right now. You're in a lot of trouble, son," the officer said. Mo craned his neck, struggling to see C.J. as the police escorted him out of the room. He could feel it in his soul that this would be the last time he would lay eyes on his family and the hurt he felt was tremendous. As they stuffed him into the back of a squad car he felt caged, like an animal that just wanted to roam free. First, they had separated the men from the women in their family, and then they had divided the women from their children. Now they were tearing the children from one another. The government was breaking them down to a point past repair. Things couldn't get any worse, and as the car pulled away Mo dropped his head as tears of fear fell silently down his cheeks.

* * *

Waking up had never been so hard. As C.J. laid in the hospital bed, he was conscious beneath the surface, he just couldn't quite get to the light. He lay still, hearing the comings and goings around him as he desperately willed himself to move. The social worker had come to check on his state, someone from the U.S. Attorney's office had stopped in to remind the social worker what the story was, and even the police had shown up to take an official report. He heard it all and after three days of trying with all his might, he finally opened his eyes. There was instant pain and he touched the side of his head, grimacing as he pressed lightly on the bandages.

"Hey, C.J. Welcome back, buddy. My name is Ms. Bernice."

The social worker, C.J. thought, recognizing her voice. He kept reminding himself that she wasn't his friend. She was on the side of the state, the person who had intentions of splitting up him and Mo. *Don't trust her,* he thought. Bernice sat in a chair in the corner of his room. He didn't understand her worried expression. She wasn't his family. She didn't know him. Why was she even still here? "Where is Mo?" It was a genuine question. *Is he hurt too?*

"Mo is being sent to juvenile detention, C.J. He is in some trouble. You won't be able to see him for a while," Bernice responded.

"And what about me?" C.J. asked. "Am I going there too?" C.J. wanted the answer to be yes. They had faced worse than lockup together. As long as he was with his older cousin, he didn't care where he ended up. It was the separation that gave him anxiety.

"No C.J., you aren't. You're going home."

C.J. looked at her in confusion. There was no one *home* to receive him. Death and destruction had surrounded him. Was this lady playing some type of cruel joke? "I don't have a home anymore."

"Hopefully one day you will see this new place as your home," Bernice replied. "I don't feel comfortable leaving you in the custody of the state. I could lose my job for this C.J., but I also would not be working in your best interest if I took you back to Social Services. After seeing how the U.S. attorney behaved, I fear for your safety."

C.J. was quiet partly because he didn't know what to say. Who was this lady? Making him her problem? Why was she taking the responsibility to care for him? Nobody was this nice and those who were usually had an angle. He couldn't figure out hers, but knew in due time it would reveal itself.

"To manipulate a child against their parent is unfair.

Whatever your family did has nothing to do with you. I am sorry this all has happened to you," Bernice said.

The entire situation made C.J. uncomfortable. *She's just trying to get me to talk about the family. She's the good cop,* C.J. thought as he remained silent. He remembered his mother telling him that it was easier to get your way using sugar than shit. *This is the sugar,* he thought.

"Mo's fate is out of my hands," she continued. "His file has been transferred to juvenile court where he will face charges of assault."

That revelation got his attention and C.J.'s breath caught in his throat, choking him, as emotion built in his chest. He was the younger cousin. He was used to following, not leading. Even under extreme duress C.J. could maintain his courage when Mo was at his side, but here, in this hospital room with this lady laying it on thick, he felt exposed. He felt vulnerable. He felt defenseless. He had no options. This lady was making the decisions and he had to obey, despite the warning his gut was telling him that she was leading him to the slaughter.

"Your future hasn't been written yet, and I will do all I can to make sure that the U.S. attorney never gets his hands on you. Once you're discharged, you will come home with me. This is a good thing. I think you will be really comfortable there."

She would mark up his file as a runaway. No one would think twice to question it. In fact, no one would even care. Foster children ran away all the time and C.J. would just be another one lost. He had no family on the outside to come around asking questions. It was just C.J. He was the last one standing so it was easy to make him slip through the cracks and disappear without anyone taking notice.

"I'm going to get the doctor," Bernice said as she stood and walked out of the room.

C.J. laid his head back on the pillow, overwhelmed. Even when Baraka had taken him, he had never been completely isolated. Mo was always there, always reminding him that although they were far away from home, he would always watch his back. He would rather be locked up in juvenile with Mo than live in some stranger's house. Trust was simply not extended to any outsider. Bernice could smile and make promises of security all day, but there was a void behind her eyes. It was as if the sentiments she expressed were shallow and C.J. could see right through her. Normally when a person was too friendly it meant they really weren't friendly at all and C.J. was filled with dread as he pondered the rough days to come.

CHAPTER 4

Carter and Anari sat next to each other as they rode in a golf cart that was steered by one of the servants from the emperor's mansion. The property had a full eighteen-hole golf course, full of nothing but healthy green grass and sand bunkers. They were followed by a few more carts with the rest of the team in them as they traveled to the rear of the property where there was nothing but woods and bushes.

"Where are we going?" Anari asked as she looked at the forest and then back at Carter.

"Your guess is as good as mine," he answered nonchalantly as he shrugged his shoulders. Ghost was in the front of all the carts, driving his own as they came to a complete stop just before the green grass ended and the wooded area began. Ghost stepped off his cart, wearing another well-fitted Italian suit. He then waited for everyone to get off the carts and signaled for the servants to head back to the house before he began to address his team.

"I know what it looks like. Like a bunch of woods, right?" Ghost said as he showed his signature smile. He then buttoned his suit jacket and nodded in the direction of the forest. "Come on, let me show you what's really going on." Ghost headed toward the woods and eventually onto a dirt trail that led into the abyss of the dark shaded area. Everyone looked at one another, trying to make sense of their walking into the woods, but everyone shrugged their shoulders and followed him into the unknown.

Carter was the youngest of the bunch and seemingly the bravest because he was right behind Ghost as their journey began. They all followed carefully and the sounds of twigs breaking and leaves being ruffled filled the air. The deeper they went, it seemed like the darker it got. The tall trees and an abundance of leaves seemed to block out the sunlight, only allowing small beams of light to break through the cracks and crevices of mother nature. After about five minutes of walking and no one saying a word, Brick was the first to talk.

"Yo homie, how long do we have until we get there? Scuffing up my loafers and shit," he said arrogantly as he shook his head in disappointment.

"It's just ahead! Up here," Ghost said as he pointed while steadily making his way up the path. Everyone's eyes shot forward and a huge brick building sat oddly in the middle of the woods. It seemed totally out of place and random. However, they all knew that it was their destination. The huge building had no signs and no windows. It was unlike any other building that they had ever seen. Just a brick building with a steel door entrance. The outside of it was filled with shrubs, trees, and dirt. There was absolutely no landscaping whatsoever and that was by design. This location was meant to be top secret and off the radar. The intention was to not attract anyone that wasn't involved with the doings going on inside.

They finally got to the front door and it was a ten-foot mass of steel and had no door handles or peepholes. There was just a keypad with a red backlight. Ghost stepped in front of the keypad and commenced typing in a sequence of numbers that seemed to take him forever to do. Finally, the keyboard's backlight turned green and Ghost stepped back and stood with his hands crossed in front of himself. A single beep sounded and almost instantly the steel doors parted, opening into the world of tomorrow.

As soon as they stepped into the cold building, the sounds of their footsteps echoed throughout. They all looked around in confusion, wondering why he had brought them into a big empty warehouse.

"I know what you guys are thinking. Why is it so cold? Why is it empty, right?" Ghost said slyly as he led the way through the building. He clasped his hands together and turned on the spurs of his heels so he was facing the group.

"This is where the magic happens. We have gathered the top scientists in the country and invited them to be part of this creation. After years of trial and error, we have finally created the perfect drug. As I said before it's a 'super brain' drug that gives you a rush of cocaine and, as it fades, a feeling of euphoria, which helps relaxation and your libido. At its final stage, it works as a strong melatonin that puts you to sleep like a baby. This drug totally regulates your life and will give you the most productive day while allowing you to sleep like a baby to do it all over the next day. This is literally the perfect drug. No other drug can give you all three of these phases with a single pill. Ladies and gentlemen, we have discovered a rare flower that produces this phenomenal substance. It's a slice of the devil's pie, without the downfall."

The sight of the multi-million-dollar facility was mind-blowing to them all. The frosted-glass floors and walls were impeccable. The place looked like a brand-new hospital without the patients. It smelled so clean and fresh and the silence was relaxing. Only the sound of the gushing air-conditioning unit hummed throughout the corridor. The bright lights almost strained their eyes. Everything was so bright and transparent. It almost felt as if they stepped into the future. The immaculate, well-lit lab had five rows of tables all filled with test tubes, boiling pots, and other substances that they had no idea what they were. Various scientists of Indian descent were scattered throughout the spacious room at the steel tables creating, testing, observing the creation of the drug. Ghost motioned for a scientist to come over and a male that looked to be in his late forties came over, wearing a full doctor's robe and a face mask. He approached the team and pulled down his mask, displaying his cleanly shaved face.

"Hello all. Hello Ghost," he said as he nodded at them. "My name is Dr. Ishban. We have been waiting on your arrival for some time now. We are at the final stages of a batch now. Allow me to give you guys a tour and show you what we've been working on. Shall we?" he asked as he began to stroll down the aisles where scientists were working diligently on each side.

The entire team watched and listened closely as Dr. Ishban explained the process of turning the leaves into paste, then powder form, and finally into a pill. He led them to the back of the facility where a large greenhouse was. They entered the all-glass room and a beautiful row of reddish flowers bloomed and gave the air a sweet smell, like jasmine. The sea of red was an amazing sight. The large flower bloomed widely and had traces of purple near the center, giving it an exotic appearance. They walked and listened closely as Dr. Ishban explained the life cycle of the flower all the way until its final stage. Carter and Anari walked side by side, both listening very closely while the others asked questions and randomly talked among one another. At the end of the tour they were led to a back room. A projector and screen were at the head of the room and the seats and tables resembled a college classroom.

"Have a seat everyone," Ghost said as he walked to the front of the room where a podium sat. He then lifted the laptop that was placed on the podium and turned it on. Everyone took a seat and all eyes were on Ghost as he used the remote control to dim the lights. The projector began and he started the briefing. The first thing that appeared on the screen was the map of the United States and some sections were colored in red and some in orange.

"This is the United States map and as you can see, some areas are tinted in red. These places are the launching points of the distribution of this new drug. We have about eighteen months before the FDA approves this and it will be open season to any pharmacy in the country. During this eighteen-month span we plan to move 200 million dollars' worth before the millionaire investors and the medicine world even get wind of it. As you can see we are starting where you guys have done well. These targeted areas are your stomping grounds. Each one of you will have a region. The Detroit, Flint, Chicago, South Florida, and DMV areas." Ghost used a red beam to highlight each area of the map as he spoke. "You guys have proven that you know how to distribute and control these areas and that's why you guys were hand selected by my partners. Each of you stands to make at least twenty-five million over this span. Just enough for each one of you to retire and ride into the sunset unscathed," Ghost explained.

"This sounds good, but what about the law? What if we get caught, do you guys step forward and get us out of the jam? You mentioned political connections at the Vatican. Would these connections and resources be utilized?" Brick asked as he dug deeper into different scenarios.

"Unfortunately, we theoretically don't exist. If one of you gets caught or jammed by any authorities, we will have no affiliation with you whatsoever. At that point, our relationship would be instantly terminated. This is the risk that you take to be part of this thing of ours. The bright side is that this game has a due date. Eighteen months is all that is needed to complete our goal. After that, the corporate world will have this drug and it is open season for knockoffs and copycats. We have the source and in return, we have no competition," Ghost explained.

"What are the blue areas?" Anari asked as she frowned in puzzlement.

"Good question. These are the cold zones. These are the areas where law enforcement has special drug units focused specifically on stopping narcotics. We have highlighted these areas so it cuts the risk of getting heat from the feds nearly in half. We have studied each area throughout the States and narrowed it down to five cities that would be lucrative and the least likely to get attention from the feds," Ghost replied.

"I see, I see," Anari said as she nodded her head, understanding the infrastructure of the elaborate operation.

"This is absolutely genius," Millie said aloud as she also nodded her head while rubbing her hands together. She could see the money piling up in her mind already. It was just the lick that she had been praying for. Everyone had been waiting for an opportunity like this. This is something that drug dealers never had: an exit plan. This was their one-way ticket to paradise and it was in the near future.

Carter, on the other hand, remained quiet and listened closely. He had no choice but to participate, knowing this would be the only chance to ever get his wife and son back. He was going for broke. He had made all the money in the world, more than he could ever spend, so money was no longer his motivation. He honestly just wanted to live a normal life with his family. He had been involved with the Cartel for years and was tired. He was drained and the weight on his shoulders was that of the world. He could see the excitement in everyone's eyes and he couldn't share their sentiments because his heart ached for his family. It was so bad that he literally felt pain in his chest thinking about them. He was a man broken and it was starting to weigh on him physically. He clenched his chest, feeling a slight pain on his left side. He knew it was from his previous injury, when he got shot. His body wasn't the same as it used to be and he never felt full strength.

Anari noticed Carter wince and leaned over and whispered to him. "Yo, you good?" she asked, with genuine concern.

"Yeah, I'm good, it's just heartburn," he said to avoid showing weakness. She nodded and focused back on Ghost as he began to discuss the route and pipeline of the drugs. Carter zoned out, only thinking about his love. However, the plan was under way. They would be the new regime and connection to the States for the new drug. They concluded their meeting with everything they needed to know to take over. After a few hours of breaking down the logistics, pickup points, and syndicate they were ready to dismiss for the day.

"One more thing: cell phones and laptops are in each of your rooms," Ghost said as he smiled widely.

They all laughed, feeling like they were at a strict camp and finally got a little bit of freedom.

"We had to make sure you guys were fully on board before we could trust you. But I think it's safe to say that we all are business partners and hopefully will grow to be great friends," Ghost said. "Over the next two weeks we will go over and over the plan so when you return to the States you guys can hit the ground running. We have already set up dummy transportation businesses to cater the drug directly to your hub in your particular city."

"You guys have every base covered," Brick said, as he was thoroughly impressed.

"As I said before, we have been working on this operation for years and have thought about every possible scenario to make this successful. This is a win-win for everybody," Ghost said.

He then raised his hands and clapped loudly twice and almost instantly the door opened and two waiters came in with trays with flute glasses on them. "I believe it's time for celebration," Ghost said as he grabbed a flute and raised it in the air. "A toast," he said. "To the beginning of something great." Everyone else followed suit and joined in on the toast.

"To the future!" Ghost said.

"To the future," everyone repeated in unison as the sound of glasses clinking echoed throughout the room.

Anari and Carter locked eyes as they toasted and it was as if they shared a connection. It wasn't a sexual energy but more of a real connection. They both knew something was unusual about the entire situation. However, it seemed as if they were playing chess and withholding their moves from the rest of the team. They were on the same wavelength and wanted to know more about this grand scheme.

Chapter 5

Mo sat with his head down, waiting for his case to be called. He had never been in this kind of trouble before and knowing that he was facing the dilemma alone terrified him. If he could just get his heart to stop thundering inside his chest, he would be able to calm himself. If only . . .

He had spent three days in juvenile city lockup going crazy. It had been so cold inside the holding cell that he was grateful for this warmth inside the courtroom. Detective after detective had tried to get him to divulge information about Carter's whereabouts, but Mo had kept his mouth shut. He didn't know much, but the one thing he knew was to never go against his family. He worried about his cousin. No one would tell him how C.J. was and he had no idea what fate lay ahead for either of them. They had hauled him to court each day and made him wait all day, handcuffed and afraid, only for his case to be postponed until the following day. Finally, he heard his name and made his way to the podium that sat directly in front of the judge. "Next up on the docket, Monroe Diamond versus the City of Miami.

"You are charged with aggravated assault. How do you plead?" the judge asked.

Mo didn't even know what aggravated assault was. He looked at the public defender who stood beside him. Mo didn't know where the man had come from. He had shown up out of nowhere claiming he would help Mo. So far, he hadn't helped much at all.

"Do you need a moment to confer with your client?" the judge asked, noticing Mo's confused expression.

"Just a brief one, your honor," the man replied. He pulled Mo aside and said, "This is where you plead guilty?"

"Guilty?" Mo asked. "He hurt my cousin. I was just defending—"

"Look kid, you plead guilty and the judge will take it easy on you. You can take this to trial but there are witnesses and footage that will show you stabbing a U.S. attorney in the eye. You take a plea, it will be much better for you." The court-assigned lawyer was trying to close cases at a rapid rate. He had a hundred cases of juvenile offenders on his desk. None of them would go to trial if he had anything to do with it. He was just turning cases over, convincing his clients to take whatever crap deal was being offered without even considering the pursuit of justice by trial and jury. "Just trust me kid. If you fight this you will have much worse coming to you."

Mo felt it in his gut that listening to this man was the wrong move, but he hadn't learned to trust his intuition yet. He was only twelve years old and this adult was talking over his head.

"Counsel are you ready to proceed?" the judge asked with intolerance.

"Yes, your honor."

Mo inched back to the podium and faced the judge. She was a stern-looking woman with red hair and dark eyes that were hidden behind wire-framed glasses.

"On the charge of aggravated assault, how do you plead?"

Mo looked at his lawyer once more. The man nodded. Mo felt sick to his stomach as he opened his mouth to speak. "Guilty." His voice wasn't much bigger than a whisper. He was unnerved as his chin began to quiver and his shoulders sagged.

"And you have reached an agreement with the people, correct?" the judge looked at him, waiting for an answer. Mo shrugged his shoulders, unsure of how to respond.

"I don't know," he said. "I don't understand."

"Where are your parents, young man?" the judge asked.

"I don't have parents," Mo responded. "They're gone. They died."

"Counsel, have you advised your client about the deal he is entering into?" the judge asked.

"Yes, ma'am," counsel replied.

Mo looked back at his lawyer and then up at the judge. If advising meant pushing him toward a plea then sure, the lawyer had done his job, but Mo hadn't gotten any helpful information from the overworked, underpaid, court-appointed attorney at all. Even when Mo asked questions, they were dismissed, shrugged off. "Do you want to get more time?" the lawyer had asked. "Keep your mouth closed and do as I say." That was the gist of the advice. The judge looked at him skeptically before speaking.

"Okay, well, Monroe Diamond. You are hereby sentenced to seven years. Six of which will be served in juvenile detention and upon your eighteenth birthday you will be transferred to Dade County Department of Corrections. You will . . ."

Mo didn't even hear the rest. Everything seemed to move in slow motion as the bailiff came to escort him out of the courtroom. "Hey . . . wait! Wait, man!" Mo shouted. He looked at his lawyer, eyes wide with fear, but the man wouldn't even look at him. "You said it would be okay!" He had been railroaded. Tricked into pleading out his case, because it was much cheaper for the state if they avoided trial. It was the way of American justice, or rather injustice, and Mo had just fallen victim to it. Mo's stomach went hollow because he knew that his life would never be the same. Seven years might as well be life. It was an eternity. He was being locked up for defending his family. "This isn't fair!" he shouted. "This isn't right!"

The ominous feeling of loneliness he felt made him

emotional. All he wanted to do was cry but the eyes of the other juvenile inmates watching him caused him to hold in his tears. He couldn't display fear or weakness. Not where he was going. He was passed to an awaiting guard, who escorted him outside. He was put on a white bus and shackled to the seat. Things had spiraled out of control so quickly that it felt unreal. It wasn't long ago that he was in Baraka's clutches. He had just gotten readjusted at home when the feds came raining down on the Cartel's regime. Now everyone he had ever loved was gone, either dead or locked up. They had been erased from his life as if they had never even existed. It seemed to be a generational curse that came with his last night and predictably, he had followed the same path straight to imprisonment.

He hoped life treated C.J. more kindly. *If he is even alive,* Mo thought sadly. The knot in his stomach tightened as the bus rolled away. No one spoke. A daunting silence filled the space as each boy on the bus battled with himself to be brave. How easy the notion of courage was when it wasn't tested. He remembered this feeling, of insecurity, of trepidation. He had felt it when he had been taken away from his family and he felt it in this moment. He was walking into the unknown and all he could hear was his aunt Breeze's voice in his ear saying, "Your names are all you have but if you use it right, it's all you'll need." He wasn't so sure that it would be enough to see him through the seven years ahead of him. Through the eyes of a twelve-year-old boy, that amount of time felt like an eternity. It was a punishment that would change him . . . harden him. Mo would be raised by bars and steel, sectioned off from the outside world. The idea shook him to his core.

The bus stopped and Mo looked up at the daunting brick building. The anticipation of what waited inside frightened him. He wouldn't walk back out of these gates until he was a grown man. It was a long punishment, an unjust punishment, but it was his to serve all the same. The circumstances that had landed him there didn't matter. With the bang of a gavel his fate had been ordered. He had been condemned and there was no changing it. He was stuck and there was no way out.

* * *

"Let me out of here! Please! I just want to go home!" C.J.'s voice echoed against the stone walls as he pounded his fists frantically against them. Terror seized him. He didn't know where he was or who had taken him, but he knew that he was in danger. He wanted to cry. Emotion swelled in his chest, making it hard for him to breathe, and his eyes stung as he tried his hardest to hold his tears at bay. His heart had never felt this heavy. It was like an anvil weighed down his chest as he struggled to breathe in, then out, in, then out. Bravery was hard to hold on to in the face of fear, and he tried to think of what his father would do in that moment.

He knew that Diamond blood coursed through his veins. He had heard stories of his father, his uncles, and even his grandfather. He came from a long line of gangsters, men who lived by the gun; some even had died by it as well. Carter and Miamor had tried to keep his lineage from him. Immersing him in private schools and speaking in hushed tones whenever family business was the topic. They hadn't wanted to choose the lifestyle for him, but instead he had inherited it. His family was legendary in the city of Miami and fear wasn't part of their DNA. His father wouldn't break if he were in his shoes. His uncles wouldn't cry. They would fight until the strength left their bodies. He was bred from that. Right? He wanted to make them proud, to uphold the expectation that came with his last name, but it was almost impossible to fill the empty pit that had formed in his stomach.

He didn't understand why he felt so afraid. He couldn't stop the tears from falling down his face if he tried. One minute he had been playing basketball and buying ice cream with his cousin, Monroe, and the next he was taken. He wondered if Monroe Jr. was still alive. They had separated them. Three days had passed since they had been kidnapped and he had been thrown into a basement. He hadn't eaten and his stomach churned as hunger pangs tortured him. The unsurmountable terror that seized him made him wish that he would die. A quick demise would be better than the fear of the unknown.

The locks on the steel door clicked and he looked up hopefully. He held his breath as a man walked in. He was cloaked in the finest clothes that C.J. had ever seen. His eyes were dark, menacing, vengeful, and C.J. braced himself, half-expecting to be shot down by the armed men that entered the room behind their leader.

"My name is Baraka. I am the man who is going to decide if you live or if you die."

C.J. didn't speak. He couldn't find his voice to respond. The lump in his throat blocked the pleas that were running through his mind from ever getting out. His body shook involuntarily.

"Your family took my daughter from me. Your mother buried her in the dirt. She died slowly in the middle of the desert, wondering why I wasn't coming to save her. An eye for an eye would mean that I do the same to you," Baraka said.

C.J.'s bottom lip trembled. He had never seen the side of Miamor that Baraka spoke of.

"Stand him up," Baraka ordered. His men moved on command and pulled C.J. to his feet. His legs were so weak that his knees buckled. He hadn't had water or food in days. He couldn't hold up his own body weight. "You stand or you die," Baraka said.

C.J.'s head hung low as he grit his teeth and pressed his hands against the dirty concrete floor. He pushed himself up. It took all he had to get to his feet. His skinny knees knocked and he looked up into Baraka's menacing eyes. Behind the glaring stare was a hint of remorse.

"I am sorry for what I am about to do and for what you are about to see. It should not be the burden of the child to pay for the actions of the father, but it must be."

C.J.'s eyes welled with tears as he was pushed out of the room. He was escorted down a long hall, passing steel doors that were shackled with heavy locks. His young imagination ran rampant as he wondered what or who was behind them. He wondered if Lil' Money and Aunt Leena were behind any of them. His heart ached for them. He desperately needed to see the face of someone he knew. The amount of terror he was experiencing was too much. He was afraid to even breathe so he found himself holding his breath, only remembering that he needed air when his chest began to plead with him to inhale.

He begged God. He had prayed before with his mother and even though it felt silly to speak to someone he couldn't even see, he did it more than he ever had before in this dangerous circumstance. Suddenly, the God that his mother made him put his hands together and give thanks to felt like his only hope.

Baraka stopped at the end of the hall and opened the last door. C.J. paused, but was pushed so forcefully that he fell, skinning his knees. He scrambled to his feet and was nudged forward. "Aunt Leena!" he cried. She was hanging from the low ceiling rafters, her neck bent in an awkward position and her eyes swollen shut. Her entire body was black and blue. She was bound by her wrists and had been stripped naked as she swung slowly back and forth. He couldn't contain the tears. He lunged for her, but was held back by one of the burly men. "Auntie Leena!"

"Bring the other boy," Baraka ordered. C.J.'s heart stopped as he turned and looked for Lil' Money. Mo walked into the room, his chest poked out and his lips fixed in a grimace and C.J. instantly recognized the fearlessness that he had tried his hardest to muster. Mo had it. He was a Diamond and C.J. looked up to his cousin in that moment.

"Ma?" he whispered as he finally noticed Leena. "Ma!" he screamed as he violently fought to shake out of the grasp of his

captors to reach Leena. Mo's voice seemed to stir Leena and she groaned.

"Please . . ." Her words were barely audible. She was so weak, so defeated, and the pain she felt from the beating she had endured over the past three days was immeasurable. The fight they had tortured out of her had been reignited with just the sound of her son's voice. "They're just kids," she whispered. "Please . . ."

"The children are the pawns on the board," Baraka stated. "Your very own king and queen sacrificed them. One life. Miamor's could have spared yours and theirs as well."

"This has nothing to do with them!" Leena's pleas were full of pain, full of anger. "You're an honorable man. I'm sorry about Yasmine. I'm sorry it has come to this, but Yasmine was a grown woman. She made choices. She slept with a married man! What choices have these kids made to end up here? None! This is war! This is no place for children. Please," Leena sobbed heavily. "Oh God!" Her desperation was palpable and hopelessness thickened the air. "I don't care what you do to me. I made my choices too, but they are babies." Leena's head drooped once more, her chin resting on her chest. She had used what strength she had left to declare her piece and silence was the reply. It was eerily quiet as C.J. looked at Baraka, his heart pounding, his mouth hanging agape as he as well as everyone else waited for Baraka to speak.

C.J. and Mo looked at each other as they were restrained. Baraka stood in front of them, measuring the value of their lives in his mind. C.J. felt invisible as if Baraka could see through him. It didn't matter how well he maintained his emotions or how brave of a front C.J. could muster, Baraka could see his fear.

"They will watch every second until the life leaves your body. Then they will pledge their allegiance to me. They are mine now. A small price for the Cartel to pay for what they have taken from me," Baraka stated.

"I'm a Diamond! I don't belong to you!" Mo shouted.

Baraka chuckled. "You are rambunctious. That Diamond bloodline is strong, but even Diamonds can be destroyed. You have spirit, I will give you that." He turned toward his men. "Break it. If they look away or close their eyes, kill them."

The men retrieved heavy metal chains that hung from the walls. For the first time C.J. noticed the torture tools. The chains were rusted and old. Axes and knives accompanied them and he looked at Leena, then at Monroe, in distress. His young mind couldn't quite fathom what he was about to witness.

The first blow was yielded with such force that it split the flesh on Leena's back. She yelped in excruciation.

"Agh!"

"I'm going to kill you! Don't touch my mama! Ma!" Mo yelled as he fought to get to her.

C.J. was frozen where he stood. His eyes were wide as Baraka's threats played over and over in his head. "If they look away, kill them." So, he didn't. C.J. forced himself to watch as the men took the skin off his aunt's bones, blow by blow. His stomach clenched, the empty pit now filling with hopelessness as he watched Baraka's hired hand strike once more. The sound of the chain dragging mercilessly across the ground made the hair stand up on the back of C.J.'s neck. It was like a metal snake, hissing before it prepared to strike.

Leena's screams could peel paint off a wall. She was a wounded animal and the blood that dripped from her body covered the floor around her. The beating didn't stop until there was nothing left of her. She was unrecognizable. Like a piece of butchered meat, she hung there, swinging left to right, bone and flesh.

* * *

C.J. jolted out of bed, the images branded in his mind so fresh that he looked around in horror, half-expecting to be confined to Baraka's captivity. He had the same nightmare every night. He had never spoken of the things he had seen while he was with Baraka. To witness his aunt being murdered, so brutally, at such a young age, was traumatizing. He lived in fear every day for the three years he was taken. Baraka never laid one hand on C.J. In fact, he treated them well, but like a slave master handled his favorite slave, it was still bondage all the same. The mental chains that Baraka had placed on both C.J. and Mo were strong enough to keep them from disobeying. The promise of death to the rest of their loved ones kept C.J. and Mo in line for years. Not once did they try to run; not once did they fight. After witnessing Leena beaten to death, they simply complied, breaking off all allegiance to their family to survive. No one, but Mo, knew what they had seen. They never told anyone. Not Miamor, not Carter, not Monroe. It was a secret they shared. Ashamed of the fact that they had switched sides without putting up a fight, they thought their family would abandon them if they knew the truth.

So, when they returned, they lived a life of pretend. C.J. pretended to be happy, he pretended to be normal and unafraid, but he lived in terror every second of every day. He tried to blend back into his family, but not only had they changed, so had he. He felt disconnected from his parents and he couldn't tell them why. He loved them but at the same time he felt like he didn't belong. Mo was the only person he felt completely comfortable around. He had been happy to be reunited with his blood but still he didn't seem to fit the way he used to.

The silence of the house made him hold his breath in anticipation as he listened carefully, trying to determine if Ms. Bernice was still awake. It felt odd being in her home, sleeping in this bed. It was all pretend. They weren't family and C.J. was conditioned to question the motives of anyone unrelated to him. He was uncomfortable here and his weary soul unsettled. He was being traded off from person to person and each time he woke up in a new place he lost a piece of his security. Losing Mo made it all seem so final. He had no family. There was no one he could rely on. Now he was out in the world alone, filled with insecurities. The solitude of his new existence made him feel small and unimportant. Somehow, he was falling through the cracks of society without anyone taking notice.

He opened the bedroom door and peeked down the hallway cautiously before daring to step out. He didn't want to face Ms. Bernice. There was expectation in her stare. Every time he looked in her eyes he felt pressured to perform for her. He was like the puppy she had rescued from the pound. The growl in his stomach urged him toward the kitchen and he opened the refrigerator, being careful not to make any noise. The light illuminated the dark room and he reached inside, pulling out sandwich meat and bread. Even though Bernice had told him to make himself at home, C.J. didn't want to get too comfortable. *What does she want from me?* he thought. *She's not my family. She don't know me. Why would she bring me here if she didn't want something?*

C.J. couldn't make sense out of this situation. Strangers weren't this kind. He hurriedly tossed together the sandwich and stuffed the belongings back inside the icebox. He felt like he was stealing and would be caught at any moment.

When the light clicked on, it flooded into the kitchen all at once, leaving him no time to retreat with the disappearing darkness.

"C.J., it's three o'clock in the morning," Ms. Bernice said. Her eyes went from the sandwich on the table to the guilty look on his face. "You don't have to sneak around, C.J. You can eat what you like, as much as you like."

C.J. was like a deer caught in headlights. Vulnerable, exposed, the grumbling in his stomach reminding him he needed a good meal, but too prideful to admit the words aloud. She was a stranger, in more than just the sense that they weren't very well acquainted. She was strange. Who welcomed a kid they didn't know into their home, the kid of a kingpin, a kid from a history of violence and lawlessness? Her willingness to bring him home made her suspect to C.J. and his instincts told him not to trust her. That funny feeling that made him feel like he had to throw up was constant around her and it was something about the look in her eyes that told him there were hidden motives behind her stare.

"Have a seat," Bernice said as she walked over to him and removed the bread from his hands. She pointed to the small dinette table, motioning for C.J. to sit as she pulled food from the refrigerator. C.J. noticed how she removed bacon, eggs, butter, and pancake mix without even looking inside the fridge. Her eyes never left C.J. She examined him as she moved around the room from memory and with expertise. Her disarming stare caused him to lower his gaze as he fidgeted uncomfortably.

How does she know where everything is? he thought.

"I've done some research on your family, C.J. I know you come from a very different way of life. It will take some getting used to living here. I'm not rich but it's safe. You will have a warm bed, a roof over your head, and food in your stomach," Bernice said.

She spoke the way mothers were supposed to speak. She moved around a kitchen the way a woman should, with love. His mother flashed through his mind. Miamor never cooked. She never knew where anything was, often cursing in anger when she couldn't find the eggs or the sugar. He was used to personal chefs and expensive takeout, but for some reason the idea of someone preparing a meal especially for him made his bottom lip quiver. Children of the Cartel grew up differently, wanting for nothing but at the same time wanting for everything. Anything money could buy was fair game; it was the things that a dollar couldn't attain that was lacking. Security, compassion, the image of a woman taking care of a family, taking care of a husband, doing homework with her children . . . C.J. didn't have the mother who baked cookies or the father who coached his peewee team. His family were royals and they held court in the street. His mother and father, the king and queen. No one was whipping up pancakes in the middle of the night.

His parents, his aunts, his uncles, and, from the stories he had heard, even his grandfather controlled the streets of Miami. The entire city was their playground; every illegal dollar made, the Cartel got a piece of it. There simply wasn't time for the little things. Cooking breakfast was easily delegated to personal chefs, nannies, and housekeepers. It wasn't until this very moment that he wondered, *Why do the little things feel like the big things?*

"There are some things you will have to do around here," Ms. Bernice said. "To earn your keep, but overall you will still appreciate your time here much more than if you were to be placed in the system."

She placed a plate of food in front of him that smelled so sweet, his mouth watered instantly. He found it odd when she sat next to him. He avoided looking at her, focusing on covering the sweetness with butter and syrup.

He tore into the plate, eating so fast that he forgot to chew before swallowing.

"Let's fill you up," Bernice said. He froze and let the fork linger midway in the air when he felt her hand on his thigh. It wasn't the fact that she had placed it there. Many people had pat his thigh in encouragement before. A teacher or an elder, but the way she let it linger and the way she gave it a squeeze as her eyes hooded with ill intent made him fill with instant shame. These were the types of bad touches that he had learned about when he was younger. He pushed back from the table.

"Are you done?" she asked. "You haven't finished eating."

"I'm full," he lied, scuttling away, wishing he had never ventured out of the room in the first place. His nostrils flared in a mixture of embarrassment and anger. This woman was a wolf in sheep's clothing. The way his body responded to her confused him and he just wanted to disappear inside the temporary solace of the room because it had a lock and locks were supposed to keep out the bad.

* * *

Bernice couldn't look at herself in the mirror. It always happened this way. She would take in some child, mostly boys, but she wasn't impartial to girls, and she would tell herself that she was saving them. Her logic convinced her that without her generosity these kids would be lost in a system where no one cared and few made it out. She always started with such good intentions, but it never failed, even when she fought with herself internally her urges always won out in the end. Guilt plagued her when she heard C.J. turn the lock on the bedroom door. She wanted to go to him, to soothe his worry, and ease his suspicions, but it wouldn't stop the process she had already put into motion. *I acted too fast. He wasn't ready. I have to make him more comfortable so that it feels good and he won't go telling. The last one that tried to tell . . .*

Her thoughts drifted because she didn't want to think about that time. That time when things had gotten out of control. She had stopped for a long while after that. She had been too afraid of getting caught, but when she saw C.J. walk into her office it sparked a desperate flame inside her. Her job gave her access to fulfill her sick desires. With a clean record she was easily hirable, but she had a long history of inappropriate behaviors with minors. *Nobody gave a fuck when I was the minor. There was no rescue when I was on the receiving end. I had to take it and then I had to like it and then I really liked it. He'll eventually like it.* Her twisted thoughts were attempts at justification for what was to come. Her eagerness had caused her to move too quickly. She knew that the most important step to all of this was the seduction. She had to woo him, the way she had done all the others. That way he wouldn't tell. That way he wouldn't want to tell. *In due time,* she thought. C.J. was in the hands of the worst type of monster. She was the kind that came in the form of help only to inflict more harm.

Knock, knock!

The light rap of knuckles against the wooden door made C.J. sit straight up in bed. "C.J., are you awake?"

Her voice was soft and rang out in a sweet melody but still C.J. frowned. It was almost too sweet like candy that made your stomach hurt and C.J. recognized the force behind the words. He wondered if he might be overreacting. Had the awkwardness he felt last night when she touched him been all in his head? *Did she mean it like that?* he wondered. Perhaps being in a strange home with an unfamiliar woman had him paranoid and on guard. C.J. wasn't sure, but if he had ever learned anything from his mother, he had learned this.

"That voice inside your head never lies. Trust your instinct. Your gut will never steer you wrong." He could hear Miamor in his ear, urging him not to trust this lady. He hated this defensive feeling that had infected him. He had lived with it for years while in Baraka's possession and had just gotten used to being home with his real family when he had been plucked out of his natural environment again. The feelings of mistrust and paranoia were back full force. It was unfair. At his old school, none of the kids his age had to worry about danger or survival. C.J., however, considered those things daily. It was the downside of coming up as a legacy of the Cartel.

He went to the door and turned the lock then backpedaled toward the bed as Bernice peeked her head inside.

"Is it safe to come in?" she asked. There it was again. That smile that was forced as if someone were holding up the corners of her mouth but forgetting to put the twinkle of sincerity in her gaze.

"Yeah, it's safe," he replied.

"C.J., I don't know what you've been through in the past, but no one is going to hurt you here. I just want you to feel comfortable, okay? I want you to feel good," she said.

The word *good* made him cringe. It didn't quite fit. It wasn't quite right.

"Now slip on some clothes and we will go down to the mall to pick up some things for you. How does that sound? Maybe get some ice cream and pizza on the way back? That cool with you?"

He nodded because, well, what choice did he have? Besides, the clothes he had were days old and unclean. He would need some things to get by. He couldn't stay barricaded up in this room forever.

He waited for her to leave but when he realized she wasn't attempting to exit he slowly began to peel off his clothes. He turned his back to her, moving quickly, feeling exposed, throwing on the stuff so fast that he didn't care that his shirt was inside out.

"Come here," she said. "Let me help."

He walked over to her and she rolled his shirt up over his arms. The places where her fingers touched his skin almost burned. It wasn't that he was afraid. He was weary and the way she obliged herself to touch where she pleased bothered him. He felt dirty. He remembered being touched like that, back in Saudi Arabia, when everyone was asleep; one of Baraka's men would come into the room where C.J. was kept. His hands felt like her hands, unwelcomed, inappropriate, and made him withdraw into a shell so deep that he almost had to ask himself if it had happened at all. He was thankful for the day that Baraka walked in on his hired hand trying to force himself on C.J. The punishment had been death and C.J. and Mo had been treated with decency from that day forward.

The incident was never spoken of, not by Baraka or C.J., but after that day everything had changed about his imprisonment. He and Mo were no longer pawns in a war, but guests of Baraka, whom he protected and had grown fond of, like the sons he had never had. C.J. had never told anyone out of fear that he would be judged, out of fear that it would mean something more than a child being abused. He only thought of it when the man haunted his psyche at night and now, with Ms. Bernice's hands rubbing his shoulders. He wasn't a man, not even a young man, he was a child and his discomfort was measurable by the tension she insisted on rubbing out.

He felt her hands move lower and lower until . . .

The feeling of her cold hands inside the band of his underwear caused him to react. He grabbed the first thing in his reach. C.J. didn't realize he was swinging it until it connected with a loud thud. Everything went black as he pulled it over his head and brought it down with all his strength. He knew she was stronger than he was so he kept swinging and kept swinging. His hands were wet and everything was black. All he saw was the face of the man who had made him feel so low and then he saw her face, with that haunting smile, that devious, sinister tool of trickery that she used to try to get him to trust her. He never wanted to feel the confusing, pleasurable, miserable, filthy, shameful feelings ever again and he wouldn't let her or anyone else touch him without his permission.

He snapped out of his fugue and when he saw her lying there, blood all over the bed, his stomach absorbed his heart. *I'm in trouble. What did I do? Is she . . . is she dead?* His gut was screaming, *run.* This time he didn't second-guess it. He took off running through the house and pulled open the front door, only to bump headfirst into three men. He was snatched off his feet so fast that he had no time to protest. Before he could put up much fight he felt the prick of a needle as it was jammed in his neck. It only took seconds for him to realize what was happening. His lids slowly closed but not before he saw a man stepping out of a black SUV. *Estes?* That was the last thought that crossed his mind before the curtain closed to black.

* * *

"Where is my great-grandson? There should be another boy inside," Estes said as he crossed the threshold into Bernice's home.

"This is the only kid here and he did quite a number on the lady in the back room," Estes's henchman returned.

Estes's brow furrowed in curiosity as he made his way through the home, careful not to touch anything along the way. After being contacted by Einstein, Estes knew he had to intervene with Mo. He risked coming to the States to purposefully ensure that nothing went wrong with retrieving Mo. He had no intentions of rescuing C.J. Blood was the only connection Estes recognized and C.J. wasn't family. He made his way through the house and stopped when he saw the woman barely conscious on the bed. She was bloody and moaning softly as Estes entered the room.

"There's no one else here?" Estes asked in surprise as he looked back at his men. "The boy did this?"

"Looks like it. The rest of the place is empty."

"What the hell?" he whispered. He walked over to the woman and gripped a fistful of her hair, pulling hard enough to cause her pain, bringing her to life again.

"Agh," she winced through broken teeth. "Please, please, I didn't touch him." Estes frowned and thought of a shirtless C.J. It wasn't hard for him to put two and two together.

"Then tell me what did you do?" Estes asked, suddenly repulsed. C.J. was a child. There was no purpose a boy could serve a grown woman sexually. Only a person with the sickest mind could think otherwise.

"I . . . I . . . please," she moaned as she rolled over on her side. It was clear that C.J. had inflicted much pain. He had mustered up the strength to defend himself even though she could have overpowered him. "I was just giving him a massage. He misunderstood."

"Where is Monroe Diamond the second?" Estes asked.

"He's in juvie! Please, just leave! Take him and leave!" she screamed as she writhed in pain. "I think he broke my nose."

"I'm going to keep my eye on you. If I even get wind that you have another child in this home or that you are touching another child in any way, I will come back here and I will end your life. In the meantime, you will make sure Monroe has everything he needs inside." Estes paused as he stared the woman in the eyes menacingly. "Everything. Do you hear me?" he asked as she nodded her head frantically. "Protection, commissary, privileges, and a glowing review on his records. Is that understood?"

Estes pulled a gun and forced it in her mouth, breaking even more of her teeth in the process. "Nod your head if you understand," Estes said. She nodded frantically as fear filled her widened eyes.

Estes turned on his expensive shoes and headed out the door. As he passed his hired hand he paused. "Leave her with a bullet to remember what she agreed to. She can spare a finger or two," Estes said with the overwhelming desire to inflict pain on this woman. He walked out and approached his other goon that stood watching the front door. C.J. was laid on the living-room couch. "Get the boy and let's go."

Estes was disappointed that he wouldn't leave with Mo, but after seeing what had taken place he couldn't just leave C.J. in the hands of the system. "Call the pilot. Tell him we are on our way back to the clear port."

Chapter 6

C.J. came to somewhere over the Atlantic Ocean, coming out of the fog from the induced sleep that Estes's men had placed him in. Confusion overwhelmed him as he took in the sounds around him. *I'm in the air,* he thought as he sat up and looked around the small room he had been placed in. It was a luxury bedroom aboard the G5 jet Estes owned. He scrambled to the window, crawling across the bed, until he was at the window shade. He pulled it up and gasped when he saw the white clouds. The blood on his hands reminded him of what had occurred and his breath caught in his throat. *Is she dead?* he thought, tears filling his eyes. He didn't know how he had gotten here. It wasn't long ago he was able to just be a kid. It seemed that things never stayed normal for long in his life. It was extreme after extreme, highs and lows, with no middle ground. It was no way for a young boy to live.

Now he was in this jet on his way to who knows where and he was too afraid to even walk outside the closed door to ask. He stood, unsure, as he wrung his fingers nervously, his eyes on the door like a hawk. He heard Estes's voice. He remembered him but not well. All he knew was that Estes was Mo's powerful old grandfather, that everyone rolled the red carpet out for him. He had heard Carter refer to him as the connect so C.J. knew he was an important man, one his father respected. He crept out of the room slowly and noticed Estes sitting with his legs crossed, glasses perched on his nose, as he perused a newspaper in his hands. He looked up as C.J. came into his line of sight.

"Is she . . . did I?" C.J. couldn't quite ask the right question.

"No, you didn't. She's alive," Estes replied. He didn't divulge any other details, but C.J. was relieved to hear that he hadn't done the undoable. That much blood on his hands would have haunted him for life. He was too young to start a body count. He didn't need the guilt on his conscience. Estes surmised that C.J. didn't need to know the gritty details of what had happened, but Bernice wouldn't be taking advantage of any more children. Estes had given her a one-way ticket to hell.

"Have a seat and buckle up. We'll be landing soon."

"Landing?" C.J. looked out the window at the shades of turquoise and blue ocean water below them.

"The Dominican Republic. My home is there. It's where you will stay until I figure things out and get in touch with your father," Estes said.

Relief flooded C.J. It didn't matter that Estes wasn't his blood, he was close enough and the sight of someone familiar provided him a sense of security. He nodded and chose to remain silent for the duration of the flight. He could tell Estes only spoke to him out of obligation and C.J. didn't want to get on his bad side. The possibility of seeing his father, of being with family, or close to it in Estes's case, made C.J.'s fears dissipate.

As the plane hit the tarmac with a gentle thud, C.J.'s heart raced in a mixture of uncertainty and contentment. He followed Estes off the plane and then immediately got into an awaiting vehicle that took them directly to Estes's ocean-side estate. C.J. had never seen anything so grand. He was born into money so he wasn't a stranger to fine things but the way Estes lived was nothing short of pure opulence. He looked around the villa in amazement as soon as they entered.

"A room is prepared for you. Go upstairs and clean up. I'm expecting associates. If you're going to live here, you're going to earn your keep. You can help set things up for the evening. Get yourself together and then head out back—the rest of the men will tell you what to do," Estes said with no emotion in his voice. He was disappointed that Mo was rotting away in some Miami juvenile facility. The fact that he had only been able to save C.J. filled him with guilt. He had no affection for C.J. They weren't family and Estes owed no debts, but something about leaving C.J. out in the world felt wrong.

Carter and Estes had shared a tumultuous relationship

over the years. Carter had been a source of pain for Taryn and Estes had noticed it in her eyes long before Carter ever stepped foot in Miami. From the day Carter was born, Taryn had been heartbroken; no matter how well she disguised it, Estes could see her melancholy. It was because of this that Estes had never taken to Carter. Even after his beautiful daughter's death, Estes still held a grudge.

It was only after Carter proved that he was incomparable in the drug business that Estes even considered getting involved with him. Carter was simply an irreplaceable asset to anyone's team and although Estes hated him, he needed him all the same. In all his years of supplying the streets of Miami, no one, not even the late, great Carter Diamond, had been able to run through product the way Carter did. Estes owed Carter nothing, and he had half a notion to leave C.J. where he found him, but Estes knew how valuable Carter's son may prove to be. He didn't know how he would use him, but C.J. was the seed of a powerful man. Leaving him in the hands of the foster system was really no option at all.

Estes looked out over his beachside villa as his staff prepared for a grand evening. Estes had worked for decades to build this haven for his family. The massive estate sat on a bluff, overlooking the Caribbean Sea. It had been the place where he planned to retire with his family all around him, but things hadn't gone according to plan. Street wars and battles for power had diminished his dream slowly over the years. The idea of a peaceful and full life had eroded inevitably. Death and incarceration had plagued his family, leaving only him and oddly, a boy that wasn't even his blood as the last men standing.

Estes climbed the stairs and noticed the door at the end of the hallway was slightly ajar. His chest grew tight with anxiety as he approached the room. He hadn't opened that door in years. Only the housekeeper entered that space and even that was limited to once a week. It was his son's old room and Estes hadn't stepped foot inside since the day his only son was murdered. He pushed open the door, hitting it with his palm loudly. "Get out of here now," Estes said sternly, his eyes ablaze with anger. C.J. was thrown off guard and stood up defensively.

"Get out of here," Estes said, his eyes burning with passion as he grabbed C.J. roughly and pulled him off the bed. He dragged him down the hall and opened the guest room door before storming back to his son's room.

Sammie had died years ago, but the unresolved emotions Estes held came rushing at him as if a flood had been waiting behind the closed door. He closed the door for privacy and looked around the room. At the time, the villa had been Estes's vacation home. It was where he had taken his family when he wanted to get away from Miami and all the ills that dwelled there. Estes had kept Sammie's room at the villa the same. He didn't want to throw the memory of his only son away and although he had hidden his pain well over the years, it had never gone away.

Estes looked around. It felt like a shrine. He picked up a baseball that sat on the dresser and held it tightly in his grip. Estes was an old man, rich beyond measure, but poor in his soul. He had spent his years in the game, running empires, supplying the streets with cocaine, and amassing more money than he could spend. Yet, here he stood, yearning for the one thing money couldn't buy. Young men sought power, old men sought peace—and with both of his children in early graves, peace was elusive.

Estes sat down on the bed and gripped the ball between the palms of his hands as he leaned over on his elbows while resting his chin on his fists. He gritted his teeth as he fought the urge to cry. He placed the ball back in its place and then stood. A part of him wanted to stand in this space for a while, to soak up some of the essence that his son had left behind. Instead he cleared his throat, containing his hurt in a compartment inside his heart that he let no one bear witness to. Guilt ridden over the way he reacted, he retreated from the room and sought out C.J.

Estes found him in the back of the villa, setting up just as he had been instructed to. Estes watched from afar as C.J. carried tables and chairs, following the instructions of Estes's hired hands. Estes watched him carefully. There was no entitlement about C.J. Even though C.J. came from power and money, he had humbled himself when the odds were stacked against him. *He's smart, he adapts to survive,* Estes observed.

Estes watched C.J. closely as he stood on the veranda and sipped his cognac slowly. C.J. never slacked. Even in the burning heat C.J. worked diligently without complaint, until the job was complete. Estes summoned C.J. to his side.

"Tonight, you will be seen but not heard. Some of the most powerful men in Santo Domingo will be here with their families. It's important to break bread and commune with the people I have done business with over the years. I must know their wives, their children. That way I know the vulnerabilities of those around me. You don't speak unless spoken to. Do you understand? You will keep my guests full of good whiskey and clear the plates from the table when dinner is complete," Estes said. "Is that a problem?"

"No sir, I got it," C.J. responded.

Estes wasn't C.J.'s grandfather. It wasn't required that he embrace the boy with open arms. C.J. would have to prove himself useful if he wanted to stay around.

* * *

This wasn't the first time C.J. had played servant to a powerful man. Baraka had turned him into one before and as C.J. walked around the party pouring water into the guests' glasses, it reminded him of the time he had been taken by his father's enemy. C.J. refused to complain. Being under Estes's thumb was better than being in the system, so he kept his head down and did as Estes had instructed.

No one at the party spoke to him. It was like he was invisible. His smooth, dark complexion made the pure-blooded Dominicans view him as unworthy. There was an undertone of racism in the air as all the workers were darker skinned while the guests were of fairer complexions. In the eyes of Estes's guests, C.J. was just another hired servant that Estes had employed.

C.J. sat back in the shadows, watching Estes speak as he hosted the five-star beachside dinner. His guests sat at a long fifty-person table. The men were arranged closest to Estes, then the wives, and the children at the very end. Everyone was dressed in their finest threads and the string quartet that played soft music set the formal tone. Estes had spared no expense as they sat with tiki torches burning around them, illuminating the beach as the waves gently washed ashore.

C.J. was amazed that this was no special event. It was just a way of life for a man of Estes's stature. C.J. had always thought his father was the biggest gangster alive, but Estes was next level. Everything from his home, his clothes, his stature, and even the company he kept was elite. There were no street soldiers. All of Estes's men, even his pawns, dressed in suits. He had never seen a group of people that looked so carefree.

He wished he could relate to the feeling. Ever since his father went away and his mother was caged, all C.J. did was worry. He never knew how long his next situation would last. The instability of his life made him feel like a tumbleweed, blowing in the wind. He never knew where he would end up. Even now, among the comforts of Estes's estate, uncertainty dwelled inside him.

C.J. watched as Estes and the rest of the men rose from the table. He quickly made his way over to clear the plates they left behind. Four children sat at the table as their mothers carried their wine and conversation over to the shoreline. C.J. worked around the kids, but as he reached in to grab a dish, one of the boys pushed over his glass.

"Clean that up, mutt," the boy said, causing the rest of the kids to burst into laughter. C.J. gritted his teeth, but didn't react as he picked up the glass. The kid knocked over another one. "That one too."

C.J. felt his heart begin to beat rapidly but he kept his composure. He turned to take the dishes into the villa. The kid stuck out his foot and tripped C.J., causing all the good china to fly out of his hands as he came crashing to the ground.

C.J. jumped up and pushed the boy so hard that he fell back against the table setting. C.J.'s reaction was a shock and he left no time for the kid to react. He grabbed the taunting boy by his expensive necktie and threw repeated blows to his face. The kid had a slight weight advantage over C.J. but C.J. was swift on his feet. He ignored the feeling of his bones aching as he punched with all his might.

"Oh, my goodness! Boys stop! Estes!"

C.J. heard the screams as the kid used his weight to push C.J. off. He charged at C.J., trying to scoop him below the waist and put him on his back, but C.J. kept his fists flying. His blows were vicious as adrenaline urged him to fight harder. When the kid slammed C.J. on the sand, his breath left him. The impact knocked the wind straight out of him. C.J. rolled over on his side and gasped for air, but before either of them could escalate things further they were pulled apart.

"I'm going to kill you!" the boy shouted as he spit blood from his mouth. Judging by sight it was obvious that C.J. was the victor. A woman rushed over to him.

"*Mijo,* look at your eye," she cried as she cupped his hands in her face. The kid moved his head out of her grasp.

"Let your mommy take care of that," C.J. said as he breathed heavily. "He started it. I was clearing the table and he jumped bad at me," C.J. stated.

"Don't baby him. You lost a fight?" the kid's father shouted angrily. "How am I supposed to make money off you if you're losing to some fucking black kid!"

The kid burned a hole through C.J. he was staring so hard.

"Go get some ice for that eye. What am I supposed to do with that?" the man asked as he turned toward Estes. "He's in the pit tomorrow night. He can't go in like that. You either owe me money to forfeit the bout or you put someone in to replace him. Until then, put the fucking kid on a leash."

Estes shot C.J. a stern look as the party cleared out. "Already, you're costing me more than you're worth," Estes stated. "I hope you like to fight because you will be taking the place of that young man tomorrow evening. You'll be fighting at the pits."

Chapter 7

Mo felt like a caged bird as he lay on the cot, looking up through the skylight above him. He was grateful for that window. Not every bunk had one and it reminded him of the light he had to look forward to at the end of this dark tunnel. The next few years of his life, the most influential ones, would be spent inside. No mama, no daddy—he would be raised among the wolves. The lap of luxury that he was supposed to inherit had been toppled and instead he was now a gutter rat, just trying to fight for his piece of something . . . anything . . . that would help him get through the worst time of his life.

The juvenile detention center tried hard to disguise itself as something other than a prison. Bunks were only locked at night and the boys had "privileges" that they earned until they gave a reason to have them revoked. To a boy who came from a kingdom, no amount of privileges would make this feel like anything other than what it was: captivity. Mo sat up abruptly as another kid walked into the room. He was heavyset; his stomach was round and tested the buttons of his blue uniform. His hair was long and unruly. Mo noticed the black eye that was now turning green as it healed on his face. *Damn that had to hurt. He's dark as hell and that bruise is even darker,* Mo thought. The kid didn't speak. In fact, he kept his head down as if Mo wasn't even in the room. *Cool with me,* Mo thought.

Mo didn't have anything inside. Everything had to be purchased and with nobody looking out for him on the outside he knew he would have to come up with a plan. Three boys entered their cell and circled around his roommate.

"What up, Fat Boy? Ya mama came and stacked up your account today. Let's go shopping," the kid said. Mo said nothing. He was silent as he waited to see what his roommate's reaction would be. It wasn't hard to see he was intimidated and Mo quickly did that math, knowing that the black eye had come from this crew.

"Nah, man she didn't. She couldn't afford it this time," his roommate replied.

"Well you got to pay me something. Fuck you got up in here?" the boy asked, rifling through his roommate's things as if they were his own. Anger flooded Mo. He had a temper and Mo wasn't too fond of bullies, but if his roommate wasn't going to stand up for himself, Mo felt like it wasn't his place to intervene. "All you got is books nigga! You a fat mu'fucka, but you ain't stupid, huh? Soft ass," the boy mumbled as his sidekicks laughed, one of them even going so far as to push the roommate down on his cot. The loudmouthed kid moved over to Mo's side of the room.

"Nah, man. Ain't shit this way for you," Mo said.

"What?" the kid challenged as he got in Mo's face.

"I ain't stutter," Mo stood. He was always down to shoot a fair one. He had the heart of a lion inside him and once challenged there was no backing down.

"What do we have here, gentlemen?"

The woman that walked into the cell interrupted the confrontation before it could even get started.

"Do I need to write up some infractions? I know those books must have fallen on their own. Right?" the blond woman asked as she looked around the room, searching for answers. "Monroe Diamond? You want to tell me what's going on here?" the lady asked.

Mo didn't speak. He wasn't into snitching. He didn't need anybody to come to his defense. The woman grew frustrated and pointed toward the door. "If you are not assigned to this bunk, make your way out," she demanded.

"I'mma get you," the kid said.

"You know where to find me," Mo answered. Hostility was in the air.

"Here is your package. These are the only things you will be given in here. Everything else going forward must be purchased. You can remove your clothing and place them in here after you remove the uniform and essentials that are inside," the woman informed.

Mo nodded and took the burlap bag she extended. Before she left the room, she said, "Stay out of trouble."

He didn't respond because he knew that trouble would come looking for him.

When he was alone with his roommate Mo bent down and helped the kid pick up his belongings. "Why you let 'em dog you like that?" he asked.

"That's Roach. He's on B block with the rest of the fourteen- to sixteen-year-olds. Everybody pay for peace in here. You either let him spend on your commissary or have a problem with him," the roommate responded.

"You scared of him or something? He need them niggas behind him because he can't stand on his own. You got to stand up to him and he'll stop fucking with you," Mo said.

"Ain't no standing up to Roach. Last one that tried got caught in the mess and ended up with thirty stitches. Roach split him from ear to ear," the roommate replied.

"He knows who to try that shit with," Mo replied as he shook his head in disbelief. "Hey man, what's your name?"

"I'm Joey," the kid said.

"Mo," he replied as he handed him the books and stood to his feet.

"Your last name is Diamond? Like for real?" the kid asked, intrigued. Most people were never allowed to get close to the family and their last name rang so loudly in

Miami that many people claimed affiliation without even being part of the family at all.

"Yeah," Mo replied, casually.

"Damn, man. Yo' family is made. . . ."

"I ain't trying to spread that around like that though so that's between you and me," Mo said.

"You got it," Joey responded.

"Nigga and unbutton your shit," Mo said. "Ain't nothing wrong with being a big boy but at least be fly with your shit."

Joey laughed as he unbuttoned the uniform shirt and let his white T-shirt show through.

"There you go, big boy," Mo said with a smirk. "Next time them niggas press you, you get them up off you too. Don't bitch out. You got them on size alone. Got to put some heart up in you. Them niggas ain't gon' be walking up in here like they own shit. This half my shit too." Mo tapped Joey's chest in encouragement and then changed out of his clothes. He kicked back on his cot. "Yo you mind if I borrow one of them books? I'm dry in here," Mo said, referring to his lack of personal belongings.

"Yeah man. You good," Joey said. He reached into his stash and tossed Mo *The Autobiography of Malcolm X.*

"Man, this look like a schoolbook. You don't got nothing good?" Mo asked.

"That is good. It makes you think. Try it," Joey said.

Mo knew beggars couldn't be choosers so he nodded and put the book under his pillow for later use. He wished he had gotten paired with someone who wasn't so weak, but then again, he had to be grateful because it also could be worse. At least with Joey, Mo wouldn't have to sleep with one eye open.

* * *

Word spread overnight that Mo was the son of the infamous Monroe Diamond. By morning, every kid in his unit walked by his bunk just to peek inside.

"Yo Joey, what up boy?" a slim kid greeted as he sauntered into their bunk.

Joey wore a perplexed look as he slapped hands with the kid. "What's up," he replied.

"Just stopping through to show love. What up, man," he said to Mo.

Mo nodded in acknowledgment.

"Make sure you check me on the yard during rec. We got a game going on the hoop court, Joey. Bring your man through," the kid said.

"Yeah, okay," Joey replied, his eyebrows raised in utter confusion as the boy left just as quickly as he had come.

"You don't even know that nigga, do you?" Mo asked with a laugh.

"No!" Joey responded. "The thirst is real though! That's the fifth dude that has come in here to chop it up with me today. I been in here for six months and ain't never had this many people speak to me the whole time. Bro, this shit wild! You got them going crazy like you the pretty girl at school and they trying to shoot they shot." Joey was in stitches as he laughed jovially.

"I told you not to say nothing to nobody," Mo said.

"It wasn't me. Roach or his boys must have spread word. He heard your last name yesterday and everybody in Miami knows it's only one Diamond family," Joey stated. "You crazy for not wanting people to know anyway. Niggas showing you mad love in here."

"Yeah, it's a lot of love, but it's a lot of hate too that come with my name," Mo stated.

"Yeah I hear you. I'm about to grab chow. You coming?" Joey asked.

"Chow? Like food?" Mo asked.

"Yeah, if you can even call it that, but if you don't eat now, next meal ain't until late," Joey said. Mo's stomach rumbled. It had been two days since he had eaten. He hopped up from his cot. "Lead the way."

Mo walked out of the bunk and joked with Joey the entire way to the common area where breakfast was served. "Bruh? You really eat this?" Mo asked as he grabbed a tray and he turned up his face in disgust. He was accustomed to a standard of living and the slop that was being thrown on his plate was far beneath it. As he eyed the runny stuff that resembled eggs and pinched the bread that appeared stale, his stomach turned. "I ain't eating this," Mo said.

Joey shook his head. "That's what everybody say until they stomach start touching they back."

"Bruh, your stomach ain't never touched your back," Mo teased jokingly, all in good fun as Joey laughed.

"Fuck you, nigga," Joey said in between chuckles.

They cursed like sailors, partly because they could, and

partly because it made them feel like grown men. Joey eased into a seat but before Mo could sit down, Roach entered the commons.

"Here go this pussy looking mu'fucka right here!" He was always loud, always attracting too much attention. Mo was slowly learning his characteristics and he knew they weren't going to vibe. It would be a long sentence living in the same space with this kid. Roach stepped right up to Mo. "We got a star in here. Hey, y'all, this is Monroe Diamond!" Roach announced in grand fashion. The sarcasm wasn't missed as Roach gave Mo a slow, hard round of applause. Mo's jaw tightened as he stood toe to toe with Roach. Roach was two inches taller than Mo but size never mattered to Mo. The adage was true in his book: The bigger they were, the harder they fell.

"You think you hard?" Roach taunted. "I don't care who yo' daddy is little nigga, fuck all that Cartel shit. Them niggas done. Everybody know that shit is over. Miami for everybody nigga, your family fell the fuck off. My daddy used to be out there and he said your people wouldn't let nobody eat. Shit done changed now. Cartel don't run shit no more. As a matter of fact, your punk ass don't eat shit in this bitch unless I say you can eat. Since your people wanted to starve niggas out there, I say you starve in here." Roach smacked Mo's tray out of his hands, sending food flying all over the cafeteria. Roach was grandstanding, testing Mo's gangster and Mo gritted his teeth to control his temper because he knew in this moment he had to take the L. The kid was older than him by at least three years.

He loomed over Mo menacingly, waiting for him to accept the challenge so he could give Mo the fade.

Mo wouldn't allow himself to fall for the trap. He was outnumbered and outsized and even though there wasn't an ounce of fear in him, he wasn't stupid. He didn't fight battles he couldn't win, at least not directly. He would have to go for the smart victory and if he jumped stupid right now they would drag him simply because the numbers were on their side. He knew Joey wasn't jumping in to help get some of Roach's crew off his back so he was on his own. *Walk away,* he told himself.

A loud whistle blew as a guard looked over in their direction. "Break it up, shut it up, and clean it up," he yelled sternly. "Now, or I'm writing infractions!"

Mo put his hands up in temporary defeat. "You got it," he conceded. His mouth said the words but his feet didn't move. He wasn't walking away until Roach did. If his father had ever taught him anything, he had taught him this . . . he knew better than to turn his back on his enemy.

"I know I got it," the kid boasted as he strolled away, continuing to loudmouth with his friends along the way.

Mo knew he looked like a sucker, but he would have the last laugh. He would simply bide his time and wait for the opportunity to present itself. When it was time to get even he would know it, but until then he had to just stay out of the way. He bent down to clean up the mess.

A guard came up behind him. "Get a mop from the kitchen."

Mo stood, slightly perturbed that he was the one

cleaning up when it was Roach who had made a mess and caused a scene. He was trying to keep his head down, however, so he held his protests as he found his way to the kitchen. It was empty as all the boys on kitchen duty were now serving the food. He grabbed an old mop then hesitated when he saw the mess of dishes waiting to be cleaned in the sink. He rushed over and searched for a knife, but found none. He had no time to mess around and grabbed the first thing he could find, a fork. He looked around to see if any eyes were on him and when he was sure the coast was clear he tucked it in his waistline then rushed back out to clean before he aroused suspicion.

"You good?" Joey asked when Mo returned to the table.

Mo sat, silently plotting his next move. "Yeah, I'm good," he said. The growl in his stomach matched the growl in his heart and he stood to his feet. He leaned over Joey.

"I need you to do me a favor," Mo stated.

The look in Mo's eyes told Joey that he didn't want to be a part of it, but it also told Joey that he didn't have a choice. They were bunkmates and Mo was the first person who treated him with respect.

"I'mma put some heart in you yet," Mo said as he walked away, headed for his bunk.

* * *

Mo sat in the back of the class, half-listening as he looked at the back of Joey's head in the front row. The state tried to make the juvenile detention center a positive environment by providing classroom instruction. It was going to make Mo a productive member of society and give him a tool he could use toward success. At least that was the speech the entrance counselor had given him when enrolling him. Mo only signed up because Roach participated solo. His goon squad hadn't passed the aptitude test to enroll with him so every day for an hour, Roach was separated from his pack. Roach sat on the other side of the classroom, a few rows up from Mo. Mo had made sure he walked in late so that Roach wouldn't notice his presence until it was too late.

The woman who taught the course rattled off facts and statistics up front but Mo was retaining none of it. He had come for one reason and one reason only: to make an example out of Roach. Oddly, he wasn't rattled. He didn't feel an ounce of nervousness as he sat, with his eyes fixed on his enemy, as he felt the fork rub against his arm. It was covered by the sleeve of his shirt and Mo waited patiently to put it to use.

Don't back out on me, Mo thought as he waited for Joey to play his part. He had to stop himself from laughing when Joey fell dramatically from his chair and began convulsing on the floor.

That nigga is an actor, Mo thought as he created a scene that was straight out of a movie. If Mo didn't know better he would have thought the kid was having a seizure.

"Oh, my God! I need help. I need help in here!" Mo

had timed it perfectly. There was a small window of opportunity where the guards switched shifts and the classroom went uncovered. The teacher looked around in dismay. It was against protocol to send a juvenile out of the classroom without an escort and Mo could see from the look on her face that she didn't know what to do. The other boys had started to circle around Joey, who was still on the ground going for broke. He had even rolled his eyes into the back of his head for good measure.

"I'll be back. I'm going to get help," the teacher said as she rushed out of the room. When she was gone, Mo stood and turned the lock on the door and then walked up behind Roach, who was standing with the crowd. He slid the fork out of his sleeve and before Roach could react Mo stabbed him with it, repeatedly jamming it into his side fast and forcefully.

"Agh!" Roach yelled as he fell to his knees.

Mo stood and to his surprise Joey did too as they mashed him out and the other boys instigated the attack.

"Who you gon' starve? Huh?" Mo said as he stomped Roach's head and face relentlessly. The two boys beat Roach ruthlessly until the guards burst into the room, popping the lock off the door to enter. Mo didn't stop and Joey didn't either. Roach had the beatdown coming. None of the other boys intervened because at one point or another, Roach had made them victims too. This was revenge for them all and by the time the guards pulled Mo and Joey off Roach he was a bloody mess.

"Every time I see you, I'm mashing you! It's on sight!

Talking about shit done and nothing changed! It's Cartel forever! Don't play with me," Mo shouted. He had never been so angry. He saw red and he lunged for Roach repeatedly, making the guards work for their paychecks as they could hardly contain him. Mo was in rare form. He didn't know he would explode like that, but as soon as he pressed go it was hard to stop himself. He was so full of anger that he took it out on Roach. Some of it hadn't been meant for him, but Roach caught the brunt of it anyway. The guards pinned him facedown on one of the desks and pried the fork from his hands. He had dug it into Roach's body so deep that it had bent. He hadn't killed the kid, but it wasn't for lack of trying. Joey was pinned on the desk across from him and they were cuffed before they were thrown in solitary.

"How long you think we gon' be in here?" Joey asked, talking through the closed door of the torturous cell.

"I don't know, but it was worth it," Mo replied. "Yo your big ass was wiggling like a mug on that floor!" Mo yelled out with laughter. "Then when you got up and mobbed dude with me? That was real. For real, until the day I get out of here, I got your back man. I know you scared of dude so that showed a lot of loyalty. Watch what I tell you. Now that you showed that you not a punk, ain't nobody gon' try you no more."

Joey was quiet for a while as an awkward silence filled the air. "Thanks, Mo," Joey finally said.

Mo didn't respond. He simply turned in the cell and took in his new quarters. It was so small that Mo almost couldn't breathe. The air was thick and hot. The concrete slab that he was expected to sleep on was covered in a wet puddle from the leaky ceiling above it. He extended his arms out and touched the walls on both sides of him, that's how tight the space was. He sighed but still he had no regrets.

Mo didn't care how long they left him in there because when he came out he would have his respect. He had watched every man in his life carry themselves like a boss. There were no workers in the Diamond family. Every one of the men in his life held a position of power and he wouldn't allow Roach or anybody else to ever chump him. His pride wouldn't let him and his bloodline didn't call for it.

* * *

Mo and Joey sat in confinement for six weeks before they were released back into the general population of the juvenile center. Mo didn't forget his threat, however. He didn't make empty promises, so on his first day out he spotted Roach and it was war on sight. He mashed him again, with Joey never leaving him hanging. Joey never started a fight, but he wouldn't let Mo finish it alone and together they were carted right back to the hole. They made it through, however, with conversations through closed doors. Sometimes they talked about everything, with Mo reminiscing about what his father and uncles were like. Other days they talked about nothing at all, playing dumb games and making bets on which bugs on the dirty floor would crawl the fastest. They survived and a strong friendship was forged amid the fire. It was one they wouldn't soon abandon.

Chapter 8

Carter grew frustrated as he got the voice mail for the fifteenth time. "Breeze, call me back," he whispered harshly into the phone, knowing that the feds most likely had her lines tapped. He never left messages for fear of her being targeted as an accomplice and/or abetting a fugitive. He had grown so worried and frustrated he had to leave a message, feeling like he had no choice. He hadn't been able to reach Breeze, who he thought was caring for his son. This was making him uneasy. He had been calling her phone for the past three days and hadn't heard anything back. *This isn't like her,* he thought as he looked at his phone in disbelief. All types of negative thoughts began to run through his mind. He knew the feds had made an impromptu visit to her home, but he had assumed they were on a fishing expedition. They shouldn't have been able to pin anything on Breeze. They had kept her cleanest of them all. *Did they dig up enough evidence to arrest her? Did one of my old enemies come back for revenge?*

He sat on the bench on the emperor's property and watched as the birds swooped down and fed off the birdseed scattered on the pavement. He looked just across the property and saw Brick, Millie, and Ghost playing a game of golf while smoking cigars and conversing. They offered for him to participate, but his frequent chest pains or worries of his family wouldn't allow him to join in on the festivities. He had other things on his mind, like Ghost's assurance that he could pull strings to make his problems go away. He couldn't wait to hit the streets again and create favor with Ghost and his partners. The promise that Ghost had made about helping with Miamor was enough reason for him to sneak back into the U.S. and begin to make things shake on his old stomping grounds.

"Feel like having a little company?" Anari asked as she stood behind the bench. Carter quickly twisted around and looked at her. He didn't even notice her creep up behind him.

"Sure, why not," Carter said as he scooted over to one side of the bench, giving her room to sit and join him. She quickly sat next to him and looked on at the others continuing their golf game. Carter reached into the bird food dispenser that was to the right of him and then tossed the seeds onto the ground.

"There's something about this guy I just don't trust," Anari said as she squinted her eyes and focused on Ghost.

"What do you mean?" Carter asked calmly, trying to understand Anari's angle.

"It just seems kind of odd for something this powerful and it's only niggas in the room. That doesn't seem strange to you?" she asked.

"I was thinking the same shit to be honest," Carter confessed as he looked around. He knew that where there was money, a white guy in a suit wasn't far away. It was the way of America to be quite honest.

Anari repositioned her body so she was facing him directly and looked around before she began to talk. She spoke in an exasperated whisper, "We have to be honest about the entire situation. Call a spade a spade. There is something that he isn't telling us and I want to find out what it is." Anari's tone was full of incredulity as she continued her theories. "Is there more money being made that we don't know about? Is this nigga the feds trying to suck us back in, only to give us all life sentences? So many fucking thoughts. I haven't slept comfortably since they snatched us."

"I don't think he's the feds. The nigga moves too smooth to be honest. He's not a cop. I'm almost sure of it. I can smell them from a mile away and he's not that. Yet, I do feel the same way. We don't know everything. But sometimes that's not necessarily a bad thing, ya know?"

"True . . . true," Anari added.

"Maybe some of us have no choice but to take this offer. The stakes are different for everyone," Carter said, indirectly letting Anari know that he had no more options.

While others' motivation might have been money or an escape from the drug game, his was much more. He was fighting to get his family back and this was the only option on the chessboard. Anari nodded as she was reading his mind. She saw the pain in his eyes and knew that he was going forward with the proposition no matter what. On the other hand, she wanted to know more. It was the boss in her that demanded a clear understanding before she dove in headfirst. Only time would tell.

* * *

Carter was sleeping in his suite and it was just past 2:00 A.M. It was the last night of their stay in India and the eve of their massive takeover. The following months would be them setting up shops in various cities in the U.S. and releasing the Rebe drug onto the streets.

Carter's issued cell phone began to buzz, which woke him up out of his light slumber. He slowly rolled over and watched as the phone buzzed and the screen lit up. He sat up, wiped his eyes, and reached to grab the phone. When his eyes could finally focus, he saw that it was a message from Ghost. It read:

Urgent: COME OVER. I HAVE SOMETHING VERY IMPORTANT TO DISCUSS WITH YOU. IT CAN'T WAIT UNTIL THE MORNING.

Carter frowned in confusion, wondering what it could be that was so important that it demanded his presence in the wee hours of the night. Carter's heart began to race and he wondered whether Ghost had anything new on Miamor and her case, or if it was something wrong with his family, who he hadn't been able to get a hold of? So many things were going through his mind at that very moment. He didn't know what to think, but he did know that he had to go and find out. He quickly slipped on some clothes and headed out across the field where Ghost was. He saw the small villa from afar and noticed that the inside light was on, which made it look like a lighthouse on land. Carter approached the villa and knocked on the door, but to his surprise, the door pushed open when he made contact.

"Hello, Ghost?" Carter said as he pushed the door completely open. He slowly stepped in, looking for Ghost. He grew more suspicious by the second as he crept in and looked around.

"Ghost?" he repeated as he stepped a few feet inside of the house. He noticed someone move across the room and looked closer and saw that it was Anari. She held a bloody knife and was standing over a bloody body that laid sprawled on the floor.

"What the . . ." Carter whispered as he inched closer, only to realize that it was Ghost lying there dead in a pool of blood. The maroon-colored puddle began to make a small river that traveled slowly across the hardwood. The smell of blood invaded Carter's nostrils. Carter looked at the corpse in disbelief and then he looked up at Anari, who was breathing heavily with Ghost's cell phone in her left hand and a bloody knife in the other. Anari had an emotionless expression on her face as she stepped over the body and looked at Carter square in the eyes.

"We need to talk," Anari said as she walked past him and into the kitchen area. She set down the phone and began to wash her hands over the sink, rinsing the blood off her hands and knife as it flowed into the drain. She took deep and slow breaths as she closed her eyes for extended amounts of time, trying to remain calm.

"What the fuck did you do?" Carter asked as the harsh reality began to sink in. She had just killed the only chance he had at getting Miamor back. He stormed over to her and grabbed her by both of her shoulders, twisting her around to face him. He aggressively jerked her after she didn't respond. "You don't know how you just fucked my life up!" he said as he clenched his jaw tightly and the veins in his forehead and temples began to protrude. His eyes were becoming bloodshot red and water began to form as well.

"First, get your motherfucking hands off me before I put you to sleep next," Anari said calmly with the small but sharp kitchen knife still in her hand. Carter looked down and saw the sharp object just inches away from his gut. He then shook his head in disbelief and unleashed her. He placed both of his hands on his head and began to pace the room, knowing that Anari had just ruined any chance of normalcy that he possibly had.

"You shouldn't have done this. Why? Why?" he asked as he continued to pace the floor.

"He did this to himself. I came over to talk to him

about the truth and he denied it at first," Anari said as she put down the knife, realizing that Carter wasn't her enemy. She then made her way back toward the body. She knelt and picked up a small laptop that was a few feet from the dead body. The computer had been tossed to the floor after she showed him what was on it. There was a little bit of blood splatter on it from the incident, so Anari wiped it off and then walked back toward Carter. She flipped open the computer and typed in a few things before she gave it to Carter. She had an e-mail open and clicked an inbox message.

"This is what I showed him and he completely flipped out and tried to go for his gun once I told him what I knew. I told him I would tell the rest of you and that's when he tried to kill me. But I had a knife tucked that I swiped from the kitchen. I poked him a few times and I guess I hit an artery because he was gone within a minute. He bled out like a pig," she described. She then handed him the envelope.

Carter frowned as he tried to make sense of it all, but he was lost. "This isn't making too much sense right now. What is this and what were you threatening to tell us? What am I looking at?" he asked as he held up the laptop and watched as a video started to play on the screen. Two white lab rats were running around what seemed to be a complicated maze. A camera was set in each corner and switched views every time the rodents got close to them.

"Look closely," she said as she nodded her head once, urging him to discover what she already knew. Carter placed the laptop on the countertop and looked closely. Anari watched along and began to peel back the layers of the truth.

"I knew something was up. I knew it! So, while we were in the warehouse being briefed, I snuck in and swiped one of the flowers. Before anyone noticed it, I slipped it into my pocket. I then sent it home to a scientist I know and asked him to test it for me. I explained the entire process. I told him specifically how it was broken down and created. He copied the process, breaking it down to its rawest form. He then gave it to lab rats and observed them closely for a week. What he found was mind-blowing. This drug did everything that Ghost had promised. First, it gave the rats an extreme rush so they were excited, running around the maze and interacting with each other. The second phase was the aphrodisiac stage and the lab rats began to become very sexually active and frisky," Anari said as she pointed to the rats on the screen. She paused the video that was showing the rats climbing on top of one another, gyrating rapidly. They were obviously in a state of heightened sexual arousal. She looked at Carter, who still was frowning, trying to understand.

"I know. He told us this is what the drug did already. We learned everything that you are telling me already. I'm not understanding how this is relevant to what we have—no, excuse me, what he had going on. You fucked up big-time," Carter added again as he looked over at Ghost's body and then again at Anari. He clenched his jaw tightly and shook his head in cynicism.

"But peep this. This is two hours later," she said as she sped up the video and jumped ahead a little. Carter looked closely at the video and noticed the rats beginning to act strangely. They began to have sporadic twitches and run into the walls of the mazes, displaying their lack of memory. Carter watched closely as the rats frantically ran through the maze, stopping and smelling and nibbling at every corner. They continued to do it and it became clearer as to what was going on. The rats were looking for something.

"As you can see, they are searching for something. Remind you of anything?" Anari said. At that moment, Carter began to understand that they were feigning for the product. It reminded him of the effect of crack. The rats were in dire need of the very drug that was eating them alive.

"Are they tweaking?" he asked, as he stared closely and watched as the rats kept sniffing each corner, even the same places twice.

"Bingo," she said in a low tone as she watched right along with him. "Sounds familiar, right? They are acting like—"

"Crack heads," he said as the picture started to become clear to him.

"That's right. This is exactly what they did to us in the eighties. They created a drug and put it in our communities so it could break down our families and put our men in jail. The cornerstones of our communities were all being locked in the box. A blow that we still haven't recovered from. Then the thirteenth amendment was implemented, making it legal to make us slaves again using mass incarceration. This shit is deep," Anari said as chills began to go up her arm and behind her neck. Carter felt the same chills at the very same time as the harsh secrets began to show themselves.

She continued, "I knew something was wrong when all of the targeted places had one thing in common: they were all areas with a high number of African Americans and impoverishment. They were using us to repeat what had happened in the Reagan era," Anari continued to explain more in depth. Anari pressed Play and let the tape run. It was a lapsed time video showing the rats moving frantically for an extended amount of time. They even began to fight and snap at each other out of frustration over not being able to find the drug. They both watched as the rats began to fight and fight until eventually one of them killed the other. The second rat eventually died, not being able to recover from the fight with one of its own.

"This is literally our community in a nutshell," Anari added.

"Reaganomics," Carter said as chills went up his spine once again, thinking about how deep the elaborate scheme was.

"Right. If you remember correctly, a few people from the communities got rich in a short period of time when crack hit the scene. But in return, the low-level dealers were all tossed in jail, getting more time than murderers and rapists. Mothers were forced to raise kids on their own and doing that with a crack addiction was detrimental. It tore down an entire generation and set us back years. We were merely pawns and were positioned to handicap our own people," Anari said.

"This is some heavy shit," Carter said in disbelief as he folded his arms and leaned on the sink. His mind was completely blown.

"If you remember correctly, they marked the suburban areas in the country as no-fly zones, making sure that it never touched white America. The writing is on the wall. They tried to play us. They even got that token nigga Ghost to lead us into our own demise," Anari stated.

"They set this play up beautifully. Who are 'they' though?" Carter asked as he rubbed the bottom of his chin and squinted his eyes, trying to fully understand.

"The government. I did more research and look what I found," Anari said just before she messed with the mouse and keyboard and opened another inbox. She then opened a link and showed Carter what was on the screen. A picture of a man popped up and the headline read, CORRUPTION IN POLITICS: POLITICIAN ARRESTED FOR CONSPIRACY TO USE FEDERAL FUNDING FOR PERSONAL USE. "Look closer at the picture," Anari instructed. Carter looked closely and thought the man looked familiar, but couldn't really put a name to the face.

"It's Ghost. Look!" she said as she placed her hand over the laptop screen, covering half of the man's face. "This is what he looked like before the plastic surgery," Anari explained. Carter looked closely and saw that she was right. It was Ghost without the skinny nose and thin lips that he possessed at that moment.

"He was being used as a pawn to recruit and persuade us. We all got played. They probably offered him a deal in return for him recruiting us," Anari insisted.

Carter shook his head and buried his face in his hands.

"They probably were going to set us up to get nabbed as soon as we got the drugs into our community and it could begin to sell itself. At that point, they wouldn't need us anymore. I have something else to show you," Anari said as she walked over by the body and grabbed the envelope that was on the floor. "This is what else I've found," she said.

Carter sat up as she walked over and handed him the envelope. He looked inside and then pulled out the small stack of papers. As he turned the pages, he saw pictures of himself, Anari, Brick, and Millie with all their personal information listed. Age, height, weight, and a list of family members. He looked at his and they had listed everyone he had contact with over the last seven years. He then looked at the top heading and he read, FBI MOST WANTED.

"Not all of the Most Wanted make it to the headlines. They keep stuff like this top secret to avoid alerting people that they are watching closely, waiting for them to slip. A simple phone call to the authorities and they would have been on us like white on rice. They were setting us up for our own downfall. They just needed us to penetrate the slums for them. This shit is crazy."

"Yeah, it's inconceivable but you don't know what this

opportunity just cost me. It cost me everything," Carter said as he shifted his focus back to his family.

"There's more than one way to skin a cat. No one knows Ghost is dead. Let's go through his notes and study them closely. We have to use him as a pawn just like he attempted to use us. I know about your wife. I think I know how to help. I have his phone, so that means I have his connections. I don't believe he truly knew that he was just a puppet as well. All his business was worked through his cell phone and he probably didn't know exactly who he worked for. I'm going to continue to communicate with his 'partners' and see how we can work everything into our favor," she said as she nodded confidently.

Chapter 9

"You might want to tuck in all that pretty hair, light skin." Breeze felt someone tug her long ponytail as she sat on the bench during recreation hour. She turned to find two Hispanic women standing behind her. "You're new booty in here. There's plenty bitches in here that will chop that shit off and flex on you with your own shit. You might want to try a little harder not to look so pampered in this motherfucka. People might think you think you're better than them. You know, one of them bourgeoisie hoes. Ain't no room for that in here. We all on the same level," the woman said.

"I'm not . . . I don't think . . . I'm just minding my business," Breeze said, stumbling over her response as she tried to decide how to approach these women.

"Hmm, hmm," the woman said as she sat down. "That's even worse. Nobody walks around here alone. You link up with your people. After a while family don't visit no more. The people that look like you, talk like you, come from where you from, we become your new family."

"I'm not into the whole gang thing," Breeze replied. "I don't want no problems. I'm just doing my time."

"We all just doing our time and it's not about gangs. It's about heritage mami. The only color that matters is the color of your skin. You can walk around here and alienate yourself if you want, but that makes you an easy mark. What you in here for?"

"Bullshit," Breeze responded. She didn't want to give more information about herself than what was needed.

The woman smirked. "What's your name?"

"Breeze."

"You're not Breeze in here. What's your last name?" the woman shot back. "I'm Sanchez, this is Rezzie."

Breeze looked at the other woman. "Rezzie?" Breeze asked.

"Short for Perez. We stick together in here," Sanchez stated. "So, who the fuck are you?"

"Diamond," Breeze responded.

"Well, Diamond. Tuck that hair and let me know if you need anything," Sanchez said as she stood and walked across the yard with Rezzie right by her side.

"What the hell was that?" Breeze whispered to herself as she watched them stroll away. Breeze looked around, noticing that all the inmates were cliqued up. Everyone belonged somewhere, except for Breeze. She was one of the only women sitting alone.

If you weren't cliqued up you were singled out and with this many women in one place, jealousy quickly surfaced. Breeze's silence came off as arrogance and she was slowly becoming a target. Suddenly, it felt like malicious stares were aimed her way. She didn't know if she had been too naïve and had missed them before but now that she was aware, an uneasiness settled in her stomach. She was like a sheep among wolves.

Breeze stood and tucked her ponytail inside her shirt before making her way back to her cell. At least inside there she only had to battle her thoughts. Out in the yard she was exposed to danger. Anyone could get to her from any angle and the problem was she didn't know exactly who her enemy was. In that moment, Breeze hated that she was so delicate. She hadn't been in one single fight growing up. Her father's army of goons always handled her problems. She had been the only kid throughout school to be escorted each morning by armed men for her protection and those same armed men would pick her up afterward. She had gotten so used to it that she never thought the day would come when she would have to be her own protection. The thought scared her because she didn't know if she had it in her. As she held her bulging belly she knew that she had more to fight for than just herself, but what could she do in her current state? *I'm nine months pregnant and helpless in here.*

Breeze sauntered back to her bunk and as she passed the TV room, she paused. She noticed Sanchez and Rezzie sitting with four other Hispanic women inside. A part of her wanted to go to them and ask for protection. Life inside would be a lot less lonely with allies, but Breeze had been taught to live a certain way. Her blood had been her team for as long as she could remember. She wasn't a girl who had friends, or ran in a crew of women that was placed together for superficial commonalities like looks or money. Her crew had been her family. Linking up with these women would feel different because she knew at the end of the day, none of them would hold her down like family. Besides, nothing in prison came at a fair price. She didn't know how expensive the price may be. Accepting protection from the wrong people could cost her in the end, so she would hold herself down as long as possible to avoid owing a debt. She was learning slowly but surely that nothing was free on the inside. If you received something there was an expectation of repayment and the exchange wasn't always equal. The most manipulative usually came out on top. It was like a prison stock market—deals were made every day. The last thing Breeze needed was to incur a debt with the wrong person inside. That could be deadlier than having nobody to watch her back at all.

Sanchez looked up and Breeze briefly locked eyes with her. In the split second they stared at each other, a million things crossed Breeze's mind. She lowered her gaze and hurried away, knowing that the day would come when she would cross Sanchez's path again. She just didn't know if she would be a friend or an enemy.

Chapter 10

Carter patiently waited in the bushes, crouched down out of sight. The sun was just rising and provided a faint light as he waited in stealth. He then heard the ruffling of the bushes as two people were having a conversation. The voices got clearer as they got closer. Carter looked down at the gun in his hand that once belonged to Ghost. He watched closely as Dr. Ishban and another scientist approached the door to the lab that was hidden in the woods. They had no idea that Carter was waiting in the cut for them. They never saw him rise from the bushes and creep up behind them. Carter pressed the gun directly to the back of Dr. Ishban's head, making him cringe with fear. The other doctor yelled in terror. Almost immediately, Carter removed the gun from the back of Dr. Ishban's head and pressed it to the forehead of the other man.

"Quiet down, my man," Carter said calmly as he winked at him. The man threw up his hands and his lips were zipped closed in sheer fear. He wouldn't dare make another sound, especially staring down the barrel of a chrome .45-caliber pistol. Anari came from the side of the building, slowly clapping sarcastically.

"Young nigga got some scrap in 'em," she said, looking at Carter and smiling. She hadn't done any gangster shit in years and she felt right at home during this ambush.

"Punch in the code," Carter said as he focused his attention back on Dr. Ishban. Carter nudged him with his free hand, pushing him toward the keypad. "Go ahead, put in the code or one of these bullets is going to park in the back of your head, playboy," Carter said, still using a calm, even tone. Dr. Ishban was shaking like a leaf in autumn as he held his hands up and scooted to the keypad. His hand was shaking vigorously. He could barely punch in the correct numbers. After a failed first attempt, the low buzz sounded, signaling that the wrong code had been entered.

"Calm down. Take your time and punch in the code. No one will be hurt if you do what I say. You have my word on that," Carter said, giving the scientist a brief moment of optimism. Dr. Ishban pushed the numbers in and moments later the doors opened. Carter swiftly ushered the scientists in and knew that they had to get down to business before the other scientist came in for the day. They also had to get in and out before Ghost's body was found.

"Let's go!" Carter said as they swiftly moved through

the corridor, making their way to the back of the lab. Anari had instructed Carter that they would need the female and male seed of the flower and once they had possession of that they could take that back to the States and duplicate it and start their own harvest. They also needed all the notes and trial studies that had been done on the drug. This would give them everything they needed to re-create the drug and begin their takeover.

"I need the male and female strand of the Rebe and I need it now," Carter said as he continued to hold them at gunpoint. Anari brushed past, heading directly to the room where the files were held. She was looking for files to take back to her scientist. She disappeared to the back and Carter followed Dr. Ishban to the spot where they kept the seeds. He did exactly what was asked of him and after studying the labels on the small compact pouches, he gave Carter the seeds. Carter quickly snatched them and placed them into his pocket. At that moment Anari came from the back with a few files.

"Got 'em!" she yelled as she came out of the back. Carter glanced at her and then focused back on the scientist. Carter then hog-tied the scientists with the ties they had gotten from Ghost's villa. Carter secured the ties and left the two men squirming on the ground as they exited the lab with everything they needed to relocate the entire operation and start from scratch. However, this time it would be with their own scientist and their own game plan. They had devised this plan in the wee hours of the night and in the company of Ghost's dead body.

* * *

They were on their way back home with the keys to the future. Anari and Carter exited the property without any problems and without anyone knowing what their plans were. They had a game plan to flood the streets with this new drug but instead of following the original plan that Ghost had presented, they decided to do the opposite and put it in the suburbs of America. Pills were the new crack and they had the best illegal pill known to humankind. It was a new day and the beginning of a new era. Anari set up transportation and then set up Carter with fake documents to get him back into the States undetected. Carter soon found out that Anari was shaping out to be most likely the most resourceful partner he had ever had. She was well connected and well respected.

Carter's main goal was to get back home and see what was the problem with his family. The fact that Breeze was unreachable had him worried. He still hadn't heard from Breeze and was determined to get to his family, even if it cost him his freedom. He was a wanted man back in the States but he didn't care at this point. He was prepared to go out swinging. However, he had to find out what was wrong. Breeze was his safety net and with her not responding, it sent his entire world into a frenzy. He was determined to get back home and get to the bottom of things. He also knew that to make power moves, he had to be in a position of power, which meant being financially ready for anything. He wasn't as wealthy as he had been previous to the federal government being on his tail. He knew that this move with Anari would strengthen his financial health, which would enable him to do more. He was about to step back into the game, two feet in. All gas and no brakes.

* * *

Carter's heart pumped furiously as he walked through customs with his phony paperwork. It was a week after they had killed Ghost and they were heading back into the United States. They had to stay in the country for a few days so that Anari's connections could send Carter over his fake documents. In the meantime, Anari and Carter were making calls setting up a pipeline and setting up shop for their new drug. The plan was for them to be up and running within a month and the drug Rebe would make its street debut.

The crowded customs terminal was hot, muggy, and loud from all the various conversations and movement going on. People hastily pulled their luggage and speed walked through the terminal, everyone having their own agenda. Police were scattered throughout the place, some walking K-9s, letting them sniff their way around and about. They were obviously looking for drug traffickers or anything out of the norm. Little did they know they had two of the biggest ones in America's history passing through. Carter casually looked around, trying to blend in as best he could. He wore cheap clothes and had a camera around his neck. The straw hat that sat on top of his head was far from his style; however, he needed to look as much like a tourist as possible. The passport said his name was Dean Griswold but little did they know he was one of the FBI's Most Wanted. He watched as Anari slid through customs without a problem. She looked back at him and quickly moved her focus past him, not wanting to give any indication that they were together.

Carter approached the officer who was checking people's documentation and his heart began to pump faster and faster the closer he got. Carter grimaced as he felt a sharp pain shoot through his heart and stopped walking momentarily as he squinted his eyes, hoping that the pain would subside.

"Are you okay, sir?" the police officer asked as he frowned in concern.

"Yes, I'm fine. Too much spicy Indian food," Carter said as he felt the pain going away. He smiled and passed the officer the fraudulent passport. The officer held it up and put it next to Carter's face and his eyes went from the passport to Carter's face, back and forth. He studied closely and Carter tried his best to look calm and unbothered, even though he was growing uncomfortable. After a few seconds of examining, the officer smiled and gave Carter his documents.

"Come again," the man said as he smiled. Carter quickly passed through and saw Anari waiting on the other side. They were scheduled to be on a commercial flight back to the States and it was the safest option. Anari explained that the border patrol had been very leery of private jets coming into the U.S., so she suggested that they try to blend in with the crowd and be as normal as possible. Within an hour they were on a steel bird in the sky headed back to their home—the streets.

* * *

"I've never seen anything like this in all my years," the young scientist said as he held up the test tube and shook the milky contents around. Anari looked on as she crossed her arms in front of her. She listened closely as the scientist stood there in disbelief. "This substance has a melting point substantially higher than that of the purest form of cocaine documented here in the U.S. Cocaine melts at about 208 degrees Fahrenheit. This Rebe, once in powder form, is at about 230. You, my friend, have a monster."

"Okay, talk so I can fucking understand you," Anari said as she tried to get a better understanding.

"Basically, you have the rawest shit that this country has ever seen. This can get stepped on five times and still have the same potency as the highest grade of drug on the streets," the scientist said, stripping away all of the scientific terms and getting straight to the point.

Anari smiled and saw dollar signs. She was about to set up shop in different suburbs across the nation and retire at the top of her game. By the time the feds got a whiff of what she was doing, she would be retired. The plan was coming together nicely.

Carter sat in his car and watched closely as he had been

doing every day for a week straight. There was no sign of Breeze or the kids. He continued to call but he always got the same result: voice mail. He didn't know where to start. He was lost and his faith was slipping away.

He felt the burner phone buzz in his lap and looked down, seeing that it was the private investigator that Anari had plugged him with. He hired him to help him find his family and make sense of it all. He looked at the phone screen and it simply read,

Meet me at same spot. I have an update for you.

Carter responded back immediately, texting,

On way.

He quickly started up the car and headed toward the small coffee shop just outside Dade County. Carter set up the place as a meeting spot, because it had no cameras and had relatively low traffic. Anari had connected him with one of the most respected P.I.'s in the country. He was a brown bag customer, meaning his services only were to be paid in paper bags, no trace. Carter loved that business model, seeing that it fit his circumstances perfectly.

He headed onto the freeway and rolled down the window to feel some of that fresh Miami air. It had been a long time since he had been in his old stomping grounds and he had to feel that salty, humid air as he zoomed down the interstate. He took a deep breath and inhaled as he enjoyed the scenery and tall palm trees that hovered over the highway.

I beat this highway up, Carter thought to himself with a smirk as he thought about the Cartel days and how much weight he used to move up and down the interstate. He thought back to the first day that he stepped foot in Miami and that was to see the father he had never known. He met his father at his funeral and that image always stuck with him. It was the day that changed his life forever and he found out that he had brothers and a sister. It was the day he was thrust into a position he wasn't ready for. Although Carter didn't truly know if that day changed his life for better or worse, he understood that it started a roller-coaster ride that he couldn't have imagined.

A tear dropped down his cheek as he thought about the life he had created for himself. He had never imagined that he would have made millions and owned casinos in Vegas. He also never imagined being on the FBI's Most Wanted list or going to war with some of the most powerful men in the country. It was all surreal to him. He wiped away the tear and looked down at his phone, which was buzzing. It was from a blocked number and he quickly picked it up.

"Hello," he said with optimism that it would be Breeze. He longed to find her so he could reunite with his only son. Every moment away from him broke his heart and he knew how it felt to not have your father around while growing up. It pained him, but he knew that he was continuing the cycle that he'd vowed to break.

"Yo, we got one," Anari said calmly as she hinted about what the scientist had explained to her. Carter closed his eyes in disappointment. Anari wasn't the voice he wanted to hear.

"Oh, yeah," he said as he gathered his composure.

"Yeah, it's so potent, we can moonwalk all over this mu'fucka," she said with the utmost confidence.

"Sounds like we on to something then," Carter said as he turned the wheel to get off on his exit.

"No doubt. But dig this. I think we need to expand and see if some of my old friends want in. I have some heavy hitters out in the Dominican Republic. I can see this being worldwide, rather than just here. I really think I should set up a meeting. You game?" she asked as she walked into her condominium, undressing herself. Although Anari was in her forties, her body was still toned. She talked business as she locked eyes with her husband who was waiting for her naked with an erection in his hand. She hadn't had any dick in weeks and had instructed him to get ready right before she got on the phone.

"I'm game, set it up," Carter confirmed just before he closed his phone and pulled into the small coffee shop just off the freeway.

Anari, on the other hand, ended the call but started her ride on the dick of Von, her husband. She kissed him passionately and whispered how much she loved him in between the wet sloppy kisses. He gripped her buttocks and squeezed them as he slowly guided her up and down on his shaft. Not even thirty seconds into the lovemaking session, Anari exploded all over his pole and her body quivered from the orgasm and tingling throughout her body. She smiled and stopped grinding and rested her head on his shoulder.

"I'm so sorry," she said.

"You ain't shit," he said while smiling.

"I know," she said as they both burst into laughter. Years of marriage had made them best friends and they were both glad that she was back home.

* * *

"So your nephew seems to have gotten himself into a bit of trouble," the private investigator said as he slid the court documents across the table, detailing the assault that Mo was charged with.

"Damn," Carter said as he picked up the paper and studied it.

"They have him locked up in juvie as of now and it doesn't seem like he's getting out anytime soon. He is declared a ward of the state," the man explained. The P.I. reached into his briefcase and pulled out another court document with a picture clipped to its right corner. It was a small photo of Breeze's mug shot.

"What the fuck is this?" Carter asked as he felt like an apple was in his throat when he tried to swallow.

"She was picked up for tax evasion. She's in a federal prison serving her time now," he explained as he pointed out her charges on the paper. Carter's head dropped as he felt despair, thinking about where his baby boy was.

"What about my boy? What about C.J.?" Carter asked as he looked at the man sitting across from him in desperation.

"That's the thing. Nobody can locate him. He is listed as a runaway," the man explained.

"Wait. What? A runaway?" Carter said as he tried his best to take in all the information.

"Yes. The last known place of residency was with a woman that worked for the state as a social worker." He then reached into the bag and pulled out a piece of paper. "Here is her last known address, number, and address of her workplace. This should be a good place to start," he said as he got up and extended his hand. "I hope this helped."

"Yeah . . ." Carter said halfheartedly as he tried to wrap his mind around what was going on. He shook the man's hand and reached into his pockets to pull out the money wrapped in a brown paper bag, but the man quickly signaled for him to stop.

"No worries. Anari has taken care of me already. Good day, sir," he said just before he walked away and out of the café, leaving Carter there with a table full of papers.

Carter had to think wisely before he approached the lady, knowing that she was a government employee. However, he was on a mission to find his son and even if he had to be on the run with him, so be it. But first . . . he had a trip to the Dominican Republic to take. He had to get his ducks in a row so he could knock them down. First, establish a money flow, get his son, and approach the DA with the threat of blackmail. He decided to use his trip to the Dominican as his planning period and on their return, he would go hard and get his family back once and for all.

Chapter 11

C.J. was silent as he sat in the back of the tinted Mercedes next to Estes as they were driven through the streets of Santo Domingo. As C.J. looked outside his window he saw the poverty that had taken hold of the people who lived there. Not everyone lived like Estes and C.J. wondered how Estes had gotten rich while the rest of the people in his native country seemed to be starving. A tense knot settled in his stomach and his chest ached from the anxiety of what was waiting for him ahead. He wasn't afraid of the fight to come, but the possibility of losing and getting further on Estes's bad side worried him. There was money on the line and C.J. didn't want to disappoint.

He stayed silent for the entire drive and when they pulled up to an old tobacco factory he was surprised at how big it was. He had pictured a small fight with small fuss, just some old men who had too much money who had created a small ring. This was the size of an arena. The building had closed long ago yet the scent of tobacco leaves still filled the air. Its broken windows and rusting exterior made the place a perfect location to conduct dirty business.

"I used to come here as a boy. My papa threw me in this ring when I was ten years old. Whether I won or lost, I built character over the years I fought here," Estes reminisced.

C.J. didn't respond as the car rolled to a stop. He stepped out and looked up at the tall building. Intimidation filled him, but he tried hard not to show it. He followed Estes inside, stomach queasy and legs shaky.

It looked like a coliseum inside. The middle of the factory had been barricaded off, forming an arena. Men stood on the outside of the barricade boisterously cheering as two young boys went to war on the inside. C.J. felt sick to his stomach as he watched the boys tear each other apart. This wasn't the type of fighting C.J. had in mind. There were no gloves, no referee, no rules, just savagery.

"You're up next," Estes said. The words rolled off his tongue so casually that C.J. looked at him in shock.

"Put your game face on, kid. You go out there looking like you want to run home to your mommy and you're going to be swallowing your teeth," Estes said. He bent down and stared C.J. straight in the eye. "You aren't ever in that pit with anybody that's better than you. You don't fear any man. Your enemy bleeds just like you bleed. That feeling in your heart, making you feel like you want to run, your opponent feels that too. That's not fear, that's fuel. You use that," Estes said. C.J. nodded and gritted his teeth as Estes pushed him into the pit.

Two men carried the losing boy out of the pit as the winner walked off. C.J.'s eyes widened as they carried the loser right by him. The kid moaned, barely conscious, his face bloodied to the point of unrecognition.

C.J. looked up as a Dominican boy stepped into the pit. He was taller than C.J. and about twenty pounds heavier. The look in his eyes held no fear. A loud bell rang and the boy charged at C.J., who dodged the first punch and then the second, only frustrating his opponent. C.J. was swift.

"Stop running!" a voice shouted from the crowd. The whoops and hollers only seemed to incite the kid. His fists might not have been connecting but the wind that came behind them was so strong that C.J. could almost feel the knockout coming. C.J. was just a boy but he wasn't a fool. If he squared up with this boy he would lose. The kid had a size advantage over C.J., but C.J. had stamina. The kid couldn't land a punch on C.J. if he tried and with every swing his frustrations grew. It only made the boy exert more energy trying to land one knockout.

When C.J. found his opening, he threw a punch, connecting with the kid's face. Dodging the kid's counter, he faded him again, landing one to the boy's eye once again. C.J. wasn't technical with his attack, but he had sparred with Mo enough times to know how to handle an older kid. He had taken losses fighting Mo to prepare him to give one out when he was tested by an outsider.

The crowd erupted in surprise. C.J. was the underdog. It was his first fight and everyone expected him to lose. Grown men had big money on his opponent but C.J. wasn't proving to be an easy win.

C.J.'s adrenaline had turned him into a beast and he was executing each punch with precision, completely frustrating the boy. It was obvious he couldn't outswing C.J. but when he delivered a blinding head butt, C.J. was stunned as he stumbled backward. Blood leaked from his nose as a ringing filled his ears. C.J. bent over and the kid followed up with a knee to C.J.'s face.

"Get up!" Estes shouted. C.J. was dazed and the blood in his eyes stopped him from seeing well. He scrambled backward but the kid was coming at him too fast. The boy lifted his foot but C.J. rolled out of his path, barely avoiding the kid's wrath. He struggled to his feet, squinting his eyes as he wiped the blood away with the back of his hand. The kid swung, and C.J. dodged left and came back with a hook to the jaw that buckled the boy's legs. C.J. kept attacking because he knew if he stopped, the boy would get the best of him. He didn't want to give this kid any opportunity to strike back. C.J. kept waiting to hear some type of bell that signified the end, but no one stopped the fight. The kid fell to his knees and C.J. punched him. His fists were so sore that with each strike it felt like his knuckles would break. C.J. stopped when he heard the kid yell, "I'm done."

"You're not done!" a man in the crowd shouted as he jumped into the pit. He rushed over to the kid and pulled the boy to his feet, only for the kid to fall back to his knees. C.J. stood, unsurely, his hands up, ready.

The kid wasn't tapping back into the fight, however. The man pushed the boy down onto the ground in disappointment and C.J. finally relaxed as the crowd erupted at the unexpected defeat. C.J. backpedaled, not wanting to take his eyes off the kid. He retreated to Estes, who stood with a proud smirk.

He placed a firm hand on C.J.'s shoulder and they walked through the unruly crowd of men.

It was a blood sport. It was a fight to the finish and C.J. had proven more than anything else that he had heart.

* * *

Estes chuckled to himself as C.J. tore into the meal that his personal chef had made for him. He had certainly earned the dinner.

"Are you sure you don't want anything else? I tell you my chef can make you anything in the world and you choose a burger and fries?" Estes was amused by C.J.'s humility. It was honorable and rare.

C.J. chewed sloppily and didn't respond. He had worked up quite an appetite. Estes was surprisingly proud of C.J. The kid wasn't his blood but he was something special. His grandson Mecca had been a beast, Monroe had been sharp as nails, but they had their faults as well. C.J. seemed to possess an inner monster that he brought out when needed, but he had self-control too. He was smart and most important he possessed a level head that allowed him to assess a situation before reacting. *If Mecca and Monroe had been anything like him, they both would still be alive,* Estes thought. *If my Sammie had been more like him . . .* Estes stopped the thought. He didn't want to let his thoughts lead him down that path.

Nevertheless, he was impressed with C.J. He was young and had no one, yet somehow each time he fell, he landed on his feet. His resilience was remarkable and the young boy intrigued Estes. The way C.J. fought, fearlessly, Estes knew he could make a lot of money by putting C.J. in the pit each week. With a bit of training, C.J. would be unbeatable.

"I underestimated you when you first arrived, C.J.," Estes admitted. "This is your home now. You have access to anything here. The room that you walked in before . . . it belonged to my son. He died a long time ago. That is the only place in the house that I ask you to stay away from. Other than that, you have free rein at the place. You have a gift with your hands, C.J. You're young and your instincts are good. I would like to put you back in the pit. You stand to make a lot of money. You can shape your own life, C.J. Every fight you win, I will put money away for you, in an account that belongs to you. You'll have the best trainers, the best diet. I can turn you into a machine if you let me," Estes said. "What do you say?"

C.J. nodded. Working out his anger in the pit had felt good. After the fear had dissolved, he felt liberated. Every punch he threw was about more than just winning. Since he was five years old he had felt vulnerable. From the day

Baraka had taken him from his family, C.J. felt powerless and displaced as if he would never truly be safe anywhere, not even with his family. In the pit, he felt in control. With every blow his hands delivered he released a bit of the hurt he felt inside. He didn't need to speak about his emotions, he could just fight through them.

"Okay," C.J. agreed. Estes went to the freezer and retrieved a bag of frozen vegetables. He tossed them to C.J.

"For your hands," Estes said. "Get some rest. You went into the pit unprepared today and you still came out victorious. In the morning, you'll train."

CHAPTER 12

Just wash your body as fast as possible and get out of here, Breeze thought as she stood outside the running stream of water, staring at the disgusting shower stall. The stained tile made her think it had never been cleaned and the fact that she had nothing to cover her feet made her cringe. Still, she stepped inside, knowing that her options were limited. She gasped in surprise at the coldness that hit her skin. *Apparently, warm water is a luxury too,* she thought. She held the tiny piece of bar soap in her hand that they had given her upon her arrival and tried her best to create a foamy lather. It wasn't much. In fact, the cheap soap didn't lather at all, but it was all she had so she didn't complain. Breeze wet her hair, letting the water rinse through it. She wished that she could rinse her worry away, but anxiety held her captive and there was no escaping it.

She heard the chatter of girls around her and she tried

to drown out the noise. She tried to allow the power of her mind to take her outside these walls. She was so alone. No allies, no family, no friends. Inside, all she had was herself.

Breeze scrubbed her body as best she could, using her hands as the towel since she couldn't afford to purchase one. She had the bare necessities, but when the tiny, sample-sized bar disappeared, she cut off the water. An eerie feeling swept over her as she frowned. There was no gossip, no loud singing from the fat lady who always put on a concert during wash time, not even the sound of the other showers running. She reached to pull back the shower curtains but before she could, she was bum rushed. Breeze was pushed against the wall as blows rained down on her. She tried to block the assault, but being cornered didn't leave her room to defend herself. She curled up in a ball and tried to shield her stomach, to no avail. The kicks to her bulging stomach vibrated through her entire body and fear filled her.

God please make it stop, she thought. She caught a blurry glimpse of her attacker as she fled away. She was shaking, bleeding, and as she came up on all fours she crawled across the grimy floor. "Help me," she cried, blood leaking from her mouth. She stood slowly, surprised that her legs would even carry her, but the stabbing pain that shot through Breeze made her double over. She placed a hand on her swollen belly as thunder seemed to strike within her. Something was wrong. It felt like someone was tearing her in half. She drew in a sharp breath as wetness seeped between her thighs. She shuddered as she waited for the feeling to pass, but it only intensified, making her hold her breath to try to ease the sharp discomfort.

"Agh!" she whispered as she gripped the mold-covered shower wall. She stumbled out of the tiny space, bumping into another inmate. Where had she come from? Where was she when Breeze was being beaten? Confusion and fear caused her words to jumble as she tried to speak. Everything hurt. Her face was swollen, blood was everywhere, and through it all she noticed that her baby wasn't kicking.

"Watch yourself," the girl said as she nudged Breeze hard with one shoulder before rushing out. Inmates had seen it all. It wasn't uncommon for someone to catch a beatdown when the guards weren't looking and even though Breeze needed help, the girl wasn't fazed by the scene. Breeze gripped the sink as she grimaced in excruciation. *This isn't right. Something is wrong. This can't be happening,* she thought as her vision blurred with tears and blood. The feeling was too familiar. She remembered how losing her first child had felt. Every second of that horrible day had been burned into her memory. She stood there, sweat forming on her brow as she tried to manage the pain, fearing the worst. It was happening all over again. No one even batted an eye. The other inmates walked by her as if she were invisible.

Breeze reached between her legs and when she pulled back a bloody hand her heart dropped. She tried to stand upright, but another jolt of pain caused her to double over.

If it weren't for the sink acting as her crutch, she wouldn't have been able to remain on her feet.

The perverted male guards were constantly patrolling the showers. She usually cringed at the thought of them passing through the bathroom when she was in such a vulnerable state. Now she hoped they came. Where were they when she needed them? Where were they when she was getting her baby beaten out of her? She growled as she leaned over the sink, trying to manage the pains that seemed to be coming and going so quickly that she didn't have time to catch her breath. "Agh, help me," she whispered to an inmate that waltzed up to use the sink beside her. "Please . . . I think . . ." Breeze reached down, as if she were trying to plug the hole that was widening between her legs. She squeezed her thighs tightly. Horror was in her eyes. "I'm losing my baby."

The woman looked down at Breeze. "What I look like to you, a doctor?" she snapped. She started to walk away.

"Please—please help me," Breeze stammered, grasping the girl's wrist. She was weak and her legs threatened to give out at any moment and when the girl snatched away she collapsed onto one knee.

No one wanted to get involved. They were heartlessly ignoring her, seeing her swollen eye and busted lip, no one wanting to get in the middle of whatever beef Breeze had. Each woman that walked into the showers callously walked by her as if she were invisible. The stabbing sensation that filled her was paralyzing. She looked up and saw Rezzie come around the corner.

"Yo are you a'ight?" Rezzie asked. "Oh shit, who did this to you?" Rezzie turned to another girl. "Yo go get some fucking help! You don't see her bleeding over here, bitch?"

"I didn't know she was one of us, my bad, Rezzie," the girl replied as she rushed out.

"One of us?" Breeze asked.

"I told you. We look out for our own in here," Rezzie said. Sanchez rushed in urgently. "Oh shit, she's going to have that baby right here on the bathroom floor," Sanchez said. "Sit her down, sit her down."

"No—the girl . . ." Breeze stammered. "She went to get help."

"I am the help, ma," Sanchez replied.

"What?" Breeze was scared. "I need a doctor."

"If we go get a C.O. you will deliver this baby and they will take it from you without ever giving you a chance to hold it. Now I can do this. Rezzie and I will help you. I've had two babies, all natural, at home with my *abuela*. It's going to hurt like hell, but you can trust me," Sanchez said.

"Agh," Breeze cried. She wanted to protest, but the pain was too overwhelming. She gritted her teeth so hard it felt like they would shatter. She felt pressure everywhere. It felt like every organ in her body was pressing down, threatening to explode out of her.

"Help me get her up," Sanchez said. "We'll take her to the spot."

"The spot?" Breeze asked in concern.

They led her to a door in the back of the shower room.

It was normally locked, but Sanchez reached inside her bra and retrieved the key.

A trail of blood followed them as they struggled to get Breeze inside. Breeze looked around in horror. "I can't give birth in an empty broom closet with a radio and cigarette butts on the floor," she objected. "Agh!" she doubled over in pain. "Something feels wrong."

"You're about to pass a baby through your cooch, princess. Ain't nothing right about it. It's just contractions and they are coming back to back. I know this ain't the Four Seasons, but this is happening now," Sanchez said. "Put some towels down."

Rezzie tried to make a comfortable pallet on the concrete floor and they hurriedly laid her down.

Sanchez opened her legs.

"I need medicine. It hurts," Breeze wailed.

"Just breathe, Diamond," Rezzie coached.

This wasn't how it was supposed to be. Breeze was supposed to be with her husband, in a hospital, anxiously awaiting the birth of their baby girl with the best doctors surrounding her. Instead, she was here going through the process like an animal.

She tensed as Sanchez put her hands in forbidden places.

"You measure it by fingertips," Sanchez whispered unsurely to herself.

"You don't know?!" Breeze cried.

"I got you!" Sanchez said. Breeze was terrified and from

the uncertain look on Sanchez's face, Breeze saw that her fear was infectious.

"Just push," Sanchez urged. "My *abuela* told me you push through the pain. The next time you feel your stomach tighten."

Rezzie grabbed one of her legs and pulled it back as Breeze wrapped her hands under her knees.

"Push, Diamond, push." Rezzie's voice was in her ear as Breeze mustered everything in her.

The scream that erupted from her was so loud that Rezzie stuffed a towel in Breeze's mouth to stifle her.

"Shh," Rezzie said.

"I can't do this," Breeze cried.

Breeze looked through her widened legs right into Sanchez's eyes.

"You can. I see the head. All you got to do is push," Sanchez said. Breeze heaved in exhaustion. Sanchez said the words so simply as if she was asking Breeze to do the simplest thing. The task in front of her was daunting. Breeze felt like this baby would never come out of her.

"I can't do this," she cried.

"You probably haven't had to work hard a day in your life. You're going to have to work hard for this. If you want me to call the C.O. I will but you won't even get to hold your kid after you pop it out. If you want to do it the hard way and prove that you're not some fucking spoiled little bitch that gets everything handed to her, then you push. You can do this. Now fucking push, Diamond."

Breeze placed her chin to her chest and growled fiercely as she pushed. She imagined that it was her mother beside her. She pushed and pushed. With each contraction, she pushed harder until finally the sound of tiny cries rewarded her.

"Is she okay?" Breeze asked, worried, her voice cracking from the overwhelming triumph she felt. She never thought she could ever be so strong. She didn't even think that type of strength dwelled inside her. Motherhood had suddenly given her a superpower. "Give her to me."

Breeze didn't care that her baby was covered in blood or that the cord was still attached. She received her with open arms and laid her right on her chest. Her heart swelled as Rezzie covered the baby with a towel.

"She looks a little blue," Rezzie said.

"What?" Breeze responded, panicked. "What do you mean?"

"Yo maybe we need to get a C.O.," Rezzie urged.

Breeze noticed that her baby had stopped crying but she thought it was because she had found comfort from being in her mother's arms.

"I don't think she's breathing," Rezzie said.

Sanchez opened the door to the closet. "C.O.! Somebody get help! I've got a baby in here!"

Panic erupted as a guard rushed in moments later. She didn't hear anything. It was like the world was muffled as the guard took her daughter out of her arms. A woman in a white doctor's coat rushed inside with a surgical bag. "I have to cut this cord and get the placenta out of you," she instructed, but Breeze heard nothing. She reached for her baby. As soon as the doctor cut the umbilical cord, Breeze felt the disconnection.

"Give me my daughter!" Breeze screamed. Paramedics rushed into the room and immediately prepared the infant for transport. "No! Where are you taking her? What's wrong with her? Is she okay? Is she breathing?" Breeze asked. Her pleas were heartbreaking and as she was lifted onto a stretcher she screamed, "God please!" Breeze looked at the somber looks on the faces of Sanchez and Rezzie, fearing the worst.

"We have to get her to the infirmary now," the doctor said.

"What about my baby?" Breeze slurred. She was feeling light-headed.

"She's off to county hospital. I will get you updates as soon as I hear something. I must worry about you right now."

"I can't keep my eyes open," Breeze said. "I'm . . ." Before she could finish her sentence Breeze slipped into unconsciousness.

"She's crashing! I need to get her to a defibrillator now!" the doctor ordered.

The guards rolled her down the hall, practically running toward the infirmary as the doctor administered CPR. Breeze had lost so much blood and her blood pressure was so low that the doctor feared it may be too late. She had seen many things but never had two inmates delivered a baby on their own. Not only was Breeze's life at stake but her daughter's was as well. The doctor only prayed that she could keep Breeze stable. Health care in the prison system wasn't equipped for this type of emergency and the doctor hoped that today wouldn't be the day that a prisoner died on her watch.

* * *

When Breeze finally came to she felt like she had been hit by a bus. Her entire body ached and an exhaustion she had never experienced took over her.

"Relax, just relax," a woman said.

Breeze tried to sit up. Her eyes focused on the stitching of the white medical coat the woman wore. The woman was a doctor, but Breeze couldn't help but wonder what type of doctor would separate a mother from her child. She could feel it in her soul that her daughter was nowhere in this prison. "Where is she? Where is my baby? Is she okay?"

"She was transferred to County Medical. She was having a hard time breathing and we had to rush her over there so they could help her. She's fine. She will stay there until Child Services gets her."

"What?" Breeze said, baffled. "You can't just take my baby!"

"I'm sorry, it was in her best interest to get her to the hospital as soon as possible." The words didn't quite connect with the woman's demeanor. She was cold, careless, as if they were discussing something as simple as the weather. This woman had cut the cord between her and her baby without securing a connection in another form. It was cruelty at its finest.

"I'm her best interest! I'm her mother! Take me to my daughter! You can't do this!" Breeze was irate. She was destroyed by the separation. "I didn't even get the chance to name her. She's mine. You cannot do this!" Breeze was fighting to get out of the bed.

"You've lost some blood. You need to lie down. Tomorrow you will be taken back to your cell—"

Breeze pushed the doctor so hard that she stumbled backward into the metal file cabinet. The commotion caused a guard to rush in.

"No, wait! She's just upset!" the doctor defended.

"Where is my daughter?!" Breeze shouted. She was crying and fighting so hard that the guard restrained her as the doctor shot a sedative in her arm.

"It won't put you under, but it will calm you," the doctor explained. "You need rest."

* * *

Hours passed and although Breeze settled on the outside, inside she was going through turmoil. She laid there through the night, unable to find sleep, as worry and fear filled her.

Breeze's tears were endless. Never did she think it would be this hard to let her baby go. She had only held her sweet daughter briefly before they took her away. She got one day in the infirmary and now they were forcing her back to the hellhole that was her cell.

"Let's go, Diamond," the guard said. There was no courtesy, no patience in the man's tone. It was like she hadn't even given birth at all. Breeze didn't move. She simply laid on the hard bed, facing the wall, and closing her eyes tightly as sobs wracked her body. Breeze couldn't seem to get it together. Filled with confusing emotions, she had hormones all over the place. She couldn't go back to her cell block like this. She would look like food to the vultures that awaited her.

"I need a minute," Breeze choked out.

"On your feet, Diamond," the guard persisted.

"I need a minute! I just had a baby and I'm bleeding! Can I have some fucking privacy to change my pad? Damn!" Breeze was uncharacteristically crass as she sat up reluctantly in the bed. She stared the guard in the eyes. "Are you going to watch me do it?" she challenged.

The guard backed down. "You've got two minutes."

He walked out of the room and Breeze hurriedly stood to her feet. She rushed over to the drawers where the doctor's supplies were located. She couldn't go back to her cell while they took her baby to the local hospital. A mother was supposed to be with her child. That was the natural order of things. This was cruelty. Breeze just wanted a little more time, she wanted to give a little more love, she needed to smell her baby's scent even if only for a little while. Breeze pulled at the drawers, growing frustrated as each one failed to open. They were locked and tears welled in her eyes. "Come on," she whispered. She pulled at the drawer violently until finally the flimsy lock gave. She rifled through the contents so quickly that she barely had time to read. She found a pack of razor blades and her hands shook as she opened them. The guard came back in just as she held it in her hands.

"Diamond! Drop it now," the guard yelled. Breeze didn't hesitate. She quickly placed the blade on her tongue and swallowed it. She felt it slice her throat on the way down and she was quickly tackled to the ground. The man pinched the sides of her jaws. "Let me see it. Open your mouth. Where is it?" he yelled.

Breeze didn't respond. She simply let her tears fall down her cheeks.

"You swallowed it?" the guard asked. He placed her in cuffs and sighed in exasperation as he called for help on his walkie-talkie.

The doctor rushed into the room. "She just had a baby! You can't handle her that way."

"She swallowed a razor blade, doc!" the guard shouted.

"I'll call a bus," the doctor said, springing into action as she picked up the phone. "That blade can cut up every one of her organs if it hits her in the right spots. Be gentle with her. Move her to this gurney."

Breeze laid down on the gurney and looked up into the woman's eyes.

"Why did you do this?"

"I just want to be near my baby," Breeze whispered. The desperation it took to go to such measures was one that only a mother could feel. Breeze knew that if she had slit her wrists they would have just sewn her up. She had to do something drastic, something they couldn't handle. The doctor looked at her with sympathetic eyes. She gave Breeze's hand a reassuring squeeze. Breeze saw understanding in her eyes. She could only imagine the things the doctor had seen, nursing some of the most violent women in the country back to health.

The doctor nodded subtly and whisked her away. Breeze knew they would have to take her to the county hospital to surgically remove the razor blade and that was exactly where she wanted to be.

She was risking her life. All it took was for the razor blade to touch the wrong organ and she would bleed out within minutes, but she didn't care. She was desperate and willing to take any measure to get in arm's reach of her child. Her baby didn't even have a name yet. The tiny human being didn't even know who she was yet. They needed time, even if only a little bit, to get to know each other. Breeze needed to be able to whisper into her daughter's ear and reassure her that she would come for her, even though her baby didn't understand. She hoped that the nature that connected them, the blood that flowed through them, and the familiar sound of her mother's heartbeat would be enough for her daughter to remember her.

The sound of the ambulance's sirens blared in her ear as they exited the prison and she was lifted into the back.

A sense of hope filled Breeze as she saw the sky. She looked at the hues of blue and admired the dense white puff of clouds that floated high above her. She was outside the walls of the prison and she never truly understood how good it felt to be free until this moment. She drew in that free air and closed her eyes to enjoy it, briefly. Dread quickly came washing over her because she knew the escape was only temporary. She would return and when she did, she would be empty-handed.

* * *

It felt like she was floating. Those white, fluffy clouds surrounded her as she flew high, never wanting to come down. Breeze was semiconscious as she slowly awoke from the anesthesia. Her eyes were heavy, so heavy that it was easier to not try to open them at all. So, she stayed right there, between consciousness and unconsciousness, unshackled, unbothered, and completely unaware of the six-hour surgery she had just endured. *Is this heaven?* she thought. Her entire body felt soothed. Physically, emotionally, and spiritually, she was on one accord. It was almost orgasmic.

Her entire life she had felt some type of pain. That's what living was about. Pain reminded Breeze that she was still breathing, still living; no matter how small the pain was, she lived with something on her heart daily. Perhaps it was a physical ailment, or an emotional scar, or a spiritual wound, but pain always existed until now. In this peaceful, elevated space, all she felt was bliss. That let her know that this place couldn't be real. Life never felt this good. The absence of pain meant the absence of life and the fear that came with that thought brought her crashing out of the clouds and down to reality where all the hurt awaited her.

"Hmm," she moaned as her eyelids fluttered. Hazy images came into view as Breeze blinked slowly, trying to force herself to awaken. The agony seemed to hit her all at once and she didn't even have to summon the tears that leaked out of the sides of her eyes. They were effortless, like residual raindrops that fell on windowpanes after a storm.

"Relax, relax." A soothing voice could be heard in the distance but Breeze couldn't come out of the fog long enough to see the face to whom it belonged. "You're going to feel very heavy, very confused for a little bit. Just take your time and come out of it slowly."

Breeze took a deep breath, but that only seemed to lull her back to sleep.

"Hey baby girl."

This voice she recognized. It was her father and she opened her eyes trying to find him. The heavy drugs pulled her eyes closed as if they were shutters.

"Be strong, Breeze. You're a Diamond."

She heard him again. This time she saw him and she wasn't sure if this was heaven or if she were simply dreaming but she wanted to stay. Security filled her. There was nothing like the love of Big Carter. He was her father and since the day he had been callously taken from her world, no one had been able to fill his void. Not even her brothers had made her feel as safe as her papa.

She wanted to speak back to him but she couldn't.

It was like her mouth was glued shut and the more she struggled to speak, the more it felt like she couldn't breathe.

"Be strong, Breeze."

It was her mother's voice she heard next and torment filled her. Her sweet mother, her innocent mother. Slain in the crosshairs of a war. She was a victim to the game, murdered by Miamor before Miamor became a part of their family.

Breeze was so emotional. Suddenly this dark place felt like hell. She hadn't thought of the deaths of her parents in years. Now in this heightened state of emotion their memory was being dredged up against her will. She couldn't even wake herself up to escape it so she just lay there, in darkness, listening to the ones she had buried as they urged her to be strong. It felt like a joke. She had always been the weakest link of the Diamond family. She was supposed to go away to college, to make a life outside of the streets for herself, but she had fallen for a gangster. She had fallen for a man like her father and from the moment she met Zyir, she knew that she had chosen the type of man that belonged to the streets.

"Wake up, B."

It was Mecca. Her dear, live wire of a brother. Oh, how she missed him. She wanted to tell him, but still no words escaped her.

"Breeze, get up."

The last voice was Monroe's and Breeze's eyes opened. She weakly reached for the remote that lay next to her and she pressed the Call button to summon a nurse. A part of her wanted to close her eyes and feel the closeness of her family. They hadn't come to her in years, but she knew that being close to them meant being close to death. She could stay if she wanted and they would welcome her home, but she couldn't leave her baby in the world alone. The door opened and the same soothing voice she had heard before entered.

"Welcome back," the woman said. She was a young nurse with a warming presence and a friendly smile. "Let's check your incision," she said as she adjusted Breeze's bed and lifted her hospital gown. Breeze grimaced as she saw the long incision on her stomach.

"Were you trying to hurt yourself?" the nurse asked.

Breeze rolled her head lazily to the side, the anesthesia still making it hard to concentrate. "If that's what it takes . . ."

"Takes? What does this accomplish? We had to cut you open and suture organs that had been damaged by the blade you swallowed. Make me understand this, now?" the nurse asked.

"My baby is in this hospital. I gave birth to her less than twenty-four hours ago and they stripped her from me," Breeze whispered. The pain in her voice filled the air like humidity, making it hard to breathe through the thickness of her torment.

"I'm sorry," the nurse said as she redressed Breeze's wound and then removed her rubber gloves.

"She was so little and so beautiful. I just want to see her. I'm her mother. I had this life, this extra heartbeat inside me for nine months and I feel like I'm dying now that she's gone," Breeze said. "I'm not built for this. I'm locked up because of who I am, not what I've done."

Breeze pulled her gown over her face and sobbed. She was so embarrassed that she was crying in front of this stranger, exposing her weakness as her chest heaved uncontrollably. The decorum of professionalism was hard to maintain as Breeze's sadness spread like an infection.

The nurse cleared her throat and blinked away tears. "Would you like to see your daughter?"

The nurse's voice was so low that Breeze almost missed it. She looked up at the nurse in shock, almost hyperventilating as she tried to gulp in deep breaths to calm down.

"I could lose my job for this, but if she's in the nursery, I can take you there. There is a guard on the door," the nurse said.

Breeze's sobs settled to sniffles as she gained composure. She didn't know why this woman was willing to put her job on the line to help her, but she was more than grateful. "I don't even know if I can walk right now. My legs feel a little numb," Breeze said.

"I can wheel you down there. It'll look better. I'll say I'm taking you for testing," the nurse said.

"Why are you helping me?" Breeze asked.

The woman cleared the hair out of her face and wiped her nose with the back of her hand as she responded, "Six years ago, I gave birth to a baby boy. I was addicted to pills for the entire pregnancy. He came twelve weeks early and my mother petitioned the court for custody. She took him from me and I haven't seen him since. I cleaned myself up and I finished school, got a job, but it's never good enough for her. So, I can relate to someone taking your child away. No mother should ever have to go through that," the nurse said passionately as she wiped a single tear from her cheek.

Breeze reached and gave the nurse's hand a weak squeeze.

The nurse turned her back on Breeze and cleared her throat as she composed herself. When she turned back toward Breeze, it was like the moment had never happened.

"I'll be back with a wheelchair," the nurse said.

Anxiety filled Breeze as she tried to swing her legs over the edge of the bed. She could barely stand it as she gritted her teeth in excruciation. *God, the razor felt better in than out,* Breeze thought as she grimaced. She eased down off the bed, placing her weight onto her feet, only for gravity to pull her down to the floor. The nurse came rushing back in with a wheelchair.

"Oh no! You should have waited for me. It will take a few hours before your legs feel normal again. Come on, let me help you."

Breeze held the nurse around her neck and together they managed to get her into the wheelchair.

"There is a baby Jane Doe here that was transferred over yesterday. She's under observation and a bit underweight, so she will be here for the next forty-eight hours before Social Services takes her," the nurse said. "If those staples keep opening, they will probably keep you here too."

Breeze nodded. She didn't care if she had to rip every

staple out of her belly herself, she would make sure she had as much time with her daughter as possible. The nurse rolled Breeze out of the room and they were immediately stopped by the prison guard.

"The prisoner cannot leave this room," the guard said.

"I have orders from the doctor to take her for testing. You can handcuff her to this wheelchair if you would like, but it is important that we get this taken care of."

"This prisoner is under state custody—"

"Come on, she can't even stand on her feet on her own. The test will take an hour at most. You can handcuff her to the chair and I will not let her out of my sight," the nurse insisted.

The officer reluctantly followed suit and cinched the bracelets tightly around one of Breeze's wrists before connecting it to the arm of the wheelchair. The nurse moved on swiftly and Breeze breathed a sigh of relief as they stepped onto the elevator and made their way to the nursery. Breeze thought about running. She thought about having this woman wheel her right out of the hospital, but it made no sense. Her sentence was too short to do anything other than serve it.

Breeze heard the cries coming from the nursery as they approached and her heartbeat sped up in anticipation. She sat up eagerly and the nurse stopped briefly, grabbing a blanket out of a supply closet.

"Hide the handcuff," the nurse instructed.

Breeze did as she was told and when they arrived at the window that overlooked all the newborn babies her heart swelled. Butterflies formed in her stomach and nervous energy filled her. Her eyes scanned the babies, until finally they landed on one. It was like she could discern Aurora's cries out of all the high-pitched wails. It was the sweetest sound she had ever heard.

"Please get her," Breeze whispered.

Breeze watched the nurse through the window as she bargained with another woman in scrubs. Breeze clenched her fists nervously. *God please, let her bring my daughter out here,* Breeze thought. She watched the nurse come back out empty-handed and her chest caved in.

"No, please . . ."

"I'm going to move you to an empty room up the hall so we are inconspicuous. They are going to bring her down in a few minutes," the nurse informed her.

"Really?" Breeze asked in disbelief as her eyes welled with tears.

"Really," the nurse confirmed.

Breeze waited impatiently as she was taken to a room and when she heard the knock at the door, her heart stopped. A woman came in holding a tiny bundle wrapped in pink receiving blankets.

"You've got half an hour. I'll be back then," the woman warned.

The nurse nodded. "Thanks, girl."

The woman handed Breeze her baby and tears flooded her eyes. She cried so much it was hard to see her baby's beautiful face. "What's her name?" the nurse asked.

Breeze admired her daughter's soft features. She looked

so much like Zyir that it made Breeze's heart skip a beat. "Aurora," Breeze said.

"That's beautiful," the nurse returned with a smile. "I'll give you some privacy. I'll be right outside."

Breeze shook so hard that even Aurora began to cry. "Aww, I'm sorry baby. Mommy's just so happy to see you," Breeze whispered. She kissed her daughter's forehead and inhaled her scent. She smelled so brand new. It was like no fragrance Breeze had ever smelled. It was the scent of life and it was so refreshing to her weary soul. "I love you so much," Breeze said. "And I'm so sorry that we can't be together all the time right now. I love you, oh Mommy loves you."

Aurora's lips curved up in a faint smile and Breeze knew that her daughter knew exactly who she was. They hadn't spent all that time together for nothing. Her baby knew the sound of her voice. Breeze laughed. "I can't believe you're finally here. I don't know if that was a real smile or not, but I'll take it. I'll think about that smile every day until I'm with you again," she said. "I'm going to fight to get back to you; until then you have to stay strong. We're Diamonds. We don't break. Don't forget me my love," Breeze whispered.

The tiny whine that escaped Aurora's lips was all the reply Breeze needed. She rubbed her daughter's tiny hand with her forefinger, sighing in complete bliss. Breeze had never felt something so soft or seen something so beautiful. Breeze forgot about all her troubles. In the presence of a love this grand she could only focus on her child. She couldn't believe that she had brought something so special into the world and she instantly felt obligated to protect her. This love made her question every other love she had ever known. It couldn't have been real before, because it had never felt like this. This was a level of intimacy she had never known and in that moment, she forgot about her anger toward Zyir. She just wished he was there to meet their little girl. This was a product of real love. Aurora was physical proof that a man and a woman together create miracles. Breeze savored every minute with her baby girl and when the nurse walked back in Breeze closed her eyes.

She pulled her baby away from her chest so that she could stare into her darling face. She wanted to be able to remember every feature. "I have to give her back now, don't I?" Breeze asked.

"I'm sorry. If I could get you more time with her, I would," the nurse said.

Breeze's lip quivered. She kissed Aurora's cheek. "I love you," she whispered. She held her out. "Take her. If you don't take her now, I'm not going to give her back. So just take her," Breeze said, struggling to keep herself from breaking down. When the nurse removed Aurora from her arms, it felt like someone was removing a part of her. Aurora was an extension of her—a vital one that Breeze needed to survive. She was choking on grief. Breeze's soul screamed as the nurse wheeled her out of the room and away from the nursery. Her gut churned. Her heart twisted because a mother leaving her child was unnatural and it hurt deeply.

As the nurse returned her to the hospital room, no one was the wiser that she had seen her child. The guard stood at her door and he removed the handcuffs before she entered the room.

The nurse helped Breeze into her bed and turned to leave the room.

"What's your name?" Breeze asked.

"Steph," the nurse replied.

"Steph, are you a better person since you lost your son?" Breeze asked.

"I'm clean if that's what you mean, but I won't be better until he is home with me. I'm working my ass off to prove that I am fit to be his mom," she said.

"If I asked you to take her—"

"I can't. . . ."

"Please. I'm not asking you to steal her from here or anything, but if you would foster her. Do it the right way. At least I would know who my baby is with while I'm away. I know it is crazy and it doesn't make sense, but please. I will pay you, I can get some money to you every month for taking her in." Breeze was speaking so fast, pleading her case. She had already thought of some of her father's old associates who owed her favors—favors she would cash in on if it meant her daughter would be somewhere safe. "You don't even know me, but—"

"I'm sorry, but I can't," the nurse interrupted. Breeze knew it was too much to ask, but she had to try. Breeze watched the woman exit, leaving her alone with her thoughts.

Breeze lifted her gown and looked at her incision. She dug her nails deep into it, pulling out each staple one by one. Anguish spread through her as sweat covered her body. She bit her bottom lip so hard that she drew blood, but it was the only way to stop herself from screaming. Breeze was determined to stay in the hospital. If Aurora was there, Breeze would be as well. It only gave her a couple days but if that's all she could get, she would take it.

Chapter 13

Breeze was transferred back to the prison a week later, but after days of loving up her baby girl and then having to leave her, she was no longer the same. She had someone to fight for and she would be damned if anyone stopped her from getting back to Aurora.

As soon as she entered her cell she noticed that another inmate now occupied the space. The guards had wasted no time stripping her of the special treatment that pregnancy had afforded her.

"You're on my bunk," Breeze said as she looked at the woman in frustration. The woman made no effort to move. Breeze wasn't in the mood for bitches and their attitudes. She had just lost the most important thing in her life—her motherhood—and she was looking for someone to take out her anger on. She walked over to her new cell mate and snatched the old-school Walkman she was listening to out of her hand.

"Why you all in my shit? I put my shit where the guard told me to," the woman said.

"And now I'm telling you to put it somewhere else," Breeze said. She wouldn't normally make such a big deal out of things, but she was feeling like she needed to stand up for what belonged to her. *People can't just take things from you and act like there isn't a consequence for it. They can't just take. Who just takes . . .* She felt the flutter of emotion making her heart leap painfully. *They just took her from me.*

She tossed the Walkman onto the adjacent bunk. A few awkward seconds ticked by before the woman gave in. Breeze exhaled as she collapsed onto her bed.

"I heard about what happened with your baby. That's fucked up. That's the only reason why I ain't all up in your ass right now," the woman said.

Breeze found laughter for the first time in days. "Oddly enough, it's the only reason I'm all in yours right now."

They had come to an understanding without coming to blows and Breeze appreciated the empathy.

* * *

Breeze refused to leave her cell for three days. It wasn't until the warden came to force her out of bed to eat that she found the strength in her legs to get up. She entered the mess hall and immediately found Rezzie and Sanchez posted with the Dominican girls at their normal table.

Breeze walked over to them, her arms folded across her chest. Her eyes were red and puffy, her hair was tucked into the back of her shirt. Her face was pale and sickly from all she had been through. She stood at the edge of the table.

"What up, Princess?" Rezzie asked.

Breeze hesitated before scooting in on the other side of the table.

"You don't see her trying to sit? Get your ass up. You don't know who she is?" Sanchez barked at a Spanish girl who was in Breeze's way.

"I'm down with whatever this is. I got a daughter to get home to. So whatever protection you're offering, whatever I got to do . . ."

Rezzie laughed.

"What's funny?" Breeze asked.

"Whatever you got to do? Nah, *chica,* you got it all wrong. It's whatever you want us to do, for you. We know who your people are. That trump all our shit in here. You're the queen. You don't got to do nothing for us. We for you. So, whatever you need. You say the word and that's that," Sanchez explained.

Breeze didn't respond. "Go get her a tray," Sanchez ordered the same girl, who was now standing behind Breeze.

The girl retrieved Breeze's food and Breeze ate silently, unsure of her new position. Just like that she had been placed in a position of power. These women had respect for her simply because of who she was and even though Breeze knew none of them, somehow trust was established. Somehow, they all were looking at her in admiration, waiting for her to say something, to do something. *I'm the boss?* she thought, completely perplexed. She kept her poker face strong, bluffing, as if she wasn't a ball of misery, fear, and heartache.

She looked up as they watched her and a small smirk spread across her face before quickly disappearing. It was inevitable that Breeze would come into her own. She was Carter Diamond's only daughter and that was all the protection she needed. *I'm the boss.*

* * *

The ice block that had built around Breeze's heart had turned her into a different person. As she walked down the darkened cell block her heart thundered. She could hear the emotional storm in her ears. Rage made Breeze feel powerful. It made her merciless. It took away all reasoning. She had never understood how her brother Mecca could do the things he did without remorse, or how Miamor could commit murder without thinking twice. Until now. Something had happened to them that took away their empathy for others. Losing Aurora had hardened her. She was scarred and the part of her that had remained pure over the years was now tainted.

The guard escorted her down to the kitchen. The prison had never been so silent. In the wee hours of the night when most of the inmates were asleep, Breeze had an agenda in mind. When they arrived at the mess hall, Breeze turned toward the guard and extended her wrists. The guard removed the handcuffs. "You got twenty minutes before the cameras come back on. You'll need to be back in your cell by then," the guard said.

With the promise of riches after her release, it was easy to get a guard or two to bend the rules to her favor. With a family name that carried inherited power, no one wanted to get on Breeze's bad side. Now that she was willing to use it, she made the rules on her block. She entered the kitchen where Sanchez and Rezzie stood, holding a girl at knifepoint.

"Say the word," Rezzie said.

Breeze walked closer and the girl's face came into clear view. *This bitch almost made me lose my baby,* Breeze thought. She instantly recognized her. She was the one responsible for the beating in the shower.

Breeze stood directly in front of the girl's face. They were so close to each other that Breeze could smell the fear on her breath. "You should have killed me," Breeze said. "You should have made sure I never walked out of that shower."

Breeze stepped back. "Make it hurt," she said simply. Breeze watched unflinchingly as Rezzie took the knife and dug it into the girl's back. She stabbed her repeatedly and then put the knife in the dishwasher, and removed evidence that they were ever present. Breeze bent down and looked the girl in her eyes. The girl tried to speak as blood backed up in her mouth. "This is for my daughter, bitch."

"Diamond, let's go, ma," Sanchez said.

Breeze turned and followed them out of the kitchen.

"We're family. We're riding for you, whatever, whenever. The bitch disrespected. The example is set."

Sanchez threw her arm around Breeze's shoulder and they walked out united. Revenge hadn't been as sweet as Breeze expected, but it was necessary. She knew her heart wouldn't be healed until she had her daughter back in her arms, but to get there she had to survive on the inside and this is what it took. Sanchez and Rezzie had put her on the throne. She had a gang of rough ones standing behind her and Breeze only hoped that this place didn't strip her of everything. She wanted her daughter to know her as she was, but she could slowly feel herself changing, becoming tainted, and there was no avoiding that.

Chapter 14

C.J.'s hands flew with such swiftness that he barely felt the sting as they connected with his target. The raw piece of butchered meat hung in the freezer and was the perfect punching bag for a young fighter. Estes wanted C.J. to get used to the feeling of punching flesh. He had to be desensitized to the feeling so that he didn't hesitate in the pit and allow his opponent to gain the upper hand. C.J.'s knuckles were numb to the pain as he punched, landing vicious blows. Estes sat back and watched, coaching him, training him to be a prizefighter. C.J. might have been young, but that was a plus in Estes's eyes. He had a lot of time to develop his skills. C.J. was a unique fighter. Not only was he unafraid to go in for the punch, but he was fast on his feet and his agility made it hard for other fighters to land a punch. He was good at both offense and defense. Estes saw nothing but potential in the young man.

"When you're in the pit, you're an animal. Nobody can beat you," Estes said as he stood outside the freezer watching C.J. train. The determination in this young boy was unbelievable. "You've got heart," Estes said. "That's enough for the day."

"I can keep going," C.J. said, winded, as he continued to fight. He liked the feeling of the adrenaline that coursed through him when he was in the pit. Baraka's face flashed through his mind. He saw Leena's body, his mother's face on the news, the man that had come and split him and Mo up. All his frustrations mounted when he fought, culminating into one huge ball of fury, and when his fists connected it was the ultimate therapy for him. He fought the things that he could do nothing about. Fighting gave him an outlet for the anger and hurt he had built up inside. He hid it well. Even his father never picked up on it when he called, but deep inside C.J. felt like a leaf blowing in the wind. He had no roots; therefore, he could end up any place at any time. No place felt like home, oddly enough, until now. Here with Estes, an old man, who wasn't particularly happy about C.J.'s presence, who was the most genuine and consistent person in his life right now. They shared a love for fighting. Now that he had discovered it, he only wanted to be the best. Estes wanted to teach the best and live out his childhood dreams through C.J. It worked out for them both.

Estes chuckled. "Leave some meat on the bones for another day," Estes said. "I'm calling council with a few gentlemen. I want you there. You are to be seen, not heard."

"You want me to set up, like last time?" C.J. asked.

"No, kid. I want you present. You learn the game by being a part of the game. With hands like yours you'll never have to live the lifestyle, but it's nonnegotiable that you soak up the knowledge. You come from it, so you must know how to deal with it, if it ever comes to your door. The tailor will be here in an hour. Go clean up," Estes said sternly.

C.J. rushed up the stairs. It was hard for him to hide the excitement he felt about the gathering this evening. He was getting on Estes's good side and opening a part of Estes that no one had touched since the death of his son. Even the love he had for his sweet Taryn couldn't fill the hole that had been left in his heart after the murder of his only heir. C.J. with his resilience and the heart of a lion was warming the ice walls that Estes had built. To be extended the invitation to sit at Estes's table meant that eventually Estes would break bread with him. He was just too young for the task at hand, but C.J. knew when the time came he would step into the game. Carter had always told C.J. not to follow in his footsteps, but C.J. wanted nothing more than to not only follow but surpass him.

A knock at the door startled C.J. as he pulled a T-shirt over his head. He opened the door and stood in astonishment as a team of people flooded into the room. C.J. had always seen his father and uncles in thousand-dollar suits and shiny shoes. *You dress for the position you want,* Carter had told him. It was no different on the streets. Just because they weren't corporate didn't mean they didn't aspire to power. Instead of working for that corner office and hanging degrees on their walls, the men of the Cartel worked for the throne and hung notches of respect on their belt. They were two different games, but at the end of the day, first impressions mattered.

A thin, olive-toned man with hair that was pulled up into a sleek bun entered the room. The crow's-feet around his eyes were stressed as he smiled kindly at C.J. He had the shiniest shoes C.J. had ever seen. He wore measurer's tape around his neck and barked instructions to the two women who entered the room to assist.

"You put fresh balls in a suit. Always. Go clean yourself and I'll be prepared when you get out," the man said bluntly.

C.J. shriveled in embarrassment and the assistants snickered in amusement as he retreated to the bathroom. He washed himself quickly, too quickly in fact because when he exited the shower, Estes was present and shook his head.

"Back in there," he ordered and nodded toward the bathroom. "A man must take pride in his appearance. Cleanliness is next to godliness. Don't rush."

Taking Estes's advice more seriously, he took his time the second time around. He emerged in underwear and an undershirt as Estes picked out ties and jackets. He was so particular he picked out the socks.

"I thought this was just for one night?" C.J. asked as he looked at all the options.

"There will be many nights like this. You'll need an

entire wardrobe," Estes said seriously. "The ladies will take care of your casual wear once you're sized."

"Can I wear a red tie?" C.J. asked.

"Are you a clown?" Estes replied. He normally taught with a sternness that made grown men insecure, but C.J. soaked up all the lessons without any hard feelings.

"Black?" C.J. said, seeking Estes's approval.

"Black," Estes confirmed before walking out of the room.

C.J. stood there for an hour as the tailor and the ladies worked around him. When they were finished, he was sharp in a feather-gray Tom Ford suit with a white shirt and gray tie. It was as adventurous in color as they would let him get.

"It feels too tight," C.J. said as he pulled at the collar.

"It's as it should be," the tailor said. "Be still before you catch a pin. You let me do what I do best and just relax." A few more minutes exhausted C.J.'s patience. He had been through a lot and was mature in a lot of ways, but in that way, he measured up exactly at eight years old.

When he was finally permitted to look in the mirror he felt like a man. His chest swelled with pride and he tried his hardest to contain the smile. *Men don't wear their hearts on their sleeve.* Carter's words played in his head and he wished his father could see him now.

The party was less inclusive than the first one C.J. had attended. Instead of being outside near the beautiful Caribbean Sea that played backyard to the villa, it was held inside where a poker table had been set. As C.J. entered the room, the scent of tobacco filled his lungs as smoke from freshly rolled Cuban cigars wafted into the air. The ten men sat around the table, focused, silent, as they each eyed their cards. The shiny Ferragamo shoes he wore announced his arrival before he could find his voice.

C.J. may have dressed the part, but he felt like he stuck out like a sore thumb. His discomfort was immeasurable, but his poker face was stronger than any player at the table. Each player had a man standing behind him, a bodyguard, arms folded in front of him, handgun tucked securely in the back of his waistline.

"Stand behind me." Estes's stern voice boomed and C.J. followed suit, his young heart pounding so hard that he thought the others could see it through the expensive jacket he wore.

A large man with a rotund belly tittered. He reminded C.J. of a stuffed pig. He had gotten comfortable and removed his suit jacket, but the buttons on the oxford shirt beneath were holding on for dear life. His stomach bounced jovially as he continued. "That's who you trust with your life? Against all these killers in the room?" He bellowed in laughter.

"He can hold his own," Estes replied. "Don't you worry."

"A little dark for this circle, eh?" the man pushed.

Estes folded his cards and stared intently across the table. He didn't speak but his steely gaze burned through the air. Everyone at the table tensed as they waited for him to react. Silence was worse than protest with Estes.

C.J. didn't realize he was holding his breath until his lungs began to beg him to exhale.

"I didn't mean any disrespect, Estes," the pig conceded. The temperature felt like it had been cranked up to hell and suddenly the suit felt like it had shrunk a size.

"Stand up," Estes said.

"Emilio . . ." the pig started.

"Stand," Estes repeated. His tone of voice was calm, but that stare was still so intense.

The fat man grunted and scooted his chair back as he threw down his cards and struggled to his feet. He stood and then swept his arms out as if to say, *What now?*

"C.J., take a seat," Estes said.

"I . . . um . . . I don't know how to play," C.J. stammered.

"I've got fifty grand in the pot, Emilio!" the pig objected, turning red as his anger rose.

"Then you better hope he plays the cards right," Estes said. "You disrespect my grandson in his home"—he put the cigar in his mouth and pulled the tobacco smoke into his lungs, holding it until he felt a slight burn—"*my* home, and you expect to keep a seat at this table?"

The pig wanted to object further but gruffed in displeasure instead as he looked on.

"Quit your bitching, we're at the river," Estes said, referring to the last card in the game.

The cards were nothing more than pictures to C.J. He held them in his hands, sweat forming on his nervous brow as his stomach felt twisted and hollow, his mouth dry, and his eyes stinging as if he wanted to cry. He was just starting to get on Estes's good side. If he messed this up, if he made Estes look bad, he would prove worthless.

Is he going to send me back? C.J. thought. He could feel the eyes of the other men on him and he didn't look up. He was too intimidated to look anywhere else except his cards. The most he had played was tunk, a game he had learned from Mo, and the most he had risked was pieces of candy. The sweet goodness had been their pot and it had been all in fun. The money sitting in the middle of the table made him sick to his stomach. He didn't know the rules to this game, and although he could sometimes outwit his older cousin, there was no way he could beat these men. *What happens if I lose?*

The dealer pulled the last card and the men went around the table revealing their hands. C.J. observed wide-eyed, not knowing what to expect next. When it was his turn he sat the cards on the green, velvet tabletop. He was the last to go.

"I'll be damned," Estes said.

C.J.'s eyebrows rose in worry as the men laughed around him. Suddenly, he felt the pig wrap his arms around him.

"This kid is worth something!" The man was jovial as he realized C.J. was holding three of a kind. It was a decent hand and enough to take the pot. "Ha!" he exclaimed in disbelief. "I understand why you keep him around. In the pits! At the card table! He's good luck!"

Estes sat back in his seat. "That's the kid's seat, the kid's hand, the kid's pot," Estes said.

The man released C.J. and slammed both palms on the table.

"It's the price you pay for disrespect," Estes said. "Unless you would like to cover it the other way."

The threat came out so effortlessly that C.J. almost missed it, but the way the gruff man's eyes widened in dread couldn't be lost. The other players remained silent, not wanting to get in the middle of Estes's affairs as everyone waited for the pig to respond. Nostrils flared, ire flickered in the big man's eyes, but he didn't dare protest. The man snatched up his suit jacket from the back of the chair C.J. sat in and stormed out. Estes didn't even turn to watch him leave. He had enough guards positioned throughout the villa that there was no need to worry. He always made sure his safety was accounted for, even when among those he trusted.

Estes nodded to the pot. "It's yours. We'll establish a Swiss for you in the morning," Estes said.

C.J. nodded and even though his thoughts were, *What's a Swiss?* he dared not ask.

Estes motioned for one of his men to come clear the pot and said, "Let's deal."

C.J. stood, not wanting to endure the agonizing uncertainty of another round. "Can I be excused?"

Estes nodded, already engrossed in the new cards he was receiving. C.J. hurried from the room, seeking solace, seeking relief from the tension and the inquisitive eyes of Estes's comrades. He rushed outside into the darkness that enveloped the secluded villa. His fingers pulled at the necktie he wore, releasing the tightness as he took a deep breath of relief. Everything in Estes's world was high stakes and the pressure of living up to his expectations was heavy. Perhaps if he were truly blood, if they shared relation through a deeper connection, C.J. wouldn't feel the need to do everything right. But they weren't truly family. They were affiliates and C.J. wanted to keep his spot as Estes's adopted mentee or project or whatever bond it was they were forming. C.J. simply didn't want to disappoint. He would rather live up to the hopes of Estes than to be thrust back into the hands of someone like Ms. Bernice, or God forbid much worse. He wanted to stay in this world where kings played even if he literally had to fight to belong.

The sound of someone exiting caused him to sneak off to the side of the front entrance, hiding out of sight. He wasn't ready to be summoned back inside just yet. The respite of the ocean air and the full moon was relaxing to C.J. The stakes were too high inside. He wanted to be where it was easy for a little while. He peered out from behind the bush that gave him coverage. The big man from the card game came storming out with another gentleman trailing behind him. C.J. recognized him from the table as well—he wasn't hard to remember. The long ponytail he wore secured by a rubber band and braided down his back made him stand out among the crowd.

Javier, C.J. thought, finally placing a name to the man whose money he had taken.

"Javier! Cool it," ponytail whispered.

"I'm going to kill him," Javier replied. He might as well have been breathing fire he was so irate. His eyes fumed with venom. "Who the fuck does he think he is?"

"Take a walk," the ponytail advised. "You're going to fuck up everything we have planned. The son of a bitch is living on borrowed time."

"Estes's days are numbered. I'm going to slit his throat from ear to ear and then burn this place to the fucking ground." Javier's words were so harsh that C.J. recoiled. "And that little nigger boy he has in there will be on his knees, sucking me off, where he belongs. The nerve of Estes. To sit that black motherfucker in my seat. He will pay for this."

"In due time, my friend," the ponytail responded. "For now, go home, sleep it off. We just have to be patient until the time comes."

C.J. watched in horror as the men went their separate ways, one going back in the house and the other getting into the town car that awaited him. He had become privy to a plot to assassinate Estes. There was no way he could let Estes sit among his enemies. He raced back inside where he collided with Estes. He didn't realize he was shaking until he noticed Estes's bent brow of concern.

"Everything okay, kid?" Estes asked.

C.J. opened his mouth to speak but halted when the man with the long ponytail came up behind Estes. The man gave Estes a pat on the back. C.J.'s heart raced and pounded loudly in his ears. *Should I say something? Do I tell him right now?* C.J.'s thoughts were running wild. *He might not even believe me.*

"I'm calling it a night. Appreciate the hospitality as always, Estes."

C.J.'s mouth was open to speak but the words were caught in a roadblock in his throat. *Say something. Hurry. He'll be gone soon,* C.J. urged himself but the fear of repercussion in the face of the man he would be accusing stopped him.

"Kid?" Estes called as he turned to walk away.

C.J. looked at the man who was sliding into his suit jacket by the front door and then back to Estes, who was preparing to head back to the game.

"He is planning to kill you. I heard him and the other man, the one who stormed out, talking about it outside," C.J. revealed.

Estes watched the man walk out the door and C.J. looked at him, stunned. "Aren't you going to do something?"

"You don't let the prey know they're prey, kid. You play dumb until it's time for you to move smart. You did good, C.J.," Estes said. Estes put an arm around C.J.'s shoulder and guided him back to the card game. "And fix your tie."

* * *

C.J. was roused out of his sleep as Estes opened the bedroom door, spilling fluorescent light into the darkened space. He wiped the sleep from his eyes as he looked up at the hazy image of Estes standing in the doorway.

"Get up and meet me downstairs," Estes said, his baritone voice stern and serious.

C.J. climbed from the bed without hesitating, clueless as to why he was being pulled from his peaceful slumber at this hour. *Am I in trouble?* he thought. *Did I do something wrong?* He could not help but wonder what was so pressing that it could not wait until morning. It was uncustomary for Estes to break C.J.'s rest, especially when he was due to train the next morning.

Estes met him at the front door. Even at this odd hour, he was pulled together with nothing less than perfection. C.J. looked down at himself in uncertainty but didn't have time to second-guess as Estes was already headed toward the driver that waited out front.

Silence seemed to be the standard as they rode through the darkness, up toward the mountains. The Dominican Republic was a beautiful island where multiple ecosystems coexisted. Estes resided beachside where crystal clear water washed up onto the shore in his backyard, but there were also jungles and dry areas that resembled deserts. As the car snaked around sharp curves, C.J. discovered that it held mountains as well. The elevation mixed with the darkness made him cringe with every turn but Estes sat cool and unbothered as if they weren't at risk of falling to their deaths at all.

When they arrived at the top, they drove a few more miles away from civilization and into a dense forested area.

"Where are we?" C.J. asked. He swallowed a lump in his throat. He noticed another town car and silently wondered who else was there. His gut was going haywire. There was danger in this darkness. There was death clinging in the air.

Estes didn't answer. He simply exited the car and left the door open, signaling C.J. to follow. He froze midstep when he saw the men he had overheard plotting Estes's death the night before.

"Hell of a place to meet, Estes? What is this about?" The pig might as well have had a snout. The way he spoke sounded more like snorting as he complained.

"It's about disloyalty," Estes said. C.J. was still frozen. His fear was paralyzing him, making it hard to even squeeze in breaths of the thick, humid air.

"We can take care of that for you, of course, but did we have to do it all the way up here?" the fat man snorted as he tried to laugh off the seriousness of the situation. "Who is it? I'll bet it's that rat bastard Chavez. You say the word and I'll handle him personally."

Estes stood stoically and raised his hand casually, signaling, and just like that red beams appeared on the chests of both men.

"I've shown the two of you how to build empires for the past two decades, have I not?" he posed. The men looked down at the threat that lingered over the left sides of their chests.

"Emilio!" the fat man pleaded as he put his hands up. "What is this? We are like family. I would never!"

"Only you did," Estes shot back. He nodded to the other man. "The both of you conspired to kill me," Estes said. "What did they say they would do again?" Estes looked at C.J.

C.J.'s throat was dry as sandpaper, but he couldn't back down, not in front of Estes, not when it counted. "Slit your throat from ear to ear," C.J. offered. His voice shook, but he was grateful the words had come out at all.

"Estes, this is all a misunderstanding," ponytail said, trying to keep things diplomatic.

"You're right," Estes answered. "I could never understand how two men whom I've fed for years, whose wives and children I've fed for years, could go against me in this way. You dug your own graves so you will take your own lives. Walk."

The men looked over their shoulders to the dark cliff in the near distance.

"Estes!"

Their pleas fell on deaf ears and a content mind. Once Estes came to a decision there was no changing things.

They shuffled their feet backward until their heels were on the edge of the thousand-foot drop-off. C.J. knew it took a lot to make grown men cry. The stench of death had these men sobbing as they beseeched Estes for mercy. It had been a long time since he had to put in this type of work. Estes's resume was lengthy and he was respected off name alone. These gentlemen had forgotten how unforgiving Estes could be. He was about to remind them.

C.J. tried to comprehend what was happening right in front of him. *Is he? He can't,* C.J. thought. Surely, Estes wouldn't make these men throw themselves off the top of this mountain. *Is he going to kill them right here?*

"You know the penalty for disloyalty. Nothing short of death. Not just any death: this death, in this way. You can pay for your disloyalty and walk off this cliff with your pride or I can give the signal to my men and end it with a bullet. The bullet doesn't save your family, however. If you choose that option, the death continues to your namesake. Again, the choice is yours." It was an old Dominican ritual among gangsters. The Devil's Cliff was the highest ridge on the island. A man could die with honor by selling his sin to the devil and taking the plunge or he could die by the gun. These two wouldn't be the first or the last to fall victim.

Their feet shuffled nervously as the strong wind gusts almost made the decision for them.

"Estes, por favor no hacer esto," the fat one held no shame as he got on his knees begging Estes for forgiveness. "You don't have to do this," he kept saying, in broken Spanish from the tears that wouldn't stop flowing.

Estes lifted his foot without hesitation and kicked the man backward, sending him falling unexpectedly over the edge of the cliff. The scream was so loud and fear-filled that it made C.J. close his eyes. It echoed out over the night, but the drop to the bottom was so long that the sound faded the farther he fell.

Ponytail looked in fear as Estes motioned for his driver to pull the trigger.

The shot exploded in the air and sent flashes of the day he had been taken by Baraka's men into C.J.'s mind. Anytime he heard a gunshot it brought up the unpleasant memories. The bullet hit ponytail in the center of his forehead and his body went limp, falling over into the abyss. There was no sound this time, no screams could be heard, and Estes turned away from the scene unaffected as he headed back to the car. C.J. crept to the edge and watched the turbulent ocean waters below. The ocean had served as the graveyard to the dead and made the bodies disappear instantly. It was like it had never even happened at all. A chill swept up C.J.'s spine as the dizzying heights made him stumble.

"C.J., let's go," Estes called. C.J. turned and rushed to the car, not truly feeling safe until he was inside. An awkward silence filled the air. C.J. was locked inside with a killer. He knew his family had a long relationship with the streets and that they lived by the gun, but being up close and personal with murder always made him feel weird. A part of him felt fear but the other part, the parts of him that were made up of Miamor Holly, felt intrigue. He was conflicted over what had just occurred.

"Does it scare you? Killing people?" C.J. asked, reluctantly, once they were tucked away and on the descent down the hill.

"No," Estes gave a simple reply. "Is that what you feel? Fear? Right now, after seeing that?" Estes returned.

C.J. thought about his emotions. He assessed the pit

in his stomach and the hole in his heart. "I feel bad, I guess. It feels like that will come back to me one day," C.J. said, honestly. "What I do to people matters. It's not like the pit. The kids I beat walk away at the end. This is final. Once you did it, it was forever."

"Smart, kid. You're highly intelligent," Estes said. "That feeling you have. That sickness that's telling you to throw up right now, it means you're one of the good ones. I no longer have that feeling. You hold on to that as long as you can, but never be afraid of what you must do when another man disrespects you. Once someone threatens you or the life of someone you hold dear, they must be eliminated. Do you understand?"

C.J. nodded as he sank into the plush leather interior. He couldn't get the screams out of his head. He stared out the window, noticeably conflicted about complexities an eight-year-old boy should never have to consider. Life with Estes would change him, it would harden him, but C.J. oddly was looking forward to becoming a man under Estes's watch. Witnessing the power, the influence, and the wisdom Estes had intrigued C.J. and only made him want to live the lifestyle even more. There was a hunger in his belly that he hadn't known when he was with his parents. They gave him too much, made him earn too little. Miamor and Carter had been so focused on making sure he led a life of privilege that they forgot to instill that dog's instinct that made you fight your way to the top. C.J. didn't know what the bottom felt like, but with Estes there was always the threat of losing it all so he worked hard to keep everything Estes offered. Their bond, although unconventional, was growing by the day and Estes was not only grooming a fighter, but a gangster, and, more than that, bringing out the killer instinct inside.

Chapter 15

THREE YEARS LATER

Breeze sat across from her nephew completely torn up inside. She tried hard not to show the disappointment in her eyes because it wasn't Mo who had let her down. None of this was his fault. It took a village to raise children and their village had failed not only him, but her daughter, and C.J. as well. Three years had passed and Mo had grown from a young boy to a young man. He was fifteen years old and he loomed over her, his muscular frame a result of endless days of discipline. He wasn't a kid anymore, but a young, handsome man, and with his hair grown out long and wild he looked so much like her brother Mecca. The sight of him made goose bumps appear on her forearms. It was like someone had put her in a time machine and she was looking at her brother, alive and breathing. The resemblance was uncanny. *Hell, he might be Mecca's son. Lord knows Leena popped that thang for both of them,* Breeze thought. Seeing him here, caged like an animal, paying for sins that were not his own, was like salt on an open wound.

"Don't look so sad Aunt B. I'm good in here. I'm holding it down," Mo said, his voice deeper than she remembered. He had turned into a man on her. She had missed so much. "I'm glad you out. You came back for us just like you said you would."

"I was always coming back Mo. I love you. I love C.J. too. I'm so sorry this happened," Breeze said.

The mention of C.J. hit a nerve with Mo and his expression grew grim. "You know where he is?" Mo asked.

"I don't. Not yet, but I'm going to find him. I'm here for you. I'll get a job and I'll put money on your books. Whatever you need. You hear me?" she asked.

"You don't have to worry about me, Aunt B. I get by," Mo said.

"Three years feels like a lifetime," Breeze said, growing misty. "I'm going to rebuild this family, brick by brick. When you finally come home, you'll walk out of here to a kingdom. I promise you."

Mo stood to his feet. "I've got to get back," he said. "You take care of yourself, Aunt B."

"You too, baby boy," Breeze answered. They hugged for a long time and Breeze was afraid to let him go. It was a reunion, but somehow it felt like a goodbye as Breeze watched him walk back into the custody of the guards.

Her family was torn apart and scattered everywhere.

She didn't have a clue how to locate all the pieces let alone put them back together. Mo couldn't be saved right now. He was stuck in the system at least for the next four years. Frustrated, Breeze stormed out. If her father could see the state of their family he would be so disappointed. She shook her head in disgrace as she rushed out, not wanting to miss the next bus. Life after lockup was completely different for Breeze. She didn't have access to money, her own place, or even her own car. The illusion of prison had made her forget how hard her reality would be after her release. Life had humbled her. She was so low that the crawl back to the top seemed impossible. As she emerged out on the city street she saw the bus pulling away from the corner. Breeze took off running.

"Wait!" she shouted as she sprinted full speed. She thanked God for the traffic light at the corner. If she missed this bus, she would never be able to make it downtown in time to see the social worker about her daughter. She banged her hand against the side of the bus, calling, "Wait!" Finally getting the driver's attention, she slid on, panting as she slipped the driver the fare before finding a seat.

The characters around her came from all walks of life and as Breeze sat she found herself wondering if she ever would have crossed paths with these people in her prior life. Everything had always been done at the highest level. Before their empire had come crumbling down, Breeze would have never even paid attention to the ways of these common people. She hadn't lived a regular life before, but now she was thrust in the middle of one, trying to make sense of it all. She had walked through the world with privilege that had blinded her to the struggles of the real world. Everything with Breeze had always been so high stakes. Kidnapping, murder, revenge, war. Those were the types of problems her family had faced over the years. Money had never been an issue and making a dollar out of fifteen cents was something Breeze was not equipped to do. Not many things frightened her, but figuring out how to make her own way was terrifying. *I have to contact Carter as soon as possible,* she thought. She knew that he would know what to do. *He always knows.*

Breeze was so distracted by her thoughts that she almost missed her stop. She pulled the cord, signaling to the driver to pull over. She hopped off the bus and rushed across the street, sliding into the Social Services office just before the security guard locked the door.

"They stop seeing clients at 4:45," the security guard called after her. Breeze ignored him and stepped onto the elevator. There was no way she was coming back another day. She had waited three long years for this and she wanted to get back to Aurora as quickly as she could. *I've already missed so much time with her,* Breeze thought. Each gulp of free air she breathed felt wrong without her daughter.

"Excuse me, I'm here to see Bernice Jackson," Breeze said as she stood in front of the receptionist's desk.

"Do you have an appointment?" the lady asked. She looked at the wall of employees. The smiling faces of the women and men gave her hope. They looked friendly enough. They were there to help mothers like Breeze. She scanned the wall until she found Bernice's picture. This woman was the one who would reunite her with her baby.

"Ma'am?" the receptionist called.

Breeze turned back toward the desk. "Umm, no. I don't have an appointment, but it's important that I see her today. It's an emergency."

"Every woman who comes in here has an emergent situation, ma'am. Without an appointment, you won't be able to see a caseworker."

"Please," Breeze whispered. "I just need a few minutes of her time."

"I'm sorry. You have to make an appointment," the woman replied.

Breeze's frustration mounted as she placed both hands on the counter. "I'm not leaving here until I see her," she insisted.

She was so close to getting her daughter back but still so far away.

"Ma'am, do I need to call security? Now I've told you what you need to do to see Ms. Jackson."

"You can call whoever you want, but I'm not leaving here until I see her!" Breeze said, sternly. "You do not want to be the one to stand between me and my daughter. I've waited too long for this moment to let some bitch behind a desk try to stop me."

"Is there a problem?"

Breeze looked at the woman who rushed in after hearing the commotion.

"Ms. Jackson?" Breeze recognized her. "Please, I know

you're ready to get off work but please just hear me out. My daughter Aurora and my nephew C.J. I'm trying to find them . . . please."

The color drained from the woman's face and she looked as if she had seen a ghost. She hadn't heard C.J.'s name since the day Estes snatched him from her house and she had hoped those past bones would stay buried.

"I tried to tell her to make an appointment . . ."

Bernice looked at Breeze in fear, unsure if this was another family member there to deliver a message. Bernice dreaded the day that Estes knocked on her door again. Afraid to decline the meeting, Bernice shook her head. "No, I'll take her now."

Breeze sighed in relief.

"Come on back," Bernice invited as she held open the door. "My office is this way." Breeze took the woman in, frowning as she noticed her disfigured left hand. She only had three fingers and Breeze found it hard to stop staring.

Breeze followed her to the corner office. "Take a seat."

"My name is Breeze Diamond—"

"I know who you are," Bernice said, her voice shaking. "Please, I don't want any trouble."

Breeze frowned. *Damn, just the name alone puts fear in people,* Breeze thought. She was clueless as to the reason why Bernice was shaking so hard.

"I'm just here for information," Breeze said, trying to sweeten her tone to calm the woman's rattled nerves.

"Your nephews are Carter Jones and Monroe Diamond. Your daughter is Aurora Rich. I know your case well and have followed it since it fell on my desk three years ago. I'm very sorry about what happened to your nephews. I tried to help C.J. after Monroe was sentenced. I fostered C.J. but a man named Emilio Estes came for him. He, umm, he insisted that I let him take him. I haven't heard from C.J. since. I hoped I wouldn't. I—I—have changed my life. I really don't want any trouble," Bernice stammered, stumbling over her words as her eyes misted.

"Estes?" Breeze asked with hope in her voice. She had no idea where her grandfather was, but she remembered giving the order to Einstein to find him. The fallout from Miamor's arrest had sent both Estes and Carter into a hole. "He was here in the States?" Why would he show up on this woman's doorstep? Why was fear so present in this woman's eyes?

"Yes, he came to my home," Bernice answered.

"How long ago was this?" Breeze asked.

"Three years ago."

At least C.J. is with family, Breeze thought as she sighed in relief. It was one less thing she had to worry about. *I'm almost willing to bet that Estes took him back to the Dominican Republic. As soon as I get my hands on my baby, I can go be with them,* Breeze thought.

"Where is my daughter? I need to get her back," Breeze said.

Bernice rummaged through a stack of files that sat atop her desk. She opened a manila folder and read it quietly before responding. "It looks like she is placed with a foster family."

"Who? Where?" Breeze asked. "I'm home now. I want her back."

"There is a process. You're at a halfway house, I assume. How long did they order you to remain there?" Bernice asked.

"Three months," Breeze replied.

"You can't bring children there. Once you're out, you must prove that you can take care of her. You must have taxable income and a place of your own."

As Bernice spoke, Breeze felt her frustrations rise. "She's mine! She belongs with me. I shouldn't have to prove anything. They took her from me and I did my time. Now you're sitting here telling me I have to jump through hoops to get her back!"

"It's just the way the system is built," Bernice said, apologetically.

"I can't even see my daughter?" Breeze's lip trembled as she posed the question.

"I'm afraid not," Bernice said.

Breeze leaned over in her chair as sorrow filled her. It filled her up so high that she felt like she would drown in it. She wiped away the tears that she tried her hardest to hold in. Prison had taught her not to show weakness and she was embarrassed that she was becoming unhinged in front of this woman.

"I'm so sorry," Bernice extended. "I can help you find employment and help get you a place, and as soon as you are in a position where the courts will grant you custody I will expedite the paperwork, but that's all the power I have over the situation. I swear, I will give you a glowing recommendation, just please . . ."

Breeze frowned. *What did Estes do to this woman?*

"In the meantime, you just have to be patient. You have to let the system work," Bernice concluded.

"Is she safe at least?" Breeze whispered.

"According to the reports, she is just fine," Bernice said.

Her words did little to reassure Breeze. *She's not fine. She is with strangers. She isn't with me. Nothing is fine. Everything about this is wrong,* she thought. She was pained to her core. Being locked up and away from Aurora was one thing, but being free and still not being able to get to her baby was a torture that made her want to die.

"Here is my card," Bernice said. Breeze accepted it. "You call me and I'll do whatever I can to help you get readjusted so that a judge will grant you custody of your child. Please let Estes know that I don't want any trouble."

Breeze nodded and stood as Bernice walked her toward the front. Before Breeze exited she said, "I left my wallet."

She backtracked and looked down the hall to make sure no one was coming before she flipped open the file she had seen Bernice open.

"1128 West Dorchester," Breeze whispered. She hurried and exited the building, practically blowing by Bernice on her way out. "1128 West Dorchester. 1128 West Dorchester."

* * *

It took Breeze an hour and two bus transfers to get to the address. She stood across the street from the house, waiting, watching. It took her a while to work up the nerve to walk up to the door.

She rang the doorbell and shifted nervously.

The door opened and Breeze froze. "Nurse Steph?"

A little girl in a bright blue dress ran up and wrapped herself around Steph's leg. "Mommy!"

Hearing Aurora call another woman mommy was like a punch to the gut. It knocked the wind out of her.

"Hello Breeze," Steph greeted. Breeze could see her reluctance as Steph stood guarded in the doorframe. "Aurora, go watch cartoons in your room. Okay sweetheart?"

The little girl took off, yelling jovially. Breeze's heart leaped with every inflection of Aurora's voice.

"Are you going to let me in?" Breeze asked.

"You're not supposed to be here," Steph said.

"What are you talking about?" Breeze asked. "Of course, I am. You have my daughter. She's mine. Please. You have to let me see her. I'm not asking."

Steph sighed and Breeze walked in uninvited. On one hand Breeze was thankful that Steph had taken her daughter. As she looked around the neat house it seemed that Steph was providing a good life for Aurora. There were pictures of the two of them displayed on the mantel and jealousy seared Breeze.

"I asked you to take her that day at the hospital. You told me no," Breeze started.

"It didn't feel right to let someone else take her. I applied to be her foster mother," Steph explained.

"Does she know about me?" Breeze asked.

"No, I didn't know how to explain it to her," Steph whispered.

"You didn't know how to explain it, or you didn't want to?" Breeze asked.

The look of guilt that crossed Steph's face enraged Breeze. "I want to hate you right now, but the smile on her face in these pictures is what is holding me back. You have taken care of her and kept her out of the hands of people who may hurt her. I don't even want to think of what she might have gone through if you hadn't taken her in, but I'm out now and I want my daughter back. Go get my baby."

"Breeze—"

"Go get her!" Breeze shouted.

The shouting summoned Aurora from her room. "Mommy! Why are you screaming?"

"I'm not, beautiful," Steph said. Breeze froze and bent down.

"Hi—Aurora . . ." she stammered, her words coming out with pangs of emotion. "Come here baby," she coaxed as Aurora walked slowly toward her. When she was within arm's reach, Breeze bent down and reached out her hand. When Aurora's tiny hand was safely in hers, Breeze felt a current of energy pass between them. It was the same feeling Breeze felt when she first held her in the hospital. It felt like a gift, one that God had wrapped up in this beautiful little girl and delivered to Breeze.

"Hi," Aurora replied. Her voice was so small. *She's shy,* Breeze thought. *She doesn't know me.*

Breeze pulled Aurora into her arms and sobbed as she hugged her. "Are you crying?" Aurora asked, her sweet tone sounding like music to Breeze's ears. Breeze sniffled as she pulled back.

"These are happy tears. I'm so happy to be here with you," Breeze said.

"What's your name?" Aurora asked.

Breeze looked back at Steph and then stood to her feet. She didn't know what to say. She didn't know how to make sense of the confusion. Steph was the only mother that Aurora knew. It would break her heart to learn something new, but there was no way that Breeze could let this charade continue. She picked up her daughter.

"What's your name?" Breeze countered.

"Aurora Diamond."

"That's right. My name is Breeze Diamond," Breeze said sweetly.

"Don't," Steph interrupted.

"Mommy, she has the same last name as me!" Aurora exclaimed in excitement.

"Breeze, you need to leave," Steph said. "You can't just take her. You must go in front of a judge. She needs stability. She needs—"

"Me!" Breeze said sternly. "Don't stand here and tell me what my daughter needs. She needs me," Breeze whispered.

"I'm her mother." Breeze didn't know who she was trying to convince more, Steph or herself, but seeing her daughter happy with someone other than her was heartbreaking. From her prison cell, Breeze had pictured Aurora just as miserable as she had been. She had told herself her daughter was lost without a connection to her, but it looked as if she was flourishing just fine without Breeze. She was grateful that Aurora was in good hands but it didn't stop the sting of jealousy from hurting all the same.

Aurora felt so right in her arms, so comfortable, so good. "Let me tell you something sweetheart. Look me in my eyes," Breeze said. "The reason why we have the same last name is because I'm your mommy. I'm your real mommy. Steph is my friend and she took care of you for me while you were a baby because I had to go away for a little while. I missed you every single day though. I thought about you every second. Now that I'm back, we are going to be together really, really soon. I promise you. I'm going to get us a big castle and you're going to have a big playroom filled with toys."

"You're my mommy?" Aurora asked.

"That's right and don't you forget it," Breeze said as she planted a kiss on Aurora's forehead.

"You can't do this. I'm calling the police," Steph said.

"No need to," Breeze said. She put Aurora down. "I'll be back for you," she told Aurora. She approached Steph and stood closely to her so that Aurora wouldn't overhear her next words. "The only reason I'm leaving her here is because I want to do this right. I don't want to be on the run with my baby. I want to be her mom, the right way. Dead that mommy shit with my kid. You're not her mother. I appreciate what you've done for her and as promised, you will be compensated for that, but I'm going to go to court and I'm going to get custody of her. After that your services will no longer be needed. If you try to run with my daughter, I will kill you. I'm going to have someone sitting on your house twenty-four seven making sure you don't get any bright ideas. If he even thinks you're moving wrong, I will give the order to have you executed," Breeze said. "I don't want it to come to that but it can if you push me there. Do not play games with my daughter."

With a reluctant heart, Breeze turned back toward her child. She wanted to take her so badly. She wanted to risk it all and just snatch her out of Steph's possession right now, but she knew she couldn't. She never wanted to put herself in a position to be away from Aurora again and if she handled this the wrong way, she would be sent right back to prison. Breeze took a deep breath and gazed lovingly at her daughter, then walked out the door. Every step she took made her sick to her stomach. *You didn't come this far to fuck up now. It's not like she's in danger. She's being taken care of. This is her home for now. This isn't a war that I can win with my name. I have to be a mother. I have to do what's best for her, even if it hurts me. I'll transition her slowly and once we're back together, I'll make sure no one ever separates us again.*

Chapter 16

The glamour was gone. The hair. The nails. The money. It was all a thing of the past, but the one thing that Miamor never lost, regardless of circumstance, was power. Miamor was the type of woman who always landed on her feet. They couldn't build walls tall enough to contain her. She was a giant. Mentally, she had been trained to withstand everything outside of death. Only God could touch her. Despite the physical restraints, Miamor still thrived. The prison sentence only made her legend greater. The women locked down with her worshipped her. Without even trying, she ran the prison. The guards didn't test her and the inmates respected her. Miamor walked around like a giant inside the prison. The only thing she couldn't do was walk outside the gates, but everything inside the hellhole she had free rein over.

Miamor made her way to the visitor's room, silently wondering who had come to see her. Whoever it was, she hoped they weren't expecting her to be as they remembered. The khaki uniform she wore was a size too big and swallowed her. The two cornrows she wore straight to the back did nothing to compliment her face. Miamor was rough around the edges, thugging it, and it would be a long time before she would feel like the queen that Carter portrayed her to be.

Miamor walked into the visitor's room and went down to her assigned window. Breeze sat there and Miamor rolled her eyes as she sat down, snatching the phone off the cradle.

"What are you doing here? It's been three years and I haven't seen your face, Breeze," Miamor said.

"That's because I had my own set of bars to deal with," Breeze said.

"What?" Miamor sat up, stunned by the revelation. "What are you talking about? I'm in here so that nobody else has to be. You were supposed to hold down the kids."

"Yeah, well. The government had other plans for me. I did three years, Miamor. In South Carolina," Breeze said.

"Where are the kids? Where is C.J.?" Miamor's concern was evident. She wasn't easily rattled, but the thought of her son in the wrong person's hands made her fill with dread.

"C.J. somehow ended up with Estes, Mo is in juvie, and my daughter, Aurora, is with a foster family. I don't know if I will be able to get her back," Breeze whispered. Her chin quivered.

"I'm sorry, Breeze. I had no idea," Miamor said. She felt relief that her son was in capable hands. She would have preferred if he was with Carter, but Estes was better than the alternative. For him to end up like Mo or Aurora would make every day of her sentence even worse. Estes wasn't a friend of hers, but he wasn't an enemy either. There were not many people she could say she trusted with C.J.'s life. Most would use him to make her pay for the many sins she had committed over the years. At least with Estes he would live and she hoped that he would soak up the game. The last thing she wanted was for her son to be out in the world living a false sense of security without protection. He had a killer's instinct in his blood. She just hoped he used it to survive. "Who has Aurora?" Miamor asked.

"I gave birth to her in prison and was transferred to a county hospital in Charleston, South Carolina. There was a nurse there. Stephanie Wilkes. She fostered Aurora. She's raised her since then and I don't think she's going to willfully give her back, Mia. I'm going to have to fight for my own daughter and I'm going to lose. She has a job and a nice house. I need taxable income, I need something that I've attained on my own. I'm living in this filthy halfway house for the next few months. I'm a felon! I can't win this in court. They're never going to give her back to me. I don't know what to do," Breeze admitted.

Miamor could see Breeze was overwhelmed. She had never been the type to handle too much on her own, but there was also a change that didn't go unnoticed. Breeze had made it through a three-year stretch in prison without anyone from the Cartel there to hold her hand.

"You'll get your daughter back and when you do, you bring my niece here so I can see just how beautiful she is," Miamor said. "I'm proud of you Breeze. When you see him, let him know that I love him."

Miamor knew their conversation was being recorded so she couldn't mention his name, but Breeze nodded. They both knew Carter was whom she spoke of.

"I'll tell them both," Breeze said, letting Miamor know she would pass the word to C.J. as well.

The ladies sat and chatted for an hour. Over the years, they had battled each other as well as their enemies, but they were at a place where they truly shared a sisterhood. Miamor respected Breeze's innocence. What she once deemed as weak, she now knew was Breeze's greatest strength. Breeze possessed a vulnerability that the world stripped from most people. Even now as she sat across from Breeze, after all that she had endured, she was still as delicate as the petal of the prettiest flower. Breeze hid her scars, masking her hurt, her past, and her flaws. Miamor wished she could camouflage hers so well. When their time was up Miamor felt a sadness fall upon her. Somehow, she knew this would be the last time she saw Breeze.

"You're my sister Breeze and I love you. You're going to be a great mother. Just bide your time at the halfway house, and when the time is right you will have everything you want, including your lil' mama back home where she belongs," Miamor said. "Take care of yourself, you hear me? We're all going in different directions. Even the boys have been split up. It's fucked up and it hurts but it's life. We don't always get to keep the ones we love most," Miamor said as her thoughts drifted to Carter. "It doesn't mean we love them any less."

Breeze smiled. "You're getting soft in here, Mia."

"Fuck out of here," Miamor replied as she stuck up her middle finger.

They both laughed and placed their hands on the glass. Breeze withdrew first, hanging up the phone and standing to her feet. Miamor gave her a reassuring nod, letting Breeze know it was okay to leave her behind. When she was gone Miamor sat there for a moment and lowered her head.

It felt good to see a familiar face, but at the same time Miamor wished Breeze had not come at all. Reminding her of the outside world, of her family, Breeze had triggered a yearning within Miamor that she wouldn't be able to fulfill. It only made things harder. It was a bittersweet reunion.

Miamor stood and headed directly to her cell. Being locked up limited Miamor's reach on the streets of Miami, but luckily, she had been brought up with a gang of women who followed the same code she lived by. If one of them was free, all of them had a hand in the game, so anyone Miamor needed to touch, she could. Aries had tapped out of the business and was lying low raising her son. Miamor hated to pull her back in, but she needed her to solve one last problem.

She grabbed a blank piece of paper and pen before

sitting on her bunk. She was about to send a kite to Aries. She knew it was selfish. Aries was trying to blend in and fly under the radar. She only kept coming back because it was Miamor who was calling. Miamor would do the same for Aries without thinking twice. Their bond was just that strong. Nobody knew the secrets they shared. They had been running the streets with each other since they were young and reckless. The only thing that had changed was their age. Recklessness was the characteristic that made them infamous. No one else would take the jobs they accepted. No other killers, men or women, could compare. They were the best to ever live by the gun. Miamor needed her to come out of retirement, for one final hit.

* * *

When Aries pulled the letter from the mailbox, she already knew who it was from. There was no return address, but she recognized the beautiful cursive letters. There was only one person in the world who knew where to find her. *Miamor,* she thought.

They had created an exit plan. Years ago, they had all pitched in to purchase a home for them to reside in after they retired from the streets. It was a big beautiful six-bedroom house with five thousand square feet. It had more than enough room for the original five murder mamas. Unfortunately, not all of them had made it to the end. Aries had tried to leave the game once before and had chosen a different location to retire. It hadn't felt right to occupy the house she was supposed to share with her sisters without them. This time, however, she had come home, because memories of when they had first anted up to buy the place made her feel closer to them. She had lost them all—most to the grave and Miamor to the law. Aries was the last one standing and although the past three years of her life had been normal, she was aware that one day, Miamor would pull her back to the dark side. It was just what Miamor did. Without even trying the girl was trouble but Aries loved the hell out of her troublesome ass.

The letter was addressed to her alias. Aries had no qualms about the fact that Miamor had reached out. She knew that Miamor had taken every precaution. She opened it. It was written in a way that only Aries could decipher. She was grateful for the school day because she would need a clear mind and time to decode the letter. The first character in every word needed to be put together to find the real message. Aries sat down at the kitchen table with a highlighter and pen.

It took her two hours until she came up with something that made sense. Aries grabbed a lighter and put flame to the paper, allowing it to burn in her kitchen sink, erasing all evidence that it ever existed. She didn't want to step out of the shadows. She enjoyed this pretend life she had manufactured for herself and her son. In Michigan, she was a normal woman with a normal life. Her normalcy would have to be put on pause as she dug into the deepest part of herself to bring out the killer inside.

* * *

The night was still and the only sound that could be heard was the distinct chirping of crickets as they serenaded the neighborhood. Aries sat in the stolen car, listening to the sound. Oddly, it calmed her. Her eyes never moved from the house that sat in the cul-de-sac of the middle-class neighborhood. She checked her watch. It was close to midnight. The lights had been out for over an hour so she was sure that everyone inside was asleep. She had found the woman's address with a simple Google search. Miamor had provided the name and the city, and it was enough for Aries to take care of the rest. She exited the car. Her Timberland boots hit the ground with determination as she zipped up her hoodie. She tucked the .45 in the back of her waistline and headed toward the home. "Just like riding a bike," she whispered.

She hopped the fence and made her way around the back of the house. The stealth she moved with made her undetectable. She pulled a cell phone jammer. She flipped the switch and planted it in the dirt behind the house. By the time it was found, Aries would be long gone. She then cut Internet access to the home. If there was a home alarm it wouldn't work without being online. She pulled out a lock pick and opened the back door with ease before walking inside. She stood still as she adjusted to the sounds of the house. Every house made them and she needed to be able to distinguish between footsteps and creaks.

She didn't move as she soaked up the environment. She barely breathed. When she was sure that the house was undisturbed she took a seat at the kitchen table. She pulled the gun and placed it on the table. Aries had learned long ago to wait for her prey to come to her. She didn't want to go venturing through somebody else's house to find them. Home court advantage mattered. Since this was something that had to take place inside this woman's home, Aries would control the space, deciding where and how the inevitable altercation would go down within these walls.

Aries looked at the glass centerpiece in the middle of the table and then pushed it off, causing the glass to shatter. The commotion it caused did exactly what she had intended. It woke up her victim. A yellow glow came from the hall as someone turned on the light.

"Aurora, baby? Are you in the kitchen?"

The woman stepped out into view.

"Have a seat, Stephanie Wilkes," Aries said. Aries greeted her as if this was her house, as if she hadn't just broken in. The authority in her voice made it clear that she meant business. "Or do you prefer Steph?"

"Agh!" Steph shouted, her voice a mixture of fear and surprise. Her eyes shot to the gun and then to the door. Aries could tell she was weighing her options. They all did it. Every single one of the people she had ever pulled a gun on always had the split second where they had to decide to fight or flee.

"My trigger finger is quicker than you. Don't run. You won't make it," Aries warned.

"Please, please. I have a daughter," Steph began.

"You've got a choice to make right now," Aries said, unmoved by the emotion Steph showed.

"What do you want? I don't have any money," Steph pleaded.

"That's okay," Aries said as she sat casually at the dining-room table, her hand wrapped around the handle of the gun that she let rest on the table. "I accept Diamonds."

Steph frowned in confusion. Aries was used to seeing fear on the faces of her victims. She had been doing this so long that she could smell it in the air.

"What you're going to do is go get the little girl out of the room and get her birth certificate," Aries said.

"What? No, please, she's just a child," Steph protested.

"But she isn't your child, so you won't risk your life for hers. Will you?" Aries tested. She didn't feel good about taking a kid from a safe home and returning her to a world of danger and chaos. Aries wanted to see Steph love Aurora in a way that would make her abort her plan. If this woman proved that she loved Aurora like a real mother would, Aries would walk away without disrupting the only world Aurora knew. "I can take you or I can take her," Aries said. "What's it going to be?"

Aries knew the answer before Steph even responded. She could see it in the woman's eyes that Steph wasn't the self-sacrificing type.

"Please," Steph whispered.

Aries was too seasoned to be affected by Steph's pleas.

They were just words. Words unsubstantiated were just phrases. She required action.

Aries pointed her gun. "Just take her!" Steph shouted.

Aries scoffed as she lowered her weapon.

"Go get the girl and the birth certificate. I'm taking her back to her real mother. You won't say anything about this. You'll go on collecting the checks from the state," Aries said. She reached into her jacket pocket and pulled out an envelope full of money. "That's fifty thousand. It's for your trouble over the past three years," she explained.

"The state will come looking for her," Steph protested.

"You wouldn't believe how a little bit of money makes problems like that go away," Aries said. "If Breeze hears from you again or you bother her about her daughter in any way, you'll find me sitting in your kitchen again one day. Next time, I'm only coming for one thing. I will kill you without losing sleep, without thinking twice, without regret. Do you understand?"

Steph nodded. "I understand."

Aries stood and approached Steph as she removed zip ties from the back pocket of her jeans. She roughly grabbed the woman's wrists and tied them to each other before pushing her to the floor forcefully, then tying her wrists to her feet. She walked to the back of the house and grabbed a sleeping Aurora from her bed.

"Where is the birth certificate?" Aries asked.

"Kitchen drawer," Steph replied with tears in her eyes.

Aries retrieved it and then walked out the door.

* * *

Oh, how far the mighty have fallen, Breeze thought as she cleared the dirty plates from the table and picked up the five dollars the patrons had left behind as a tip. Breeze had never thought she would find herself in this place. She had taken so many things for granted. She had been so spoiled. Breeze shook her head as she tucked the money into her apron before heading back to the kitchen. She dumped the dishes in the sink.

"They aren't going to load themselves."

She turned to see her boss, a miserable, old Russian woman who nitpicked Breeze to death.

"I'm not a dishwasher. You hired me to wait tables," Breeze replied.

"And I can fire you just as fast," the woman stated with a Newport cigarette hanging from her mouth.

Breeze sighed as she turned to begin the tedious task of loading the dishwasher. She didn't want trouble. She was simply trying to play by the rules the state had laid out for her. She was establishing employment. Since she was a felon, this was the best she could do. No one else would hire her. Breeze kept her mouth closed and did her job. Not only did she need things to look good on paper; she needed the money. She didn't want to take the risk to reach out to Estes. The feds couldn't touch Estes but they had their suspicions about his involvement with the Cartel. Breeze didn't want any criminal connections to her family to ruin her chances of getting Aurora back.

So, she struggled. Instead of taking her place back on her throne she pretended she was a regular girl. Normalcy felt strange. She had never taken orders or punched a time clock or had anyone speak to her in a way that was anything other than kind. Breeze knew the adjustment and the sacrifice would all be worth it once her daughter was back in her life. She had to keep the bigger picture in mind to stop her from walking out of this place.

Breeze took the extra hour to clean the dishes without complaint. *I'm rushing home to an empty apartment anyway,* she thought. She had transitioned from the halfway house and into a duplex house where she rented out the top unit. It wasn't much, but it was hers. No one had gotten it for her. She had worked countless hours and saved her tips to save up for it. Oddly enough, with its plain white walls, small bathroom, and itchy carpet, it made her proud. She had decorated the tiny second bedroom for Aurora to give her hope that one day, they would be a family.

Breeze finished up her shift and pulled off the apron before exiting the diner. Tired was an understatement. With the smell of grease in her hair and aching feet, she couldn't wait to make it home.

The sound of the bell above the door ringing signified the end of a slaving day. She checked the time on her phone. "Damn," she muttered, knowing she had already missed the last bus. She would have to walk the three miles back to her place.

"Need a ride?"

Breeze turned in shock. She recognized that accent.

She found Aries waiting for her, leaning against an S-Class Mercedes.

Breeze sighed in relief. "You don't even know how much you saved my life right now," she said. "I just missed the last bus."

"Wow," Aries said. "Hell must have frozen over twice. Me never thought me would see the day when Breeze Diamond sat her pretty ass on de' city bus." Aries was in her comfort zone and fell back into her natural tongue around Breeze.

Breeze smirked and shook her head as she walked toward Aries. "Yeah, that makes two of us."

Aries walked around to the driver's side. "I've got something in the backseat for you," she said.

Breeze opened the back door to the car and her heart stopped, midbeat, midbreath; her entire body froze as she stared at a sleeping Aurora.

"What did you do?" Breeze asked. "If Steph is dead and Aurora is missing they will come looking for me."

"Steph isn't dead and no one is going to come looking. You know how me work. All I's were dotted. All T's were crossed. She's yours now," Aries said.

Breeze rushed around the car and hugged her friend so tightly. She didn't care that Aries wasn't the hugging type. She held onto her long and hard as joy overflowed from her.

"Okay, that's enough," Aries said, uncomfortable. Breeze laughed as tears flowed. "Thank you."

"Thank Mia. She called the play. Me just executed it," Aries informed.

Breeze smiled. "Of course," she said. "I don't want to wake her. She's going to be so confused. How do I explain this to her?"

"Chu will be fine. I've got a red-eye out of Miami. Can you drop me at the airport?" Aries asked.

"Drop you? You picked me up," Breeze stated in confusion.

"The car's yours too. Courtesy of Miamor," Aries stated. "We planned for downfall the same way we planned for the come-up. There is a hundred thousand dollars and your daughter's birth certificate under the passenger seat for you."

"I can't take the money. It's too much," Breeze said.

"It's from Miamor's personal stash. She can't use it where she's at. If you need more—"

"I won't," Breeze interrupted. "It's more than enough to get me on my feet until I can figure some things out." Breeze was stunned at Miamor and Aries's generosity. "You didn't have to do this for me."

"We've had our differences in de past. That's water under de bridge. We're family. As a matter of fact, get your baby home. I'll catch a cab. Chu watch your back out here Breeze," Aries said.

Breeze nodded as she watched Aries walk away. She was so grateful. Breeze looked in the back of the car. She had never been so filled with love. To have a second chance at motherhood was a dream come true and as she climbed into the car she promised herself she wouldn't mess this up. She felt guilty because she knew that this was not the way things were supposed to be. Aurora was being passed from one person to the next, when all along she should have been with both her parents under the same roof. Breeze had planned to show her daughter the finest example of love. Now she could barely deliver the bare necessities to her.

She remembered how happy Zyir had been when she had shared the news of her pregnancy. It saddened her that she and Zyir hadn't reached their full potential. Love wasn't enough to keep them together, especially when disloyalty and deceit had pulled them apart. *He still deserves to know his daughter,* she thought. *Even after all that has happened. I have no right to keep her from him.* Breeze wanted to walk away into the sunset with her child, but she knew it wasn't right. She had to give him the opportunity to feel this love she felt because it reminded her that the love she had shared with him wasn't always a lie. Aurora was a walking talking example of the best parts of them and as much as Breeze wanted to, she couldn't be selfish with that type of love.

For the first time since the day she walked out on Zyir after finding out he was a snitch, Breeze made up her mind to go back. Not for herself, but for their daughter. This didn't mean they had to reunite, but she owed it to her child to give her a father. Although Zyir had broken the rules of the street she had no authority to punish him by removing his right to father their child. Butterflies formed in her stomach. Just the thought of seeing Zyir made her nervous. It was miraculous that he was still alive. After a self-inflicted gunshot wound to the head he was supposed to be dead and now she had to face him knowing that she had left him there to die.

Chapter 17

This was a day that Breeze never thought she would see. As she stood outside the rehabilitation center she tried to talk herself into walking inside. *Just put one foot in front of the other,* Breeze thought. It had been so long since she had seen his face and still she couldn't find forgiveness. This was a meeting that could no longer be avoided, however. Breeze stood frozen in place as Aurora held her hand.

"Breeze?"

It hurt her heart that Aurora wouldn't call her mommy, but she wouldn't force it. She knew that everything had happened so fast for her baby. They both needed time to adjust to their new life together and Breeze would be patient. She prayed that she could nurture her relationship with Aurora.

"Yes, baby?" Breeze answered, slightly distracted as she

stood outside the building, looking up at it in intimidation.

"Where are we?" Aurora asked.

"This is where your daddy is, baby. I think it's time you meet him," Breeze said.

"I have a daddy?" Aurora asked in shock. She put her hands on the side of her face as her mouth fell open in surprise.

"Of course, you do and he loves you so much. We both do," Breeze assured her. "You want to go meet him?"

Aurora nodded her head in excitement as she pulled Breeze down the long walkway that led to the door. Breeze was glad that Aurora was so eager. If it hadn't been for her, Breeze would have certainly changed her mind.

She walked into the building and was greeted by a friendly face. An older black woman sat behind a desk wearing scrubs and a smile.

"Hi, I'm here to see Zyir Rich." Breeze said the words in a whisper as butterflies danced in her stomach. She had spent so much time hating him that she had forgotten how much she loved him. Thoughts of the days when she used to worship him played through her mind and she drew in a deep breath to try to calm herself. There was no making sense of the many emotions she felt. It was because of Zyir that the feds had gained leverage on the Cartel. He was the weak link that caused the chain to break and Breeze had judged him heavily for it. His character was flawed and even though he did it all for her, she still blamed him for it all. So many people had suffered from the fallout from Zyir's actions. Aurora was one of them.

"Wow. Mr. Rich hasn't had a visitor the entire time he has been here. It will be good for him," the woman responded. "I need you to fill out these forms and I will let his recovery team know you are here."

"Thank you," Breeze replied. Breeze remembered the day she had left Zyir as if it had happened yesterday. It was as if years hadn't passed them by. As if the wound from his betrayal was still fresh. Breeze had left him upon discovering his deceit and when she heard the gunshot ring out as she stepped into her car, she assumed he was dead. Zyir had lived, but Breeze hadn't even gone back to make sure he was okay. She simply walked away and tried to erase him from her memory. Her family, her brothers came first and a part of her felt guilty for putting her family name over her given one. There was no way the daughter of Carter Diamond could be with a snitch; but as she sat silently waiting for this reunion, she realized how much she still cared.

A doctor came out. "Mrs. Rich?"

"It's Diamond, but you can just call me Breeze," she said as she stood and shook the man's hand. "This is my daughter." She paused. "Zyir's daughter, Aurora."

"It's very nice to see you both. I want to prepare you for what you are about to see. I know it's been some time since you have seen Zyir. He is healing, more and more each day, but he still has a long way to go. He is very lucky to be alive. He has had twelve surgeries since the shooting so there are some scars and there was damage to his—"

"Please, just take me to him," Breeze insisted. If this doctor kept warning her she might lose her nerve.

The doctor nodded in understanding. "Of course. This way," he said.

Breeze picked up Aurora. Her three-year-old frame fit awkwardly in Breeze's arms. Aurora was too big to be picked up. *My mother would call it spoiling her,* Breeze thought, but Breeze had lost so much time with her daughter that she made an exception. She wanted to feel like she could get those vital years back. She had missed so many important things and as she walked toward Zyir's room she wondered if they would ever be able to get back what they had. Breeze knew they couldn't, but she couldn't help but wonder what their life would be like if Zyir hadn't turned on the family.

The doctor led her to a room at the end of the hall and knocked once before entering.

"Zyir, you have some visitors today," he announced.

Breeze's heart felt as if it was caught in a vice grip. Her queasy stomach made bile back up in the back of her throat. She stepped inside the room and everything she had rehearsed went out the window.

"My God," she whispered. She had never allowed herself to think about Zyir. All she knew was that he had survived, but as she stood here in front of him, she felt the need to mourn. This beautiful man, who had loved her, held her, encouraged her, taught her, had suffered greatly.

She crossed the room without realizing it. She reached out to touch his face. His handsome face was swollen from the most recent surgery he had endured. White bandages covered one side of his crooked face. His eye drooped on one side. Breeze's lip quivered as her eyes teared.

"It's been three years. I didn't expect—"

"The healing process is extensive. He came out of surgery to reconstruct the right side of his face. The trajectory of the bullet left him with no bone structure around his eye socket. We had to go in and reshape his face. He lost half his tongue, and half his teeth were blown out. He had to learn to walk again, to control his bodily functions. The brain is the computer to the body. We had to teach him to recode it. He has been through a lot and has come a long way. It's been three years but it's been a very long three years," the doctor explained.

"Who is she?"

His voice made her heart flutter. It had been so long since she had heard it, but the words he spoke caused a devastation so great she had to put Aurora down. Breeze wasn't sure she could support her own weight. Her legs were weak.

"It's me, Zy. It's Breeze," she whispered. She stared in his eyes as she touched his face gently. He rested his head in the palm of her hand, leaning into her.

"His body language shows that he is familiar with you. He is comfortable with you, but he can't remember who you are. The bullet damaged his temporal lobe, which affected his long-term memory. He's fine with everything that happened after the incident, but people, places, names, everything before the shooting is lost to him. It would have been beneficial if family would have been here as visual cues to help stimulate that part of his brain when it first happened, but it's been three years."

"He doesn't know me," Breeze whispered in disbelief as she began to cry. "Zy? How can you not know me?"

He stared at her blankly.

"It's me. Zyir?"

"Don't apply too much pressure on him. Patience is important," the doctor said. "I'll give you some time with him. Just call a nurse if you need anything."

Breeze willed herself to stop her tears. They wouldn't do anyone any good. She didn't want to make him feel as if his progress so far was not enough, but finding him here, like this, was devastating. She felt empty. *All this time he's been here like this and I've been hating him. This is punishment enough,* she thought.

"Who are you, ma?" he asked.

The question made her smile. He couldn't connect to his memories of her but indirectly he still touched her soul.

Breeze didn't know how to answer the question. *How do I tell him that I divorced him because he snitched on my family? How do I tell him about the family, the drugs, the money, the wars if he doesn't remember that stuff . . .*

"We can start with your name, beautiful," Zyir said, interrupting her thoughts. It was hard for him to speak clearly with the bandages wrapped around his head and face. He sounded different, more guttural, as if talking took effort. His smooth voice was now a deep baritone that Breeze barely recognized.

"My name is Breeze and we used to be—"

Before Breeze could get her answer out a nurse walked into the room.

"Hey handsome."

Breeze frowned at the informal greeting as a beautiful woman walked into the room. Her dark skin was flawless and she had the darkest eyes Breeze had ever seen. The dimples that sunk into her cheeks as she smiled complimented her petite lips and perfect teeth. Breeze recognized the look in the woman's eyes. It's what it looked like when you were loved by Zyir Rich. Jealousy seared Breeze.

"Hey baby," Zyir responded.

His greeting caused Breeze to recoil as she drew in a sharp breath. She watched as the nurse leaned over to kiss his lips. She was so comfortable—too comfortable—with Breeze's man. Breeze was sick to her stomach.

"Let me introduce you to somebody," Zyir said. "What was your name again?"

His question reminded Breeze to breathe and she exhaled, trying to manage the infection of heartbreak that was spreading through her.

"Breeze," she said in a low tone. "I'm Breeze."

"Breeze, this is Kai," he introduced. Breeze could tell from the tone of Zyir's voice that he had no idea how badly he was breaking her on the inside. "The woman who saved my life. She hasn't left my side since the day I got here. Even on her off days she sits here, all day and all night.

She's fed me, bathed me, prayed over me. I heard her voice when I couldn't open my eyes and it kept me from walking over to the other side. She's always here when I need her." There was so much admiration in his voice. So much love in his face as he gazed at this woman.

"Stop it Zyir, you make me sound like a stalker," Kai responded. She smiled and Breeze was taken aback by her beauty. Breeze didn't even want to shake the woman's hand as she extended it. Reluctantly, Breeze accepted the greeting. "It's nice to meet you, Breeze. I'm so glad someone from Zy's family is here. Are you his sister?"

Breeze wanted to pop this bubble that the girl lived in. *Bitch, I'm his wife,* she thought. She wished she could haul the words at this beautiful, regal queen, but she couldn't. Breeze wasn't Zyir's wife. She had made sure of that, but now that she sat there looking at Zyir love someone the way he used to love her, she mourned. She wanted to be mad. She wanted to fuck this woman up and reclaim her spot, but how could she? This woman had been by Zyir's side during the most trying times of his life. She had nursed him back to health. She had stuck by him and done the job Breeze had refused. So instead of throwing her real identity into the mix, she simply smiled. "Just an old friend."

"And is that your daughter?" Kai asked.

Breeze picked Aurora up and nodded. "Yeah. It's getting late and I really should get going," Breeze said as she stood to her feet. Breeze knew she had no right to walk back into Zyir's life demanding a position. He still had a lot of healing to do and he had found someone who could help him do that. Breeze felt selfish for wanting to interrupt that. She hadn't wanted Zyir. She had deemed him unworthy of her because he had snitched. She had written him off and erased him from her life with ease. It wasn't until she saw him happy with someone else that she realized what she had lost.

Kai frowned. "I didn't mean to interrupt your visit. I can come back. You should stay and finish spending time with him," she offered.

"Yeah stay, I feel like there are things you haven't said," Zyir interrupted. "Like I can feel that we used to be close, but I just need you to fill in the blanks."

Breeze sniffled as a tear fell and she quickly swiped it away. "There aren't enough words to fill in all the blanks and all the things I want to say," she whispered. She cleared her throat. *I can't interrupt his life, his recovery, his relationship with this girl,* Breeze thought. She wanted to be bitter. No, she wanted to slap the perfect smile off this girl's face, but she held her tongue. *I made my choice. Now I must live with it.* This girl was taking her place, loving her man, and there wasn't a damn thing Breeze could do about it. To do anything other than walk away would be selfish.

An awkward energy filled the room. "Maybe I should come back later," Kai said.

"No—"

Kai stopped Breeze from speaking. "No, I insist." She bent down and adjusted Zyir's pillows before kissing his lips quickly. "I'll be back handsome."

Breeze watched her walk out. "She seems nice."

"Yeah, she is," Zyir answered.

He stared at Breeze, unflinchingly, making her look away first. It was like he was beckoning her with his eyes. Even under all the bandages he was still the puppeteer to her heart. "I used to love you," he said, in a matter-of-fact way.

"In the most perfect way," Breeze replied. "You were my very best friend, Zy. I know you don't remember what happened, but when you think of me, know this. I'm sorry." Breeze was crying effortless tears. They just fell from her eyes, like a leak from an old sink, one after another. She carried Aurora's dead weight in her arms and she was grateful that the sandman had lulled her daughter to sleep. "I love you and I'm sorry. I'm glad you found a woman like Kai. She feels right for you."

She saw the confusion in his eyes and she turned for the door. As she opened it his voice stopped her. "I don't know much, but I know I love you too. That's the only way to explain this heaviness in my chest and every step you taking to walk out right now is making me feel like I can't breathe ma," Zyir said.

Breeze turned to face him, but she didn't close the gap between them. Everything in her wanted to run to her man. She wanted to confess her love and fix things between them, but to do that she would have to explain to him where things had gone wrong. She would have to dig up the past and tell him who he was before he had swallowed a bullet. She would have to admit that she had left him there to die. Breeze had been so callous that she hadn't even gone back after hearing the gun go off. Breeze would destroy the promising love he was growing with a woman who genuinely loved him, to rekindle a flame that she had purposefully snuffed. So instead of doing what she wanted, she did what was right. "Goodbye Zy," she whispered sorrowfully. Breeze rushed out of the room before she changed her mind. She sobbed the entire way out.

When she got to the parking lot she heard a voice calling her name.

"Breeze!"

She turned to see Kai chasing after her.

"That's his daughter, isn't it?" Kai confronted.

"I don't know you. This isn't your business," Breeze defended.

"He probably can't see it because he isn't in his right state of mind. He's on pain medication and recovering from surgery, but it's clear as day. You come in here after three years with a toddler, you can barely look at him without crying. He had a ring on his finger the day he was admitted. He was married and you're his wife. This is his kid!" Kai was so spot on with her accusations that Breeze couldn't defend herself with a lie. There was no point. They both knew that everything Kai was saying was fact.

"Look, just go back in there. You're asking for something that you don't want. Just take care of him. He deserves to be happy," Breeze said.

"How can I keep this secret from him? How can I go back in there and build a relationship with this in the shadows?" Kai asked.

"Because this is the only way you *get* to have a relationship with him!" Breeze shouted in frustration. "If I tell him about who I am, about who this little girl is . . ." Breeze paused as she lowered her voice. She wasn't trying to fight with this woman. "If I bring out those emotions and those memories in him, you won't stand a chance. The love I have with him is like the sun. It burns everything up in its path. It's consuming and brilliant and intense and . . ." Her voice drifted because she could go on and on. "If I tell him, he will love me with every piece of himself and that leaves nothing for you. If he has to choose between his old life with me and a new one with you, he will always choose me. So just thank me and let me walk away," Breeze wasn't being arrogant, she was simply telling the truth. No matter if he remembered her or not, his heart could feel her and Breeze would bet her life on it.

She could tell that her words had injured Kai, but she had asked and Breeze had answered.

"If you're so sure then why are you running away? Why not just take your man back?" Kai asked. Breeze could see that Kai was threatened. It wasn't her intention, but Kai had every reason to worry.

"Because too much has happened. Some things are meant to remain secrets of the past. Don't tell him about me, about her; give me your word," Breeze said.

Kai was silent for a long time and Breeze gave her a few moments to weigh her options in her head. Breeze knew what decision she would come to. Kai did not want to lose the possibility of a life with Zyir. Self-gain always won out in the end.

"I won't say anything," Kai said.

"Of course, you won't," Breeze said. She walked away with sadness rising with each step she took. Breeze had lost a lot in her lifetime. It seemed that she could never truly find a happiness to call her own. There was always a piece missing, but she told herself that no one could have it all. She had Zyir's seed and that meant she would always have a piece of him. So, when the days grew long and her heart grew weary, she would be able to look into Aurora's eyes and know that once upon a time she had been loved and in return had loved someone. She had walking, talking proof, and as Breeze placed her baby in the car seat and walked around to enter the driver's side she took one last look up at the building. Zyir was right inside. All she had to do was go back for her man, but she knew that she couldn't. She knew that she shouldn't. It was just she and her daughter, and she realized that was enough.

Breeze was tired. She was ready to live a whole new life. She had made plans to go find Estes and reunite with her family, but she just couldn't. She didn't want any reminders of the tumultuous past. Breeze decided right then and there, as she pulled away, that Zyir, the Cartel, and even her last living brother, Carter, would remain in her rear view. She had her daughter and she had the future ahead of her. It was all she needed.

Chapter 18

Carter sat stoically as he looked out the window of the private plane. The trip had taken sixteen straight hours and Carter hoped it would be worth their while. He looked over to Anari. She was sleeping, which was a compliment to his character because she didn't trust anyone enough to close her eyes around them. Trust had been established between them. Carter admired her beauty. Her light skin and brown hair that had been highlighted blond and was cut short fit her perfectly. Faces like hers didn't usually run empires and Carter would be lying if he said he hadn't underestimated her. She was a natural born hustler and Carter knew that if she had brought them all this far, it was for good reason. The flight concierge came by and nudged Anari out of her rest.

"I'm sorry to wake you, but the captain would like to

begin his initial descent. Could you please buckle up?" the woman asked.

Anari nodded and cleared her throat as she fingered her short pixie cut before putting on her seat belt.

"How long was I out?" she asked.

"A few hours," Carter replied. "I'm anxious to hear what your people here have to say."

"There is a round table. The same families have dominated the D.R. for decades. We'll meet them all informally tonight at the pits," Anari informed. "Tomorrow, we will discuss business."

"The pits?" Carter inquired, with a raised brow.

"It's quite brutal," Anari responded. "But it's a tradition here. Men put boys in a gladiator's battle and let them fight. No rules, no holds barred, just the survival of the fittest."

"What type of shit is that?" Carter asked with a frown. "They fight people like dogs?"

"Yeah, the right man gets the right fighter and he can make a lot of money. We aren't talking friendly wagers. I'm talking about quarter-million-dollar fights. They train these kids like professionals," Anari said.

"That's fucked up," Carter said.

"It's the way of the land," Anari responded with a shrug. The plane hit the tarmac with unexpected ease and Carter looked out his window. He wanted to make sure that their entry into this country was undetected. The last thing he needed was for anyone to determine his whereabouts. He had taken great precautions to live out of the scope of the feds' radar and he wanted to keep it that way.

"Relax. I don't move sloppy. It's a private airstrip," Anari said, easing some of the tension in his chest.

"I'm getting too old for this shit," he said with a laugh as he shook his head. The amount of anxiety and turmoil he felt in his heart kept him up at night. Being away from his family was weighing on him but the only way to get to them and make things right was to go through Anari. He had to play things her way if he wanted to free his wife and find his son.

Anari chuckled softly as she made her way to the exit. A bulletproof, black-on-black truck waited for them at the end of a red carpet.

Carter looked around, his neck on a swivel, as he entered the vehicle. The dirt roads kicked up dust as they drove through the city streets. Barefoot children ran after the car excitedly, waving and laughing as they sped by.

"Such a beautiful country with such poverty," Anari said more to herself than anyone else.

"Pull over," Carter stated.

"Señor?" the driver frowned as if he hadn't heard him right.

"Right up here, pull over," Carter instructed.

"We don't have time—"

"We'll make time," Carter said sternly. He got out of the car, the warm humidity causing sweat to form instantly on his forehead. He removed his suit jacket and tossed it inside as he watched the kids catch up to him.

He pulled a wad of money out of his pocket and the children cheered as he began passing out hundred-dollar bills. You would have thought they were meeting Santa Claus himself the way they jumped for joy. The beautiful faces of these kids touched him as he thought of his own son. He would want someone to do the same if God forbid his son ever needed it. The more bills he passed out the more kids accumulated and Carter gave freely until he was out of money to give.

He was swarmed with hugs and Carter could barely walk as he made his way back to the car. They clung to him as if he had saved their lives. He waved goodbye and retreated to the air-conditioned temperatures of the truck.

"You can't save them all," Anari said.

"No, but those few won't go hungry tonight," he answered.

Anari nodded and a rare smile graced her face as the driver slowly rolled away.

Carter was a man of character and he believed there was no point in getting money if you weren't going to give a little of it back. He'd done enough wrongdoings in his attempt to acquire wealth that he had to balance it out somehow. It was what made him sleep easy at night. Lately, that had been a lost privilege anyway. With his son's whereabouts unknown and the love of his life behind bars, rest hadn't come easy and the bags under his eyes showed it. Carter had never wanted to retire from the game as much as he did now. He remembered a time when he had hung on to his throne with no thought of ever coming off it, but now he craved normalcy. He used to clown the average Joe with the average job. He had never understood the mentality of working a nine to five, but now he envied the man who lived that simple life. Living check to check meant a man didn't have to live bullet to bullet. It may not have been a grand life but it wasn't a dangerous one either. *Joe ain't never had to watch his wife take a bid,* Carter thought.

His reverie was interrupted when he noticed they were pulling into the gates of an old factory. Expensive cars lined the sides of the road as men in suits made their way inside.

Carter and Anari exited the vehicle.

"Matias will meet us at the entrance inside," Anari said. "Leave your pistol. There are no guns allowed inside."

"I bring my gun everywhere," Carter insisted.

"We are on their territory. Your one gun won't do much against the hundred men that will be inside. Just trust me. I wouldn't lead you into the darkness," Anari pushed.

Carter reluctantly left his weapon and then made his way inside.

"Anari, welcome beautiful lady." She was greeted warmly as soon as she stepped foot in the building.

"Matias." Anari beamed. "Thank you for having us. This is my associate, Carter."

Carter nodded in acknowledgment.

"First we play and tomorrow we talk business. I've got the best seat in the house for you. Will you be placing wagers this evening?" Matias asked.

"No, we're just here to observe," Carter answered sternly.

Carter and Anari would have been seated ringside, if a ring existed at all. They were front and center as they watched the crowd slowly filter in. It was like a real sport and Carter couldn't believe that these people had the stomach for this. He was all for professional boxing and could even deal with the MMA stuff, but when he saw a young boy walk out into the ring it instantly enraged him. *This shit ain't sport,* Carter thought. He felt Anari place a calming hand on his forearm and he took a deep breath.

"Their house, their rules," she leaned into him and said. "Remember the bigger picture. We can't save them all."

Carter's jaw was tense as he watched the crowd react to the vicious fight between youths.

Grown men hooted and hollered around him. It was savagery in its rawest form.

Carter stood to his feet when his eyes fell on the next fighter.

C.J.? he thought. His mind was playing tricks on him and he squeezed his eyes closed and opened them, hoping that the picture before him would be different. *That's not my son. That can't be my son. He's in the States, back home, somewhere in foster care.* Suddenly the idea of him being in the system seemed so much more comforting than this reality.

A mixture of anger and pride filled him as C.J. moved around the pit with skilled athleticism, taking no prisoners as he delivered blow after devastating blow. He was taller than Carter remembered. The years had crept by and at almost thirteen he was coming into his mannish looks and clearly, he had been conditioned for this fight.

"C.J.!" Carter shouted. His voice caused a momentary lapse in focus as they locked in on each other. A flicker of recognition reflected in C.J.'s eyes and his opponent didn't waste the opportunity to send a crashing jab to C.J.'s jaw. It staggered him and before he could recover he was hit again with an uppercut that rocked him. Carter was on the floor in an instant but Anari pulled him back.

"Let him finish. He's been trained for this," Anari said.

"That's my son out there," Carter protested, livid as pure rage coursed through his veins.

"And he was winning before you distracted him," Anari commented.

Carter shrugged her off and rushed over to the fight, pulling the boy off his son and flinging him across the pit.

The crowd erupted in protest and Carter pulled C.J. to his feet. "Get off me!" C.J. shouted. "I'm the best fighter here. I got this. I don't need your help!" Carter was taken aback as C.J. snatched his arm away from him.

"Boo!" the crowd antagonized as Carter looked on in utter confusion. "How are you here? Who the fuck got you into this shit?" Carter had so many questions. He had sent people to the Dominican Republic in search of his son and they had come back short of information. How had he missed this?

When Estes stepped into the pit, suddenly it all made sense. Carter met Estes halfway across the circular arena and before Estes could speak one word Carter leveled him with one blow. The old man was no match for Carter, not where hands were concerned. Carter pulled his backup piece. He had warned Anari that he never went anywhere without being armed. He may have left one gun in the car, but the one holstered on his ankle was readily accessible. He pointed it on Estes. Within seconds another gun was pointed at the back of his head. This was Estes's house, Estes's territory. Carter had let his temper get the best of him, but when it came to his son there were no limits.

"Ah, ah, ah. I wouldn't do it." Anari came out of nowhere, with her own small-caliber pistol aimed at the man who was threatening Carter. The entire arena was silent as everyone tried to guess how this would pan out.

"Carter, be smart," Estes said as he rolled over on his side to spit blood from his mouth. "You shoot me and what then? C.J. witnesses his father gunned down and then fed to the pigs. No harm has come to him in my care. This is just a hobby."

Carter pulled back the hammer on his gun. "You've been hiding my son from me? For what? So he could represent you in this fight? You breeding my boy like he's a slave? Putting him to work for you? Training him like an animal? Tell me why I shouldn't blow your top, old man, because I'm feeling real trigger happy right now." The threat was real. The tone of his voice said it all. Estes would die tonight if Carter had anything to say about it.

"Stop!" C.J. yelled, enraged as he stormed over to help Estes off the ground. "Nobody forced me to do nothing! I want to fight! I'm the best and you coming here messed up everything we worked for. I didn't ask you to show up here! Just go back to where you came from cuz I don't need you anymore! You're too late! I've been waiting for you to come back for years and now you want to come in like I need saving! I like it here and I'm not going with you! This is my home now! I'm a man, I can take care of myself."

Estes motioned for his goon to lower his weapon and Anari slowly lowered hers as well. Carter stormed after C.J. The amount of resentment he heard from his son was wounding.

"C.J.!" Carter shouted. He grabbed him by the elbow and turned him around. "Don't turn your back to me. I'm your—"

Before he could finish his sentence, his chest throbbed with excruciation. It felt like someone was squeezing his heart, trying to stop it from beating, and Carter's face twisted in agony. Spittle flew from his mouth as he pursed his lips and blew out a sharp breath as he gripped the left side of his pectoral.

"Carter?" He heard Anari's voice.

"Dad?!" C.J. called out, his tone going from anger to worry as Carter fell forward into his son's arms. The weight of Carter sent them both to the ground and C.J. held his father, leaning Carter's back against his chest as Carter gasped for air. His eyes were wide in desperation. He just couldn't get enough air in.

Breathe, he told himself. *Fucking breathe.*

A slow burn spread through the entire front of his body and Carter kicked his feet as he attempted to stand. He never left the ground. He just kept scooting C.J. back, farther and farther.

"Somebody help me! Dad?! Dad?!" C.J. was crying. Carter could hear his son wailing in his ears and for the first time in his life Carter was afraid. He gripped his son's hand as he tried to concentrate on the beat of C.J.'s racing heart.

Thump. Thump. Thump. Thump.

He could feel C.J.'s heartbeat as he leaned against his son. The rapid pace matched the panic and commotion around him but it didn't match his own heart that was slowing down by the second. With each beat, agony struck like lightning, and he knew his beats were numbered.

"Just breathe, Carter," Anari said as she knelt in front of him.

He knew he was in trouble from the look in her eyes. The woman who let nothing rattle her feared what was happening.

I'm dying, he thought. The intense pain never let up and he gripped C.J.'s hand, wanting his son to be the last person he felt before he took his last breath. He closed his eyes and saw Miamor's beauty behind his lids. It made him want to keep them closed forever.

"Dad! Open your eyes! Keep your eyes open! Help is coming." It was C.J.'s cries that forced him to pop his lids back open but it was so hard. Fighting this feeling, resisting this transition was impossible. He squinted his eyes in panic when he saw his brother, Mecca, standing across the pit. He just stood there, still, among the crowd and Carter blinked away the image.

Carter couldn't keep fighting for much longer and

when his grip around C.J.'s hand went limp, C.J. knew that his father was gone.

"No! Man, no!" C.J. cried, not caring who witnessed his weakness.

Anari put both hands over her mouth in shock as she knelt and touched Carter's neck. There was no pulse. There was no . . . well, there was nothing. Carter was gone. C.J. looked up at her with hope in his stare, but she shook her head letting him know that his father was no more.

C.J. hugged Carter so tightly that it brought tears to Anari's eyes. Finally, the ambulance arrived but it was too little too late. Unless they were raising the dead, they couldn't help. Carter had passed and if her eyes hadn't deceived her, Anari was sure that he had felt every tortuous second of it. Estes and Anari looked down at C.J. in sympathy.

"Come on kid, let's allow the people to do their jobs," Estes said.

C.J. stood, reluctantly releasing his father. His rage boiled over as he kicked at the dirt and flipped over the rectangular table where men placed their bets. He just wanted to hurt someone, anyone would do, even if it was himself. He sat in one of the chairs and brought his elbows to his knees as his hands rested on top of his head.

I don't know what to do, he thought. He had never thought he would lose his father at such a young age, but now that he had, C.J. was devastated.

Estes could see the steam boiling off C.J. More and more, Estes was understanding C.J. Every pain in his life was transformed into aggression. Anger and hurt went together like beans and rice in his mind. C.J. wouldn't heal from this. No one had taught him how to take the hard stuff so that it didn't fester and turn into a bigger problem later. This would be another source of rage for him. It would be what he drew on to help him win his fights. C.J. watched as they loaded up his father's body. He was underneath a white sheet and the beautiful woman he hadn't been formally introduced to was at his father's side, giving directions to the paramedics.

C.J. sat there for a long while. Even after every man in attendance had cleared the place, C.J. couldn't bring himself to leave. He could feel his father there and he knew once he walked out their connection would be severed. Estes didn't rush him. He just gave him space to feel whatever emotion he had assigned as appropriate. C.J. often got emotions mixed up in his head. He was so full of so many things that had gone unresolved that when things happened to him it was often a mystery as to how he would respond.

It took three hours for C.J. to pull himself up. "He's dead, isn't he?" C.J. didn't know why he was asking a question he already knew the answer to. Of course, Carter was dead. C.J. had felt the coldness of his skin. It was a cold that a living, breathing thing could not ever be. C.J. was glad that Carter had come back into his life. C.J. had been the one to hold him until he transitioned on, but he hated the way they had left things. His last conversation with his father had been a bad one, an argument where he had said things he didn't mean. He never thought it would be the last words they would exchange and C.J. wished he had handled things differently.

"They're saying a heart attack," Estes confirmed.

C.J.'s fists were at the side of his head as he clenched his eyes shut at the revelation. Time was always something he had more of. It was what he was banking on when it came to his parents. All he had to do was wait for time to pass and God would put him and his parents in a place where they could reunite. Miamor would be released from prison in due time and his father would return home. All he had to do was be patient. That's what he had told himself on nights when he missed them so badly that he couldn't sleep. Now nothing would ever repair their fractured family because Carter was gone.

Estes sat next to him, knowing there wasn't anything he could say to ease C.J.'s torment. He remembered exactly how it felt to lose someone so dear. There weren't words to describe the anguish. He could see C.J.'s lip quivering as the boy tried his hardest to stifle the tears. He was trying to be strong, trying to maintain the hard front that he usually put on in front of Estes but holding it inside was damaging. This type of suffering would rot a man's soul away. Estes knew because he had allowed himself to decay slowly over the years after the death of his beloved son Sammie. It was no way to live, especially for a young boy. C.J. hadn't even begun to explore the depths of his heart. It couldn't go without repair at this early age; it would stop him from ever adequately loving anyone again. The only people he had extended his heart to were his parents, his close family, and Estes, but C.J. had yet to know the tender tug of a woman's devotion. He had yet to feel the butterflies and nervousness that loving a beautiful woman could bring. If C.J. stifled his loss now and bottled it up inside, it would damage him. He wouldn't ever allow himself to open his heart again in fear of feeling this same devastating blow.

Estes was a man with an ice block around his heart, but he forced himself to pull C.J. into an embrace. The empathy he felt for C.J. made Estes uncomfortable but he didn't let go because he knew that it was what C.J. needed. "You're not alone, kid," Estes said. "I got you. Let it out. You have to let some of that water out or you will drown in it. It will be okay." His hug was firm, sturdy, supportive, and strong enough to hold up a breaking C.J.

C.J. sobbed, releasing years of detriment. He had felt so alone, so abandoned, but he always knew that one day his father would come back. Carter was godly to C.J. He could beat anything and anyone, and would, in order to return to his family. Death was the one thing that Carter couldn't come back from. It was permanent and as C.J. cried he felt the magnitude of it all. Death was a part of life; it was a passage that everyone must take eventually. The prematurity of his father being taken away made him feel like he was dreaming. How would he become a man, with no father? Who would teach him about sex? Who would show him how to change a tire? Who would dissolve his worry when he finally became a father himself? His example of manhood was on a slab in the morgue and

Estes was telling him that it would be okay. Nothing would ever be okay. Nothing would ever feel complete because the man from whom he came hadn't finished his job of molding C.J. before God stripped him of the privilege.

He pulled back, clearing his throat as he swiped a hand over his face.

"Let's go," Estes said.

"Go where?" C.J. asked.

"Home," Estes replied.

C.J. looked around, knowing that there was no point in staying here. Refusing to leave wouldn't bring his father back. If he never saw the place again it would be fine with him. "I can't fight here anymore, but I still have to fight," C.J. said. He held up his fists in front of his face as he shook them with conviction. "Fighting is the only thing I've got."

Estes nodded in understanding. "It's fine. We'll put you in a real ring with real fighters. No more street stuff. It'll be good to give you something serious to focus on."

Estes stood and extended his hand to C.J., then helped pull him from the ground. As they walked out, Estes threw an arm around C.J.'s shoulder and gave him a quick pat of reassurance. Their relationship was symbiotic. C.J. needed Estes, especially now that Carter was gone, but Estes was in dire need of C.J. as well. A fatherless child and a childless father. They filled a void in each other's lives and they would for years to come.

Chapter 19

I felt every pain, until I felt nothing and then I saw the reaction to the way I left this earth. It's fucked up the way death creeps up on you. In the most unexpected way I was ripped from everything and everyone I held dear. In front of my son, in the arms of my son, I was sucked back up into the womb of my creator. The same way that I was waiting to cradle my son as he was pushed out of the womb of the creator. The parallel between life and death, so apparent as my son ushered me into the light. It's hard, knowing that I'm leaving him behind when I haven't fully taught him how to survive in it. Seeing him cry, feeling his soul shake, but not being able to do anything except walk beside him along his journey. I hope he feels me there because I'll never leave him. It's a bruise to a man's ego to see his son cry on the shoulder of another man. I should have been there. If I could have, I would have been there and now he will never know why I was away so long.

Time didn't permit me the favor of making up for my disappearance. There are certain things that a boy never heals from and I hope my death isn't the thing that manifests trouble in C.J.'s life. The way I miss him, the way I miss his mother, is immeasurable. I'm comforted by the fact that she knew. Miamor knew exactly how deeply my love for her flowed. She was the key to parts of myself that were inaccessible before her. I hope she is able to remind C.J. of how much I cared and how hard I tried to be a man he would want to become one day. I didn't have that. I didn't know that feeling of admiration for a man greater than myself. Even without ever having one conversation with Carter Diamond, I somehow grew up to be just like him. I tried to make my mark on the world, tried to provide for my family, without doing much harm, but in some cases harm was necessary. I was a man who lived a flawed life for the perfect reasons: for them. If only I had the chance to do it all over again. I would hustle less and love them more, because at the end of it all the things were left behind. The money, the cars, the houses, even the power, all stayed on earth. They were possessions to be bought, sold, and traded. What God allowed me to take with me, what crossed over from the realm of the living, was love. The memories of those I cherish are like pieces of treasure in a heart-shaped chest and I now know the purpose of life was to fill that chest up . . . to fill my heart up. I want that for my son. I want that for my wife. I hope I get to witness that as I look down on them from above because I'll be watching, closely. I'll never be far. I know they will mourn my passing. I know my absence will make Miamor angry with God, but I'll leave her heart up to Him because I know only He can change it. He knows how much I need her, here with me, in this beautiful oasis, so I'm confident that He will repair his relationship with her. I have no doubt about that. Miamor lacks the understanding that she will see me again, that much is guaranteed. Time doesn't exist up here. So, when we are reunited it will feel like a separation never existed, but those decades that Miamor and C.J. have yet to live would feel long to them. Days will be hard. Loneliness will settle in and tears will fill endless nights. I pray that the bad days don't last long for them because I'm still right there, not in flesh, but in spirit, and I always will be.

Chapter 20

Death always seemed to be the thing to bring families back together. *Weddings and funerals,* Breeze thought. It was the only time black families got together and as Breeze stood over her brother's body she wished like hell that it had been a wedding that had brought her back to town instead. Carter looked so peaceful that she would have thought he was simply sleeping if she didn't know better.

She shook her head in disgrace. None of this made any sense. Carter was a man who had survived everything. Wars with Haitians, conflict with Mexican cartels, threats from Saudi princes . . . he had come out of all those circumstances unscathed. Or so they thought. The weight of all those things had cost him. No one knew how heavy the crown could be except for the king. Being the one to make life-and-death decisions, being everyone's protector, being the oldest child is what had caused his heart to fail him. He simply carried too much and Breeze knew that the fracturing of their family had been the thing to break him.

Carter had come into her life so late that now she wondered what life would have been like if she had known him when she was a little girl. She felt like she had been robbed. He was the brother she loved the most, but had spent the least amount of time with. Breeze had the privilege to walk around Miami without worry because of Carter's influence, because of Monroe's influence, because of Mecca's as well. All three of them were in the grave now. Prematurely, she was stripped of her entire family. She was the last of the Diamond children and the loneliness she felt being in the world without her siblings made silent tears escape her. It didn't seem real. *A heart attack?* she thought, dismally. *Not even a bullet to the chest could kill him but a heart attack did.* She shook her head in utter disbelief.

Breeze thought of Zyir and was grateful for his memory loss. For the first time, it didn't seem like such a bad thing. Losing Carter would have broken Zyir and Breeze would have never been able to put the pieces back together the same. Carter's impact on everyone around him was so magnified, so intense, that his absence would change the fabric of their lives. His death wasn't one that would be forgotten.

Time simply could not heal this wound. Breeze had tried to move on from Miami. She desperately wanted to leave it all behind. The only connection she hadn't severed was the phone calls she accepted from Mo, but Carter's death had brought her running home. Carter Diamond had left a strong legacy for his children. While being his seed was a gift, it was also a curse and an early invitation to the grave seemed to be one of them. She had attended one too many funerals in her lifetime and as she looked back to her daughter, who was being occupied by one of the funeral home's workers, she promised herself she wouldn't be next. She turned to the funeral director. "Nothing but the best for him. He was one of the good ones," she said.

"Of course," the man replied as he rolled the white sheet over Carter's face.

Breeze rushed out of the room and scooped up her daughter before racing outside. She gulped in the fresh air as soon as she exited, trying to erase the stench of death from her nostrils.

She knew that she would have to be the one to tell Miamor and that was something she was not looking forward to. Over the years, they had developed a bond that was unbreakable, but Breeze was at a point in her life where she wanted to keep Miamor at a distance. It wasn't personal. She wanted to keep the entire city of Miami and the past that came with it at bay. Miamor had played grim reaper for so long that death was attached to her. It was as natural as water or air for Miamor and Breeze couldn't allow that type of energy to infect her life. Not anymore, not since motherhood. Breeze told herself that this would be the last time she allowed herself to come back home. After she buried Carter, no one would see or hear from her again. If Zyir could erase his memories and start anew, she could too, but first, she had to make it through the funeral of Carter Jones.

* * *

Miamor's chest was weighed down by chains. It was heavy and the burden of the loss pulled at her, enticing her to crumble. She felt her legs shaking, withering in the height of her despair with every step she struggled to take. Nothing had ever hurt this bad. She wondered if others could see her pain. It felt like an ugly scar, one that caused gawkers to ridicule. It had to be the reason why all these inmates were staring at her as she made her way toward the exit. They could see it . . . the devastation . . . the heartbreak. She wore it like an accessory.

She was escorted by two guards, one on each arm as they walked her toward the light of the free world. Her shuffled steps made her feel as if she would fall as the chains at her feet tripped her up along the way and although she had worn the cuffs on her hands before, today they seemed to bite into her skin extra tightly. Miamor felt everything. On this cloudy, rainy, gloom-filled day, her emotions were magnified. She knew the sun wouldn't shine for the occasion. She was surprised it had risen at all. Not even the flowers would bloom on such a tragic day. It had taken God seven days and seven nights to create the beauty of the earth and it had only taken one thing to destroy it all for her. She would never see awe in anything of this world. With the death of one man, everything stopped. Life.

Significance. Love. Joy. Purpose. It all ceased to exist. Carter Jones, first-born son of Carter Diamond, was gone.

How did this happen? she thought. She was desperately hoping she had been misinformed. Perhaps it was Zyir who had died, or C.J. or Mo, or Breeze, or hell, just any-fucking-body except Carter Jones. Oh, she could feel the ache in her bones. It settled in deeply, penetrating her like the winter winds on a freezing day and all she could do was feel it. Miamor felt no shame that she was wishing death on all her loved ones because any one of their deaths would be easier to deal with than his. He had been the man to thaw her cold heart. He was life for Miamor and although Miamor knew there was a God, the only person she had ever worshipped was Carter.

Miamor had done so many bad things in her lifetime and she had waited for karma to circle back to fill her with regret. The prison sentence wasn't severe enough. To a woman like Miamor it was simply a waiting game, but this . . . this death, this unexplainable, unfair, and unexpected loss was unfathomable. It was her karma. To love Carter and then to lose him was the most traumatic thing she had ever felt. Had there been someone to blame, to murder, to exact revenge upon, it would have made it easier. Every hustler has his day when the grim reaper sends a shooter at his door. If he had fallen victim to the game, Miamor could have understood, she would have been able to wrap her mind around the *how* of it all.

His heart just stopped beating. It just stopped working, she thought. *How does that happen?*

She had a million questions. The who, what, when, where, why, and hows of this death plagued her, but no one had the answers. It had simply been his time. *Only it wasn't his time. We didn't get a lifetime together, I didn't get to see his beard turn gray, or watch him raise our son. He was supposed to grow old, we were supposed to grow old together.* Her thoughts were torture and her uncharacteristic tears fell as effortlessly as the rain from the sky on this ugly day.

Miamor couldn't even appreciate the free air as she stepped outside because without Carter the entire world felt like prison. The only thing that would make her feel free is if God snatched the breath from her lungs and allowed her to make the journey with him into the afterlife. If she could, she would purchase that one-way ticket without hesitation. She would lay down her life for him. Never would she have taken these years behind bars if she had known he wouldn't be there waiting for her at the end of it all. Miamor lowered her body inside the unmarked transport car and leaned her head against the window. *God please,* she thought. She didn't know what she was praying for. Death was the one thing that couldn't be undone. The way this had occurred felt like the cruelest joke.

When the car pulled up to the cemetery the pit in Miamor's stomach filled with bile. She was sick, physically and mentally. Her emotions were all over the place. Miamor saw the casket sitting high over the plot of dirt that would serve as the final resting place for her only love. She wanted to throw herself into the pit right along with him. The casket was pure gold and it shined. It was only fitting. Carter had gone through life as a king and the beautiful custom box was made just for him. There were only a few people in attendance. Carter wouldn't have wanted to make a spectacle and she couldn't help but wonder who had decided on the intimacy of the occasion. The details were supposed to be up to her. She knew him best. She was his queen, his wife. She should have been there for him to plan his memorial and cry while picking out flowers and the words that would forever be etched on his headstone.

Miamor bypassed Breeze, who stood holding the hand of a beauty of a little girl, tears staining both their cheeks. Miamor was almost sure that the little girl was only crying because of the uncontrollable sobs that left Breeze's lips. Another woman was present, someone Miamor didn't recognize, a stunning beauty who bore no tears but whose solemn expression told Miamor that she was saddened, but not grief-stricken, from losing Carter. It was like the woman was managing her pain, controlling how much she let show, and Miamor wondered how anyone could have such incredible restraint. She needed some of that restraint in this moment because with every step she took, sorrow added one more brick to her back. It wouldn't be long before she was folded over, unable to carry it all. Her breakdown was inevitable. Her feet sank into the wet grass with every dreadful step and she wished God would just open the ground and swallow her whole. *I just want to go with him,* she thought.

She stood directly in front of the casket and lifted her shackled hands to touch the top. She recoiled, surprised how cold the metal was. She shook her head. "I need to see his face," she whispered. "Open it." She turned to the groundskeeper that stood off to the side at a respectable distance. He was like a vulture just waiting for the family to leave so that he could throw Carter in this ominous hole.

"I'm sorry, it's policy—"

"Open the casket!" Miamor's voice was full of venom and suddenly tension was an attendee.

"Inmate—"

"I'm not leaving here without seeing his face. I'm his wife. I deserve to see him. I just want to see him!" Miamor was distraught. She was crying so hard that her face had taken on a shade of red as her distress plagued her.

The woman whose face Miamor was still trying to place stepped up and whispered something to the groundskeeper. Seconds later, the casket was being opened.

There he rested. Seeing his dark face, eyes permanently closed, hands folded on top of himself in a signature suit, Tom Ford, if she had to guess. It was this image that haunted her. To see the absence of life, his shell, lying before her, knowing his spirit was somewhere in the clouds, dug a hole in her so deeply that Miamor's shoulders jerked with pain.

"Hey handsome," she whispered as she touched his face, caressing it with the back of her hand as she bent to place a kiss on his lips. "I love you. My God, I love you so much. How are you leaving me right now? How could you do this? I'm so sorry I wasn't there," she wept. Miamor had always hoped they would die together, old in their home, with a lifetime of memories behind them. They were just getting started. In fact, amidst the wars and the treachery, they truly hadn't even begun. She blamed herself for not being by his side, but only because she needed someone to assign blame to. She knew her presence probably would have made no difference, but her absence placed a guilt on her that she couldn't shake. She had incomprehensible loss to deal with: the burden of her imprisonment, the inability to be there for their son. Miamor knew Carter enough to know that it was what had killed him. He had been disconnected from his lifelines and his heart couldn't function without them.

Miamor wasn't even supposed to be touching Carter but not even the guards were cold enough to stop her. It felt like they were witnessing a private moment. Everyone in attendance was a voyeur to her grief. Her world was ending as she realized her doom would be the punishment of walking through life without a world that included him. His love was what sustained her and without the sustenance of *him,* Miamor would slowly rot. She may be physically present but her soul was right there in that casket with Carter. No one would ever be able to touch her heart the way he had. Carter was her soul food and without him she would starve. He was the one who made her believe she was worthy of love, that she was worthy of a man who wanted to do more than simply possess her. Carter had shown her forgiveness when he owed her none and she had yet to repay him for that kindness. With him six feet under, now she never would.

The opportunity to enjoy this gift of a man had passed her by. She had wasted it, wasted her life, their life, behind bars. *I should have just run away with him. We could have taken C.J. and lived away from the madness. Away from the feds. At least we would have been together,* Miamor thought. She was so full of "what ifs" that she was choking on them. Miamor could feel the torturous vacuum of nothingness begin to consume her as she cried over her man. He was hers. She was his. They belonged to each other. How dare God take him so soon. Carter's death had birthed an anger with her creator that she had never felt before. She had never been close to God, because she did the devil's work, and Carter's death only widened the gap.

Miamor was vulnerable, exposing her heartbreak for the few that were in attendance, and it was a scene to see. Everyone, even the guards, felt her loss. She noticed the droplets of rain falling onto his body and quickly realized that it was her tears, staining him. The rain was picking up and Miamor didn't want him to get wet. She reluctantly let go. "Even a lifetime would not have been long enough. I'll see you when I get there, my king," she whispered. She already had it made up in her mind that she would expedite the process. Miamor couldn't breathe, didn't want to breathe; the privilege of inhaling felt selfish if Carter could not.

As she leaned over to kiss his lips she wished she could just share her air with him, let him borrow a little of hers, but life didn't work that way. Everyone was living on borrowed time and Carter's had sadly expired. *It's not fair. God please.* But there was no point in begging. Hers would be the last prayers to be answered if ever there was a hierarchy. Her sins were just that great.

"Mia . . ."

Miamor loved Breeze but she wanted to dead her where she stood for interrupting her goodbye. She turned her head, eyes ablaze, but her misplaced anger was quickly doused with the image of her son.

"Ma?"

C.J. stood, the spitting image of his father, and Miamor felt the tug of her heart. This was what Carter had left her with. C.J. was the kryptonite that would make sure she wasn't destroyed in Carter's absence.

Not much time had passed—in fact C.J. was coming up on his thirteenth birthday—but it had felt like an eternity and somehow, she could see he had changed. He was flanked by two men, both of Dominican descent, clearly there for C.J.'s protection, and she looked at Breeze stunned. She went to her son, who stiffened slightly as she embraced him, but a mother's love, no matter how distant, is undeniable. He melted eventually at her touch.

"You're so big. I can't believe I've missed so much," Miamor whispered, completely distraught. It was like the time she missed didn't hit her until she saw his face. He had completely transformed into a young man she didn't recognize. "I'm so sorry," Miamor whispered. "As soon as I can, I'm going to come for you. That's my word."

"I'm okay, Ma," C.J. said with a maturity that Miamor didn't like. It burned her that she was missing these important years with him. She would have no control over the type of man he would become and the thought both saddened and scared her. Without Carter, who would shape him? Who would he be? He was growing at a rapid rate and she felt like less than a mother for not being around when he needed her. She had banked on Carter being there to fill in for her absence but with him gone, the guilt ate at her. He lowered his tone. "I'm with Estes."

Recognition flickered in her eyes as worry filled Miamor. She didn't entirely trust Estes with her son. *I killed his daughter . . . an eye for an eye . . .*

"Leave here with your auntie Breeze. Listen to me, C.J. You cannot trust Estes. Do you hear me? Don't trust him," Miamor warned.

She could already see his indifference and the guards were stepping up, intruding on her space and her time with her seed. It was important that he listen to her. It was imperative. His life could depend on it. Miamor wrapped her arms around her child. "I love you, don't ever forget that. You're the son of Carter Jones. You best not ever forget that. I love you so much."

The guards grabbed her by the elbow. "It's time—"

"Don't touch me while I'm talking to my son!" She snatched her arm away from their grasp, but before it could become a scene Breeze stepped up.

"I've got him, Miamor," Breeze reassured.

Miamor hung her head in defeat as tears fell with the

rain. "Take care of him, Breeze. Please, make sure my baby is okay. Look at him. He's hardened. He's—"

"A son of the Cartel." The mystery woman stepped up and as if she were the one cutting the guard's checks they backed up, giving her space. "I'm Anari. I'm a friend of Carter's."

Anari noticed the looks of jealousy and wrath that crossed Miamor's face and she chuckled. "Only a friend," she assured. "I've heard about that temper of yours. You have nothing to worry about. I don't want any part of that illogical craziness that Carter loved so much. Carter ensured your freedom before he passed. Reuniting with you and his son has ordered his steps for the past year. I'm sorry he won't be here to see all his hard work pay off, but he took care of everything. I need you to stay strong in there, erase those thoughts I see swarming in your head. Think of your son and stay low. I'm going to be coming for you and when I do, I need you to be ready."

Anari stepped off and before Miamor could ask any questions the guards were escorting her away. "Wait, please, wait." When she turned back she saw her son standing in front of Carter's casket, saying the same goodbyes she had just muttered.

She went to him, walking up from behind, and placed her cuffed hands around her son's body. He didn't cry the way she had. He only stood there, quietly, solemnly. The groundskeeper stepped up. "We have to close it now. The rain . . ."

Miamor nodded and watched. Pieces of her heart broke

off as they lowered the lid inch by inch. "Wait," she said. She reached inside and removed his Rolex, then handed it to C.J. "I love you" were the last words she said before the guards insisted that she leave.

She was grateful for their tolerance on this day, but she had a feeling that some of it had to do with the mystery woman who was now being driven away in the blacked-out Bentley. Miamor didn't look back because it would only make her want to stay with her family, stay with him, and none of it was possible. So instead, she retreated, nursing a wounded soul as she headed back to her imprisonment. An era had ended and much like the conclusion of all good things she wanted to fight it.

Suddenly she regretted every single insignificant thing that had ever kept her and Carter apart. None of it had been worth it, but in the end, she was glad that he knew how much she loved him. Miamor would sacrifice it all for Carter Jones and he knew that because she had shown him. Their tumultuous love had endured the darkest valleys and reached the highest peaks. It was the most beautiful thing she had ever experienced and she was grateful to know truth and love without conditions through her connection with him. If they all were God's children, there wasn't a doubt in her mind that Carter was his favorite, because the energy he contributed to her life was almost mystical, as if God had given her a small token of love to show her that He was indeed real. Not many people experienced love like that and as she stared out her window and looked up into the sky, she felt Carter with her. He would always be with her because he had been inside her. He had rooted himself there, giving her a baby, planting his DNA. Carter had fertilized her soul so good that remnants of him would bloom every season when it rained most.

This was one of those times. The pain was present but somewhere deep inside she felt the pulse of his strength telling her to keep going. *He's here, he will always be here,* she thought as she placed a hand to her heart. She took a deep breath and when she exhaled her tears ceased. Her loss was great. They had written a story so great that without it the world of the Cartel would have no narrative. They had fought hard and loved harder. She wouldn't have minded doing it just a bit longer.

She remembered meeting him in that casino all those years ago. She remembered hesitating at the funeral when she was supposed to kill him, when something inside her told her she couldn't. She remembered the way he had entered her on that beach under the moonlight. She smirked as she thought of the many showers she had taken to get the sand out of all her creases. She thought of disappearing from his life then appearing on his doorstep, begging him to forgive her as rain poured over them. He had stepped out into that rain with her, taking her back because their love was fated. Neither of them had ever been able to resist. The birth of their son, traveling across oceans to bring her man back from Saudi Arabia, building up Vegas together as the first black family to have a majority share in a casino, and being crazy enough over him to put a girl in the dirt for trying to take her place. All of it—the good, the bad, the hood, the ugly, the crazy . . . she would do again in a heartbeat because it had been a hell of a ride. Carter had made every moment worth it.

Miamor would yearn for him every day for the rest of her years. That's just what a real man had the power to do to a woman. She had experienced one of life's gifts. He had blessed her and Miamor would never forget it. They were inseparable, even the grave couldn't part them, and she promised herself that every day with every breath, she would live for them both.

Epilogue

TEN YEARS LATER

C.J.'s heart pounded as he stood at the grave site, staring at his father's headstone. He felt so many emotions pulsing through him and he clenched his fists at his sides, used to working out his conflicts through his hands, through boxing. This feeling was one that fighting couldn't solve. "You weren't there for me, man," C.J. whispered as he swiped his hand over his full beard and sniffed away the mist in his eyes. C.J. knew his father was a great man, but so many years had passed without him that he had grown resentful. "You just left me." C.J. had been too young to understand Carter's absence in his life after Miamor had gone to prison and years without explanation had put a deep seed of hurt inside him. At twenty-two years old, he was a man with unresolved anger.

He chose to work it out inside the ring. Estes had raised him, almost bred him, like a prizewinning horse. He had spent most of his life in the Dominican Republic, making a name for himself with his skill, fighting all the demons that lived inside his head from his childhood. He had worked hard to make his exterior as hard as possible. His defined abs, his broad chest, and hard biceps were all masks that hid his interior. C.J. was fucked up, unable to trust, unable to love, and he made no apologies for it. Everything he had lived through had made him this way.

He looked at the Rolex watch he wore on his wrist. It was the only thing besides his name that he had of his father's. It was time to go. He couldn't spend too much time wallowing over the past. He had to make it to his training session or Estes would kill him. He was preparing for the biggest fight of his career, right here in Miami. He had moved back to train with a world-class team, but he knew when he stepped foot in the city that his family's past would come back to haunt him.

He could feel the legacy of his family name in the air. Like slaves haunted plantations, the Diamond family seemed to make Miami their own personal heaven. Even a decade later, the name still rang bells all over the city. He told himself that he could stay focused amid the media storm, but he had no idea of how strong the legacy of his father really was. Miami was a city that could turn even the best of men bad, and he prayed that the decision to come back wouldn't lead to his downfall. Only time would tell.

* * *

Miamor sat braiding the hair of her cell mate but in her mind, she was on a sandy beach with Carter Jones. It had been ten years and time had done nothing to remedy her heart.

"You good Mia?"

Miamor nodded and looked down at Ash. "Yeah, just thinking," she replied.

"You go off in your head a lot," Ash said. "Better be careful in here. One of these bitches in here is just waiting to catch you slipping. What are you going to do when I'm gone?" Ash asked.

"They know better," Miamor said. "And I taught you everything you know. You came in here looking like a meal to some of these women. Now you know how to protect yourself," Miamor said. Ash had been her cell mate for the past four years. When the girl had first arrived, she was young and defenseless. At eighteen years old, she was way too young to be in prison. After she had gotten into a fight with an inmate, Ash had spent two weeks in the infirmary with cracked ribs and a punctured lung. When she returned, Miamor taught her how to keep the wolves at bay. She taught her everything she knew and turned her into a monster. Ash was fearless with Miamor at her side and had caught two bodies since being inside. The guards didn't know who was responsible for the hits, but the inmates knew and once they recognized Ash as Miamor's guard dog, they never tested her again.

"You're getting out of here, I'm proud of you. I'm not telling you not to get your hands dirty, because you're a grown woman, you're going to do what you want to do, but be smart. Move smart out there. I don't want to see you back in here with me," Miamor said.

"You only have a year before you come home," Ash said. "I'm going to set up everything for when you get out."

"Tell me what you have to do," Miamor said.

"I got it," Ash assured.

"Tell me anyway," Miamor insisted.

"You want me to contact Aries and get your money, get a place, and then find your son," Ash said, reciting the instructions in the exact order Miamor had taught her.

"He will have enemies that he knows nothing about. Don't let them touch my son. He doesn't need to know I sent you. In fact, being close to me will make it harder to be close to him. So, don't even mention me. Just become acquainted. Get close to him and keep the snakes out of his grass," Miamor instructed.

Miamor knew that her son was back in Miami and there was no way she was leaving anything to chance. She had made too many enemies to not worry.

"I got him, I promise," Ash said.

Ash had become like a daughter to Miamor and although she was sending her back into the world with an agenda, she truly did care about her well-being. "And take care of yourself, Ash. Miami is treacherous. Be careful," Miamor added.

"I will," Ash assured her. "Now you can go back to your daydreams," Ash said with a chuckle.

Miamor laughed but as she continued to braid, she slipped back into the depths of her mind where Carter still lived.

* * *

"Nigga, I want my fucking money when I burn your ass," Mo said as he revved up the engine to the stolen convertible Porsche 911 he drove. He looked over at Joey, his best friend, who sat confidently behind the wheel of a 1969 Camaro.

"Bruh, get the fuck out of here. You in that foreign shit. I like that homegrown," Joey cracked as the beautiful ebony-colored girl seated in his passenger seat giggled at the witty response.

Mo looked at the exotic woman next to him with her manufactured looks and then stuck up his middle finger. "Just have my bread, my G," Mo gloated. "On three."

"1," he counted.

"2," Joey added.

"3!" the girls shouted as both men took off. They flew through the streets of Miami, lawless and without worry as the horsepower under their hoods made it neck and neck. They were playing a dangerous game, pushing 140 miles per hour down the city street, weaving in and out of regular traffic. Mo's long hair that he wore wild and free like a lion's mane blew in the wind as he pressed the beautiful machine to the limit. His face fell in defeat as Joey took the victory and the sound of his tires screeching to a stop as he did a full three-hundred-sixty-degree turn tore through the air as he hopped from the car.

"Give me my money, nigga!" Joey gloated, his boyish charm oozing out as he gave a mischievous smirk.

Mo went into his glove box and sourly pulled out three thick rubber-banded knots of green bills before tossing them out the window. "Yeah, yeah. You got lucky," Mo stated. "You know you got to give me a chance to win that back." He had just lost twenty grand in seconds, but it was worth the high of the race.

"Your ass would gamble on two ants on the sidewalk, my G," Joey cracked as he climbed back into his car.

Mo chuckled but didn't respond because he knew it was true. He lived a high-stakes lifestyle at all times. Everything was a gamble.

"Yo you still got the hookup on that fight in a few months? You putting bread on that?" Joey asked.

Mo nodded. "Absolutely."

Mo hadn't seen C.J. in thirteen years but as soon as he saw the billboards around the city he recognized him. The fight was a big deal and Mo would be ringside. They had a lot of catching up to do. Family was scarce in Mo's world these days and he couldn't wait to surprise C.J. at the fight.

Life had taken them down two different paths. Mo was getting his in the dirt and Miami was his playground. Running the streets was as natural to him as water to a fish and he took to the underworld as soon as they released him from lockup. His name rang strong and true on these streets and Mo was getting a lot of money, just as the Diamond men before him had done. He had no idea where C.J. had been all these years but he was about to welcome him back home. He hoped that C.J. wanted in because together they could take over and claim the throne that was rightfully theirs.

Mo revved up the engine and looked up at the billboard at his cousin's face before speeding off.

A new era was about to bring heat to the Miami streets and Mo was going to prove to the entire city that his family hadn't fallen off. A smirk spread across his lips because he knew what was to come and he couldn't wait to take his piece of the pie. He gripped the steering wheel tightly with one hand and rested his other on the pretty girl's thigh beside him as he thought, *Niggas thought we were done. We just getting started. Diamonds are forever.*

To be continued in
Long Live the Cartel
Coming Soon